I0722236

Court

OF

Death

AND

Dreams

USA Today Bestselling Author

MEG ANNE

"Death cannot stop true love. All it can do is delay it for a while."

— WESTLEY, THE PRINCESS BRIDE

COURT OF DEATH AND DREAMS

Empyria
Glimmermere
Mitven River
Iris Lake
Fallshade
Cragshadow Foothills
Pillar Wastes
Brillergarde
Grey Gorge
Worm Sea
Rift Blade
Darkhollow
Dead Man
The Four Shadows
Nighthaven
Nightshade Moor
The Brinewaters
The Rascal Lands
Green Brook
Midport
Spring Woods
Ravenndel
Montnau
Unora's Folly
Kendere Temple
Jeltar
Knightsgrave
Colvers
Sea of Souls
Chrendle's Lament
Fog Forest
Southorn Flats

AUTHOR'S NOTE

Court of Death and Dreams contains mature and graphic content that is not suitable for all audiences. Such content includes murder, torture, explicit violence and gore. **Reader discretion is advised.**

A detailed list of content and trigger warnings is available on my website.

CHAPTER 1

BAST

"All right, you fucker, you better cover up anything you don't want me to see. You asked for an hour, and I gave you double that, but this is ridiculous. We all get it. You can rail your woman into the ground. Bravo for you. We should all be so lucky. Now put your dick away and come back to the safety of the camp so the rest of us can get some sleep without worrying the two of you are out there dead or dying."

Despite the cavalier nature of his speech, apprehension hummed in his veins, the unrelenting buzz growing with every step. Having already walked the length of the beach within sight of the bonfire twice over, Sebastian prowled along the edge of the trees, shouting his frustration into the darkness beyond.

"Come on, Ronan! Shadow! I'm not playing games. I require proof of life!"

Since beginning his pilgrimage from Colvers across Empyria, he'd cultivated a persona born of indulgence and baptized by excess. Not only cultivated, perfected. To any who looked at him, he was a young courtier without a care in the world. The next high all that mattered, and responsibility the only sin recognized by a man who'd made pleasure his religion.

How he paid for it now.

No one took him or his warnings seriously. Instead, his sincerity was met with derision and amusement. Which was why he was out here searching for his missing friend alone.

"Leave them be, Sebastian. They've more than earned their privacy," Calypso had said when he'd asked the pirates to join his one-man search party.

"You know I'm the last person to get in the way of a man and his intimate pursuits . . . unless they impede my own," he'd added with his trademark roguish grin. "But this is hardly the place for one to wander off. Between my capture and the two separate attacks we've suffered in as many days, surely you must agree."

"I don't *disagree*, but Ronan and Shadow are more capable than most. If they run into trouble they can't handle on their own, they'll call for us."

"What if they stray too far and we can't hear them?"

Calypso's uncovered eye glittered in the firelight, the iris currently a warm amber. "They know the risks and have endured all that we have—more from the sounds of things. They're smart enough to know how far they can safely venture."

Bast had wanted to pick up the log he'd been using as a seat and fling it up into the air. Why was he the only one who seemed to realize that believing in people's abilities, whether the faith was justified or not, was what had gotten them all into this mess?

Skill and reputation were not replacements for knowledge of their surroundings. No one knew how to prepare for the unknown, not completely. How could they? It was the exact reason they'd found themselves taken hostage by sentient shrubbery. And it wasn't like he and Loren had asked to be plucked from their bed and absconded with by a small army of drakes and their ghastly riders either. These were the sorts of hazards one could not defend against.

If he'd learned anything during his travels, it was to expect the unexpected. Calm was never a guarantee of safety, only the inevitable quiet heralding an oncoming storm.

And Twilight's Cove, with its many secrets, was more dangerous by far than any other realm he'd explored. On these sandy shores, threats were not a mere possibility; they were a guarantee.

So if he, a notorious scapegrace, could so clearly see that, why in the name of all that was holy couldn't anyone else?

There were greater injustices in the world. Ones he'd personally suffered that ultimately changed the entire course of his life. But this? This arrogant naivete and willful stupidity felt like a damned crime that needed serious punishment. Nothing as painful as a public flogging, mind you, but perhaps something equally embarrassing. A naked parade while being lobbed with rotten fruit, for example. Just something humiliating and smelly enough to help reinforce the lesson.

"You'd probably enjoy that, though, wouldn't you? Arrogant bastard that you are. I can hear you now. *'Why not give the people what they want, Sebastian? When your cock's practically a national monument like mine, it'd be a bleeding shame not to share it with the public. Besides, it never hurts to show the ladies and blokes what they're missing, am I right? Har har har,'*" he mocked, imitating Ronan's rough timbre with exaggerated flair.

"You sound just like my friend. For a second there, I thought you were him."

Taken on its own, there was no reason for the soft, unfamiliar voice to cause alarm, but out here in the middle of the death jungle? He was very fucking alarmed.

Sebastian's first instinct was to draw his weapon and respond with violence. But that kind of reaction wasn't exactly in character. It was more along the lines of what Ronan or Shadow would do. Not silly, charming, utterly nonthreatening Bast—unless one was discussing virtue, then no greater threat existed. But no. This was a matter of defense, and he had one very specific role to play until his mission was achieved.

Until that day, he couldn't do anything to draw unwanted attention to himself. Unwanted being the operative word. This persona of his did necessitate a bit of . . . flamboyance, but that was the safe kind of attention. Expected, even, since it helped sell the act. But to reveal his secrets before he even knew what sort of threat he was facing?

That was a gamble he could ill afford when it would call everything he'd spent years cultivating into question.

So, even though it pained him to no end, Sebastian did not unsheathe his blade. Rather, he threw his hands in the air, spun around, and let out a high-pitched shriek.

"Please don't hurt me. I'm too pretty to die."

It was hard to tell who was more shocked, him or the petite woman gaping at him. With her flaxen curls and big blue eyes, she didn't look capable of harming so much as a fly. Then again, no one expected vines to attack either, so he wasn't about to drop his guard.

"I'm not going to hurt you, Bast. Quite the opposite. I'm here to ask for your help."

"My help?"

He slowly lowered his arms, staring at the blonde hard as he tried to place her. She was striking, her beauty the kind not easily forgotten. He was certain they'd never met before, yet she'd called him by name. Caution pricked at the back of his neck, warning him to proceed very carefully.

"Excuse me, mademoiselle, but you seem to have me at a disadvantage. It's been a wild couple of days, and I'm not quite myself at the moment, so you'll have to forgive me, but . . . have I ravished you?"

"No," she said, laughter dancing through the word and shining in her luminous eyes.

Huh. The answer to that question is almost always yes.

"We've never met. Much to my disappointment," she added. The words could have been polite frippery, but there was a weight to them. A familiarity. As if she knew *exactly* who he was and was truly disappointed they'd yet to meet.

If that was the case, she either knew him by reputation or because of his family. Neither boded well for him. The first meant she somehow tracked him from Glimmermere all the way to this darkness-forsaken island, which made her a crazed stalker. The second meant she had the ability to reveal secrets he'd long kept buried, which made her a threat.

He was *really* starting to regret not opting for the sword.

Careful to keep his suspicion from his expression, he offered her a megawatt grin. "Then perhaps you'd care to explain how it is you came to be here? Or, at the very least, how you came to be in possession of my name? Or, better still, you could offer your own. In my world, it is a crime not to know the name of a beautiful woman."

She seemed on the verge of laughter. "Perhaps I should back up."

"Back up? *Mon ange,* we've yet to get started."

"And that's quite enough of that."

Sebastian allowed a little whimper to escape as a newcomer joined them. This one was far more intimidating than the last, and Bast immediately sought escape routes. Where the woman was sweetness personified, this man was barely leashed violence. He wouldn't just hurt a fly; it would be an out-and-out massacre.

The stranger towered over the woman, his brows dipped low over eyes so dark they'd be black if not for the ring of bronze in the center. His full, kissable lips were bracketed with deep lines that the scruff of his beard did nothing to hide. He was just as beautiful as she. If one enjoyed broody, hulking, dominant males.

Which he did . . . almost as much as lush, vivacious females.

Maybe it was his lucky day and they were seeking a third?

As soon as Mr. Tall Dark and Broody opened his mouth, that tiny bubble of hope burst. "Tell him what you came all this way to say before he keeps looking at you like that and I have to kill him."

"Lucian," she said with a laugh.

"Effie," he countered, all primal growl.

Stars, what a terrible time to sport a semi.

Sebastian cleared his throat. "As nice as the pair of you are to look at, I would quite appreciate some answers."

Tossing her partner one last exasperated look, Effie returned her attention to him. "You'll have to excuse my mate. He's a wee bit overprotective."

"As he should be," Bast replied with a polite smile, because what else could he say? He wasn't about to call the man out for threatening murder over a mere expression. He refused to start a fight he could not win.

"I can see why he likes you."

"I'm afraid you'll have to be more specific, *mon chéri*. Most do."

"Stop that," Lucian barked.

"Stop what?" he asked, truly stymied.

"You may call her by her name or her title, but flirt with her again and you'll answer to me."

"Lucian," Effie chided, but there was too much tenderness in the word for it to convey genuine disappointment.

"Who's flirting? I'm merely being courteous."

"She's mine. Back off."

"Really, Luc? Are you going to piss a circle around me next?"

"No, but I won't hesitate to throw you over my shoulder and take your arse back home."

"You know why we can't do that."

"I'm glad somebody does," Bast muttered, entertained by their exchange, but at a loss as to what these two were doing here.

"It's as I told you. I—"

Lucian cleared his throat.

"*We* have come to ask for your help rescuing our mutual friend."

"Well, you see, *Effie*," he overexaggerated her name for the benefit of her scowling mate. "I am already in the middle of searching for one friend. I do not think I can spare the time to begin looking for a second."

"I know who you are, Sebastian Villehardouin of Colvers. Who your parents were. What happened to them and your sister, Marguerite."

He went rigid at the use of his sister's name. It was the first time he'd heard it aloud since he'd cradled her mutilated body in his arms. He still carried the shirt he'd worn that night, the one drenched in her blood. It had become his talisman in the days and weeks to come. A reminder of why he could not fail in his quest.

"How can you possibly know that?"

"I've Seen it."

He was familiar enough with seers to understand she did not mean literally. His courteous mask cracked, remembered pain giving his voice a furious edge. "Then you also know who I search for and why."

Compassion softened Effie's gaze. "I do."

"And yet, even knowing my true mission, you'd ask me to abandon it?"

"No, Sebastian. I want to help you obtain your justice."

Justice. Revenge. Retribution. They were but different strips of the same quilt.

"How?"

"Our paths are intertwined. Help me save Ronan, and I will lead you to the man who murdered your family."

"I already know who he is."

Dominic.

The High Lord's Vulture.

He was the one responsible for what had happened that night. For the blood that coursed like a river through his home. For the mindless slaughter of an innocent girl and her entire household, all because his parents had refused to sell her like chattel. Glimmermere's former ruler was not the pillar of honor his people made him out to be, and Shadow was hardly the first who'd had to do a sovereign's dirty work. Rugen had taken one look at Marguerite in the marketplace and had her followed, wanting her for himself. When Sebastian's parents refused, stating she was too young, Rugen sent Dominic to deliver a message not soon forgotten.

No one says no to the High Lord.

All of this Sebastian learned years later, after following a trail long run cold as he collected whatever scraps of information remained. By then Rugen was already dead. But not Dominic. The Vulture was alive and well, flourishing in the palace. It was Bast's mission to send that rutting bastard back to hell in as many pieces as he could manage. He wanted to look down upon the filth who had ripped his heart from his chest the day he'd destroyed his family as he repaid the favor in kind. He wanted to make it last. He wanted it to *hurt*.

But mostly, he wanted the murderer to die with the name of the child he'd killed on his lips. If Sebastian was forced to live the rest of his days with the sight of her ravaged body seared into his memory, then the least the monster who killed her could do was remember her fucking name as he begged for mercy.

"And where he is," he belatedly added, his hatred of the man making his voice cold and hard.

"True. But until now you haven't been able to get close to him. Join me, and I will lead you straight to him. You have my word as one of the Three."

"Effie," Lucian snapped. "We do not give our vows lightly, and we certainly don't reveal our secrets to strangers."

"But Sebastian isn't a stranger. Are you, Bast?"

"You know all my secrets, so I suppose that makes us friends. More than, actually, since not even my closest friends know what you do."

Effie smiled. "Perk of the job. I know lots of things."

Sebastian glanced around the empty beach and then back toward the forest behind him. "Is one of them Ronan's current location?"

Her smile faded. "Unfortunately."

"Unfortunately? I've been shouting myself hoarse trying to find him. If you already know, then we can get on with it."

"He's not here, Sebastian," she said, confirming his earlier suspicions. "There is a reason I said I need your help to save him, not find him."

"Save him?" Bast's heart dropped. "Why do I get the feeling he's not just trapped in the treetops like I was?"

"Because he's not. Erebos has him."

"Erebos? But . . . how?"

Effie and Lucian exchanged a look before she let out a long sigh. "Perhaps it's best we return to camp and collect the others. There's much I need to tell you, and we're going to need all the help we can get to face what's coming."

"You make it sound as though we're not going on a rescue mission but heading off to war," he said with a hollow laugh, too distracted by the buzzing beneath his skin to realize neither of them were laughing.

When his gaze found hers again, the sapphire flecks ringing her pupil seemed to glow. "That's because we are."

CHAPTER 2

BAST

The sand muted the sounds of their footsteps as Bast returned to camp with his foundlings. The flames of the bonfire had died down, but enough of a glow remained to easily make out the three figures sitting around it in a loose semi-circle. Two had their backs to them, their eyes on the crashing waves, but the third was angled straight at them.

Bast knew the second they'd been spotted. There was a warning squawk, and then all three figures shot to their feet. The tense atmosphere and aggressive body language were such a sharp contrast to the laid-back, unconcerned trio he'd left that it took him a second to realize they'd gone so far as to draw their weapons.

"Bast," Calypso said silkily, "I'm sure even you can see this is not the couple you set out to find."

"Do you really think I would mistake these two for Ronan and Shadow?" He laughed. "Even were I blind, my nose is not."

"Are you saying we smell?" Lucian asked dryly.

Bast waved his hand distractedly. "Not you. Ronan. Now, if you would be so kind, please shut up. Best not to distract me when I'm in the middle of saving your life."

Lucian quirked a brow. "Are you? What a novel experience."

"You've been saved before. By me, I might add," Effie muttered with a haughty sniff.

Affection shone in the man's dark eyes as he skimmed a finger along the side of her neck, seeming to trace something the rest of them couldn't see. "As if I could ever forget."

Bast had to clear his throat around the corresponding bolt of emotion that punched through his chest. Lucian looked at Effie the way Ronan gazed at Shadow.

The way Loren had looked at him.

Focus, Sebastian. One crisis at a time.

"Nor am I deaf, for that matter—"

"We get it, Bast. You are in possession of all your faculties. Though, I'd still wager your wits are lacking."

Bast glared at Bronn while the others snickered. Except Jagger. That man never smiled. He could give Lucian a run for his money in a brooding brooders who brood competition.

Effie placed her hand lightly on his shoulder and stepped forward. A bold move, considering, but with that beast at her back, he supposed it was easy to be fearless.

"As I already explained to Sebastian, we are here to help, not harm." After a beat, she amended. "Well, we will harm, just not you."

The captain made a considering sound and lowered her sword. "You'll forgive me and my men for our caution."

"Of course. I'd expect nothing less after the adventures you've shared."

There was a momentary beat of confusion before Calypso's expression cleared. Positioned as she was by the fire, the right side of her face was completely illuminated, allowing Bast to watch as her iris transitioned from maroon to violet. Not for the first time, he wondered if the color was dependent on her mood or if it was entirely random.

"You're a seer," she breathed.

"Where I'm from we call ourselves Keepers, but yes. I have the gift of Sight."

"Him too?" Caly asked, gesturing toward Lucian with her chin.

"He's my Guardian." Effie flicked her eyes up to Lucian, her smile soft. "And my mate."

"Damn straight," Lucian growled, almost too low for the others to hear, but there was no missing Effie's resulting blush.

"How *did* the two of you come to be here, by the by?" Bronn asked.

"Portal," Lucian answered. "Effie's vision was so specific, we were able to use it to create the link. Usually, a Guardian cannot create a portal to a place they've never been, but it seems the Mother didn't want to waste time."

"She certainly was more detailed than usual," Effie said, rubbing absently up and down her arms as if warding off a chill.

"What did you See?" Jagger demanded, surprising all of them with his gruff rasp.

The Keeper's expression turned grim. "Terrible things. A wedding—"

"That doesn't sound so bad," Bast interrupted.

"—torture—"

"That sounds less good."

"—and death. So much death."

"Okay, terrible. Terrible was accurate."

Calypso scanned the empty beach behind them. "Where are Ronan and Shadow?"

"They've been taken. And her true name is Reyna. She was once a queen of her people, enslaved by Erebos when he first captured her," Effie answered. "She is at the center of my visions. Whatever Erebos has planned, she's the heart of it."

"Taken? As in, they're no longer on the island?" Bronn asked.

"Peninsula," Bast muttered, annoyed they finally seemed to care now that a stranger showed concern, but when he'd hinted at danger, no one batted an eye.

As usual, no one paid him any attention.

"Exactly. Currently, they're en route to Glimmermere."

Caly frowned. "We're hardly in a position to follow. Without my ship and the rest of my crew, we'd have to travel by foot. What's more, we don't know these lands like we do the sea, nor do we have supplies for a trip of that magnitude."

"I know where you can get a ship," Effie said.

Calypso's brow shot up. "Oh? Are you carrying one around in your pocket?"

"Next best thing," Effie said, pulling out a small purple stone. "I can take you to it."

"I thought we were in a hurry. Why don't we just use that or one of your fancy portals and head straight to the capital instead?" Sebastian asked.

"My vision was clear. Any attack initiated before its time will fail."

"How will we know it's time?" Caly asked.

A small frown marred Effie's brow. "The bells. I see a night sky, swollen moon the color of flame, red towers, the swoop of a bird, and bells."

"What are we supposed to do in the meantime?" Bronn asked.

"Recruit the rest of our army."

"Army?"

Effie nodded.

"Lady, there are but six of us. Where exactly are we to find an army?"

"Everything we need will be found in your pirate town."

"Smuggler's Rock?" Bronn asked.

"Twilight's Cove," Bast corrected.

"Yes," Effie answered.

Bronn and Calypso shared a look. "Well then," the captain said after a beat. "What are we waiting for?"

ONCE THE STOMACH-TWISTING NAUSEA PASSED, Bast quite appreciated the convenience of travel by Kaelpas stone. One second, they'd been standing on the beach beside the fire; the next, they were on a stray dock overlooking what could only be Smuggler's Rock.

The pirate town was precisely the den of sin he'd hoped it would be. Barely lit, more taverns and gaming halls than people, curio shops tucked away in winding alleys, and all manner of irresponsible reprobates.

"Nereus, and I thought the sea could be a right bitch," Bronn said, hands braced on his knees, face a familiar shade of green.

"I should have warned you, but I thought it best to let you find out for yourselves," Effie said with an apologetic mien.

"Witch," Bronn grumbled, but it lacked true heat.

Calypso was faring a bit better, and Jagger and Lucian looked the same as ever. Which was to say, grumpy and mean.

"Well, witch, where to?"

Lucian glared at Bronn. "It's Keeper. Call her witch again, and you'll become intimately familiar with the taste of my fist as I cram it down your throat."

"Kinky," Bast said, earning himself twin glares. "What?"

Effie chuckled and twined her arm through his. "Come on. We need to find The Salty Sailor."

Bronn gave her a worried look. "The Sailor? Really? That's not exactly—"

"A place for a lord or lady of means?" Calypso offered.

"Perfect. The people we're looking for should be right at home there."

It was clear by the looks on their face that the pirates hadn't expected the Keeper's reaction, but Bast was thrilled. Who came to a secret pirate town to play by the rules? He was here to misbehave. Okay, he was here to find a way to save Ronan. But if he could have a little fun while he was at it, why not take advantage of the opportunity?

"Do they know we're coming?" Bronn asked.

"Why would they?" Effie asked.

"This is going to be a shitshow," he groaned.

"Splendid," Bast said, rubbing his hands together. "Sounds like the makings of a top night."

"You *would* think so," Bronn muttered.

For a second, he sounded so much like Ronan that Sebastian's heart lifted, only to plummet straight to his feet. The realization that he was here while his only true friend in years was locked away and doomed to spend the foreseeable future being tortured without end was a tough truth to accept.

"Stay strong, *mon ami*. We are coming for you, just . . . hold on." The words were whispered on the wind, but no less earnest for it.

There was one amusing moment where no one moved, everyone looking to Effie because until this point, she'd spoken with such authority they'd all just assumed she'd continue to take the lead.

"What?" she asked.

Calypso laughed, the first to realize their mistake. "You don't know where the tavern is, do you?"

Effie shook her head. "I've Seen the sign, but I have absolutely no idea how to get us there."

They chuckled softly, Bronn taking over as their guide. He led them across the creaking wood of the far dock they'd arrived on, the planks softly swaying beneath their feet with each ripple of the dark water. Bast supposed the location had been selected so they'd be far enough away from prying eyes when they'd appeared out of thin air, but this wasn't a place for asking questions. Even if their group drew more than a few curious stares as they made their way into the heart of the smuggler's den, they were allowed by without incident.

It was less than a handful of minutes before they reached their destination, their arrival met by an unrelated cheer from within.

"Sounds like coin is flowing tonight," Bronn said with a familiar gleam in his eye.

"Oh no, you don't," Calypso said. "The last time you went out wagering, you lost your shirt, and I was the one forced to repay your debts."

"He lost more than that," Jagger muttered.

"You're only still going on about it because I didn't let you join in."

"He was too busy with a redhead, if I recall correctly," Caly chimed in, sounding far more annoyed by the memory than a captain had any right to be.

Bast's eyes were still glued to Bronn. The gambler in him was eager to test his skill against one he might actually beat, but before he could open his mouth, Effie caught his eye and shook her head no.

"You're not the one who needs to gamble tonight, Sebastian," she said with calm certainty.

"But . . . why not?" he sulked, feeling the weight of all those lost starlings slip through his fingers.

"You'll see," she murmured with an infuriating smile as she jerked her head toward the door the others had already disappeared through.

The Sailor was everything one would expect out of a pirates' drinking hall. Weather-stained boards and parts of old ships made up the bulk of the decoration, a striking figurehead holding pride of place on the wall. Beautiful carved hair and a fish's tail protected the majestic woman's modesty. He'd heard of mermaids, but had never understood the appeal until now. But that was about all that was appealing in the place. Bast grimaced when his boot stuck to an unidentifiable spot on the floor.

"Many a man has met his end in search of the fabled sirens," Bronn warned as he walked past.

"Fabled," Calypso scoffed. "Right." She surged ahead, weaving through a throng of bodies in search of a drink and leaving the rest of them to follow or stand awkwardly in the entryway.

Bast hurried to catch up, taken aback by how few seats were to be found. This wasn't exactly what he'd consider a hot spot, but the place was packed. Despite the crowd, it was clear they'd caught the attention of everyone in the tavern because the raucous conversation died down to little more than hushed exchanges.

If not for that, Bast didn't think they'd have been able to hear the scrape of wood over the floor that preceded a shocked, "Captain?"

Bast's eyes flew wide open when his gaze landed on the owner of the voice, who wasn't a man as he suspected, but a stars-blessed minotaur. He didn't even realize his mouth was hanging open until Effie reached over and pushed his jaw closed with the tip of her finger.

"It's not polite to stare," she teased.

"But it's . . . he's . . . he's wearing fucking spectacles." The delicate gold frames had clearly seen better days, one lens cracked and the bridge between them tied together with a frayed bit of rope.

"Yes, we can see that," Lucian muttered dryly.

Bast realized the giant and his compatriots were members of Caly's lost crew when she made a happy sound and rushed over to the minotaur.

"Captain, you're a sight for sore eyes," he called out, his voice a deep rumble.

"As are you," she said, greeting others she recognized with gentle squeezes on their arms as she worked her way through the crowd of men. She gasped when she finally reached him. "Oh, Tiny, your glasses."

Tiny? There was nothing insignificant about the creature. Even the ring piercing his snout was easily the size of Bast's wrist.

The minotaur's happiness dimmed, his unexpectedly expressive face turning mournful as he tearfully sniffed. "I did what I could to salvage them."

"We'll find you another pair," Calypso promised, reaching up to pat him on the shoulder as best she could.

Lucian surprised him by stepping forward. "I can repair them."

Tears. Actual tears brimmed the minotaur's eyes as he looked over to where Lucian, Effie, and Bast stood. "You'd do that?"

"It would be my honor."

Sebastian turned wide eyes on the Guardian. Had he become possessed since they set foot inside? *Who is this man, and what has he done with the scowling arsehole I met on the beach?*

There was no need for Lucian to weave through the crowd. The people parted like the damn sea so he could reach the minotaur and the mangled spectacles cradled in his large palm. Lucian held his hand just over Tiny's, his irises flaring a blinding bronze before returning to their nearly black state.

"There you go. All fixed."

Tiny's mouth dropped open in shock when he carefully lifted a perfectly restored pair of glasses. "Th-thank you," he stuttered, his eyes filled with tears once more. Frames pinched between two massive fingers, he reached out with his free hand, reeling the Guardian in for a powerful one-armed hug. "I can never repay this debt."

Beside him, Effie snickered as her mate squirmed uncomfortably in the minotaur's hold.

"There's no debt," he choked out, awkwardly patting the pirate's back before he was finally released. "Happy to help."

Calypso beamed at Lucian, her arm around a bald man with a dark bushy beard that Bast didn't recognize. Jagger was as expressionless as ever, but Bronn had to clear his throat a couple of times before giving Lucian a grateful dip of his chin. Even Bast found himself oddly touched by the exchange.

A tearful reunion was not what he'd expected when Effie said they'd be recruiting an army. Leaning his head so his mouth was beside her ear, he whispered, "You made it seem like we were here to convince strangers to join our cause."

"I couldn't resist the surprise. And I think those three have earned a little bit of happy after what they've been through, don't you?"

Sebastian didn't disagree, but he couldn't resist asking, "What about my happiness?"

Lucian released a heavy breath while Effie let out a soft, tinkling laugh. "Oh, Bast. Please never change."

Caly waved them over, and after a few chaotic moments, everyone around the table had been introduced. Bast's head swam with all the new names he'd just been given. Tiny. Cookie. A young lad named Willie. Durgan. Temple. Adonis. And a partridge in a pear tree. There were a handful of others, too, but he wasn't going to pretend to remember who was who. While not every crew member of the *Revenge* had made it through the Lusca attack unscathed, a good number had managed to find their way to safety.

After introductions, it was another thirty minutes at least before the newly reunited crew had finished trading tales regarding what had come to pass since they'd seen each other last. As one might expect, their side of the story garnered surprised gasps and cheers for the numerous enemies they'd bested. As for the rest of the *Revenge's* crew, it seemed a passing ship had found them bobbing in the water, using pieces of salvage to keep them afloat, and had rounded them up and brought them all here.

"Where's this captain and crew that rescued you? I owe them my thanks," Calypso insisted.

Given his complexion, it was hard to know for sure, but Bast would have sworn Tiny paled as he wrung his hands together. "Well, you see, Captain, that's the interesting bit . . ."

"Oh?" she prompted when he didn't continue.

A shadow fell over the table, and it soon became clear that there was no need for the minotaur to answer when Calypso's head turned, her welcoming expression instantly souring.

"Drake, I thought I left your sorry arse to drown in the Triangle. But then, I guess not even Nereus wants a lying, cheating bastard to taint his seas."

CHAPTER 3

CALYPSO

aptain Drake Lawless. Here. After all this time. What an unexpected, wholly unwelcome blow.

Caly glared at the man who'd made off with more than her ship and her dignity. He'd taken her virginity too. He was the same handsome bastard she remembered. Better looking, if she was being honest. The years had been kind to him.

The prick.

Drake was undeniably handsome with his tousled inky black hair and jewel-bright blue eyes, their beauty enhanced by thick, sooty black lashes and sun-kissed skin. Not to mention a pouty lower lip that begged her to bite into it and a chiseled jaw liberally dusted with dark scruff. Scruff she happened to know would leave her inner thighs deliciously raw.

The pop of his dimple as he smirked down at her told her he knew exactly which memories she was replaying.

He was every inch the unrepentant scallywag she'd fallen hopelessly in love with nearly a decade ago. Age may have made him prettier, but it had made *her* wiser. And meaner too, unfortunately for him.

If he thought they were going to pick up where they left off after what he did, he was going to find himself on the other end of her father's dueling pistol. She'd kill him before letting him touch her again.

Drake loomed over the table, his stalwart first mate, Ignatius Montefortuna—Iggy for short—at his side.

"Caly, it's good to see you're as fiery as ever," Iggy said, his kind smile so at odds with his captain's. He looked the same as she remembered. His broad cheeks were sunburnt and dusted with freckles, warm brown eyes reminiscent of a love-starved puppy, and his thick black curls mostly hidden by the same red knit cap.

She spared him what barely passed as a friendly glance. "Good to see you too, Ig." Then she stood, arms crossed, as she glared up into Drake's stormy eyes. "What, not going to say hello?"

He tilted his head, never looking away as he whispered in Iggy's ear.

She hated the pang of disappointment in her belly. She'd always loved his slow, easy drawl. It made her think of melted butter and the soft scrape of velvet over naked skin. One of the things she'd missed most in those early days when his betrayal had cut the deepest was the way he'd whisper absolute filth as he climbed up her body and the reverent way he'd look down at her as he cupped her cheek and called her his pearl.

Everything about this man was a seduction. To this day, she knew he was the reason a single lover wasn't enough to satisfy the wanton desire he'd helped her discover. Maybe if he'd stayed, he could have been her one and only, but there was no going back. That ship had long since sailed.

Iggy tossed Drake an uncertain look, but at his captain's slow nod, he cleared his throat and haltingly confessed, "He said he's found himself struck speechless by your timeless beauty."

Her breath hitched. Drake had said the same thing to her once before, under a starry sky at sea, right before stealing a kiss and taking quite a few liberties with her. For one suspended moment, it was as if no time had passed at all. He was still the handsome young sailor toiling on her father's ship—or so he'd led her to believe until she'd realized it was all part of his charade—and she the naïve young girl too stupid to know better.

But as it inevitably does, the whole ugly truth came crashing back, and it was as if steel had injected itself into her spine. "Nereus be praised! The guardian of the sea has seen fit to spare me from the endless amounts of crap that falls from your lips. What a glorious boon."

Barks of laughter met her scathing retort. She could make out Bronn's sunny laugh, as well as Jagger's deeper rasp amidst the din. A quick glance to her left showed Cookie had replaced his trusty cleaver while Tiny's usual smile was nowhere to be found.

Drake might have saved her crew, but their loyalty was hers alone, and they knew no love was lost between the rival captains.

"So how is my ship, Lawless? I'm shocked you haven't managed to sink her yet."

Once again, it was Iggy who answered. "The *Lorelei* is as hale and bonny as ever."

Lorelei. He hadn't changed it.

It took everything in Caly not to hurl herself at him and rake her nails down his smug face. He knew. He fucking knew what the *Lorelei* meant to her. The ship was her legacy. Not just hers, but her father's. The beautiful galleon had been named for her mother. It was all they had of the woman who'd stolen his heart. He'd spent the rest of his days sailing the seas, searching for the beauty who'd stayed with him only long enough to birth his daughter.

Her jaw ached from the way she clenched it to keep from spewing every hateful word trying to escape her mouth.

Effie's blonde curls caught her eye, and instinct had Caly looking over Iggy's shoulder to the Keeper and her Guardian. Lucian was inscrutable as ever, but there was a weight to Effie's gaze. As if she was trying to convey some hidden message. Then she looked purposefully at Drake and gave a single slow nod.

And it all clicked.

This. This is why you brought us here.

Effie had promised to lead her to a ship. In her wildest dreams, she never would have imagined it was *her* ship.

"I'm taking her back."

Drake lifted a dark brow, not remotely threatened by her bold claim.

"Caly," Iggy said, voice rife with warning. "You don't have the men to stage a mutiny."

The clank of coins rolling across a table inspired her, and her lips lifted. "I don't need them. I'll play you for her."

She'd surprised him. Drake's eyes widened before his lips curled up. Iggy glanced to the side, waiting to see how his captain would like to respond to her challenge. Still refusing to speak to her directly, Drake waved a hand as if to say *'Be my guest'* then leaned down and began furiously whispering in his first mate's ear.

Using the momentary diversion, Bronn stepped forward, his voice pitched low and thick with tension. "Cal, you sure about this?"

"Never been more certain of anything in my life."

He gave her a wary nod but stepped to the side, likely knowing she'd never forgive him if he did anything to publicly challenge her authority.

Iggy's eyes flared wide as he listened to his captain's orders, but after a few nods and a muttered, "As you wish," his gaze found hers. "My captain's terms are as follows: since you laid down the challenge, he will pick the game. I will act as his stand-in, but you must be the one to play me. If you win, the *Lorelei* is yours free and clear. If I—he —wins, you will give him the boon of his choice without debate."

"Absolutely not," Jagger grunted.

"No way in hell," Bronn said on his heels, echoing the sentiment.

"Captain," Tiny said, his eyes filled with worry behind his newly restored glasses. "I'm not sure . . ."

She cut him off with a glare. This wasn't their choice to make. It was hers.

If she were a different woman, she might have been touched by the show of support from her crew. But she wasn't, and their doubt only fueled her determination. She would do this.

She *would* win her ship back.

Instead of answering, she tipped her chin to her shoulder and uttered, "Get up," to the men seated around the table. They were so quick to obey that several chairs were knocked over in their haste.

Flipping out her coat, she lowered herself onto one of the freshly vacated seats and raised a brow. "Well? What's the game, *captain*?" There was so much disdain in the word no one could mistake it as a sign of respect.

Iggy was ready with his response as he took the seat across from her. "Siren's Bluff."

That would be Drake's thrice-damned choice. A game of chance rather than skill.

"Fine," she growled out behind clenched teeth.

"What's Siren's Bluff?" Sebastian asked, his voice coming from her left.

Tiny was the one who answered. "A pirate's game of chance. The deck is shuffled and spread across the table. Each player chooses their card and then flips it over. Highest card wins the pot."

"That's it? Just the flip of a single card to determine whether she wins back an entire ship?"

"That's it," Tiny confirmed.

"Seems like a fool's bargain if you ask me."

Ah, sweet Bast, he'd reached the crux of it in one. The game was evil in its simplicity. There was nothing she could do, save cheating, to better her odds. The result was entirely up to fate.

The fickle bitch.

"I want a fresh deck," she demanded.

Drake's only answer was another slow, deliberate nod.

Bronn whistled, a sharp, piercing sound that cut through the jovial shouts of the crowd. A barmaid was quick to hurry over with the requested deck before she scurried off again.

"One of my men does the shuffling," she said.

Drake's brows lifted, but again, he acquiesced.

She didn't like how agreeable he was being. It was as if he couldn't care less about the outcome. But that didn't feel right. The only thing

Drake had ever truly cared about was procuring his own ship. Why risk it all now?

"Tiny," she called, knowing he, more than any of the others, would be entirely beyond reproach. "Would you do the honors?"

"Aye, captain." He deftly broke the seal and pulled out the deck. The snap and soft hiss of cards being shuffled replaced the low chatter. People were starting to take notice, and the atmosphere in the tavern was growing tense as the terms of their wager spread throughout the room.

Her eyes never left Drake's face. She trusted Tiny to do a good job. When he carefully spread the cards out across the surface of the pockmarked table, she acknowledged him with a soft, "Thank you, Tiny."

His response came by way of a warm squeeze of her shoulder.

"Ladies first," Iggy offered.

Calypso sneered. "I'm not a lady. I'm a pirate." But she leaned forward to make her selection anyway.

The skin beneath her eye patch itched, as it always did when her gift attempted to make itself known. But she couldn't risk it. Not here. Not in a place where men bartered and sold women for nothing more than existing. What she had concealed beneath that thick circle of leather wasn't just rare; it was one of a kind. If they discovered her secret, she wouldn't just be sold, she'd be killed outright, and her eye plucked from her skull as men tried to steal her power for themselves.

So she ignored the insistent prickling and took a deep breath, allowing her flattened palm to hover over the line of cards, waiting for a tickle or some inexplicable change in energy to inform her choice. Just because she couldn't rely on her gift didn't mean magic didn't exist in other forms. She had to believe that whatever force brought Effie to her would continue to guide her now.

"This one," she said, tapping a card near the far right. Easing it out from the row, she slid it toward her and waited.

Technically, Drake wasn't allowed to interfere with Iggy's choice, but when the man's hand hovered above the one her rival wanted, he let out a low cough.

Bastard.

Iggy slid his captain's choice across the table until it rested right in front of him. "Ready?"

"On three."

"One," he said.

"Two," she answered.

"Three," they said together, each flipping their card over.

There was a moment of silence, where everything felt as if it shifted to slow motion before her eyes dipped down to discover her fate.

Queen of Stars. The second-highest card in the deck.

Hope bloomed beneath her ribs, and a smile lighted her lips until her gaze found Iggy's card and her heart promptly sank.

The King of Stars. The only card capable of beating hers.

She heard nothing over the racing of her pulse. She could see the anger and despair on her crew's faces along with the slight furrow between Effie's brows, but she'd made her bed, and it was time to lie in it.

"Well?" she demanded, not trusting herself to say anything further.

Drake leaned down and whispered in Iggy's ear once more.

His first mate paled. "Captain, you can't be serious—" But a sharp look had him swallowing whatever protest he'd been about to make. Licking his lips, Iggy returned his attention to her, his face filled with apology. "Captain Lawless is willing to offer you a deal. Since you and your crew are in need of a ship, he will grant you all passage on the *Lorelei* . . ."

It was too good to be true. There was no way Drake would give her what she needed, not without demanding a hefty cost.

She was right.

"But only if you spend a night with him."

CHAPTER 4

BAST

As soon as the words left the man's lips, chaos reigned. Jagger was the first to explode forward, his fingers outstretched and reaching for the lapel of Drake's coat. The table flipped on its side, cards and coins scattering as Bronn, the one called Cookie, and two others leapt forward right behind him. Their fury was not limited to the captain; they spread their attack, also aiming for his crew.

Caly didn't stay idle either. She kicked one of Drake's men in the chest, sending him toppling backward over his chair. Then she stood and threw an elbow into the gut of another before driving her knee into the groin of the third.

Before Sebastian made heads or tails of what the hell just happened, he was thrown behind a wall of snarling male.

"Not sure this is your scene, mate. Might be best if you sit this one out, yeah?"

Bast had half a mind to tell Lucian where he could stick it but thought better of it. Another lifetime ago, he would have been right there beside the pirates. In this one? He'd be the sorry bastard having his bell rung for saying something inappropriate or, even more likely, sleeping with someone else's wife.

Voice dropping to the soft cadence he only seemed to use with his mate, Lucian asked, "Want me to put a stop to it?"

Effie worried her bottom lip. "No. This has to play out. It'll be over soon."

"You Saw *this*?" Sebastian asked, incredulous.

She gave him a sheepish look. "Not in so many words . . ."

"Still . . . you couldn't have given them a heads up?"

"I told them all that I could."

One of Lawless's men threw a right hook that had blood spraying over the three of them as his unfortunate victim spun in a circle before dropping in a graceless heap on the floor.

Bast raised his brow. "Seems a mite bit lacking, wouldn't you say?"

"You think this is lacking? Sweet summer child, you haven't a clue how good you have it, do you?"

Anger licked up his spine. "Good isn't the word I would choose, no." Jaw tight, he stared out at the writhing mass of bodies, not sure which side was winning, as it was nearly impossible to distinguish one from the other.

Effie reached out and brushed her hand against his arm, her expression soft. "We're all doing the best we can, Bast. I promise. The Mother sent us down this path, and now we must wait while fate runs her course. Everything will happen as it should."

He gave her a begrudging nod, his eyes widening when a pirate came flying at them. He ducked, narrowly missing being knocked out by the unconscious man's peg leg, when Lucian snickered. Given that his gaze was trained on the Keeper and not the full-blown tavern brawl taking place in front of him, it was clear she was the subject of his amusement.

"What's so funny?" Effie demanded.

"Nothing."

"Lucian."

He tucked one of her curls behind her ear, his expression tender. "It's just funny hearing you repeat the same assurances I once gave you. Especially when I can recall with perfect clarity how fiercely you used to hate them."

Her lips twitched. "I'm working for the other side now."

"We've always been on the same side, fledgling."

She laced her fingers through his. "And we always will."

Bast didn't know their story, but it was evident from the way they interacted with one another that they'd seen the very worst life had to offer. It was there in the way they never quite let the other out of their sight, like two celestial bodies locked in orbit, revolving around and existing solely for each other. If not for that bond, he was willing to bet they wouldn't have found themselves here today.

Jealousy curdled in his gut. He wanted what they had, but it seemed all he was destined for was a life of revenge. Needing to get his mind off the tragedy of his life, Bast searched for a familiar face in the crowd. He'd expected to find the minotaur, but with his metallic blue hair, Jagger was the easiest to spot. He had a hand wrapped around the throat of two separate men and was in the process of bashing their skulls together. He appeared so calm that if not for the trickle of blood down his temple or his split lip, Bast wouldn't know he was fighting.

Where's Buttercup? Even as the thought occurred, a flicker of orange caught his eye and he glanced up, a laugh escaping. Apparently, Jagger's protector only intervened in life-threatening matters, because the little finch had sought safety in the rafters.

"Are we really just going to stand here and watch?" Sebastian asked when Bronn spat out a tooth.

"It's almost over," Effie said, still oozing cool confidence.

"How can you tell?"

She didn't need to respond; the answer was soon evident.

"Enough!" Caly's shout rang out as men with swollen eyes and broken noses shuffled away from her. She pressed forward, bringing a familiar man in a knit cap with her. Somehow, she'd managed to get Iggy in a choke hold, a dirty fork pressed against the side of his throat.

There was a beat of silence, and then the rival captain stepped forward. Lawless wasn't empty-handed either. He held a squirming boy fast by a hand at the neck of his shirt. Bast had lost sight of Willie during the fray, but the captain must have known he'd be the ace up his sleeve because as soon as Calypso's eye landed on the dirt-streaked face, she dropped the fork and shoved Iggy away from her.

"I'll agree to your terms," she spat, her eye a glowing emerald green.

Lawless grinned and released the boy, who rushed straight to the minotaur's waiting arms, but Calypso wasn't done.

"You get my crew and our friends to our port, and then—and only then—you will have your night." A heavy scowl darkened Drake's brow, but it only made her smirk. "You never specified *which* night, Lawless. Maybe next time instead of using a lap dog, you should deliver your own ultimatums."

Well . . . that's our transportation sorted.

Effie shot Bast a knowing look he had no trouble interpreting: *Told you so.* He couldn't help but return her small smile. In so many ways, nothing about the night felt as though it went to plan, and yet, they'd gotten exactly what they'd come for: a ship and an army.

Now they just had to get to Ronan and pray it wasn't too late.

CHAPTER 5

RONAN

A roar built in his throat as the unforgiving kiss of Erebos's whip landed across his chest. Pain blossomed, the sting white-hot as skin separated, beads of blood forming only to drip down and join countless other rivers painting his shredded flesh.

"Have you had enough?"

The ability to form words had long since passed. His muscles shook, the magic-nullifying chains shackling him to the wall all that kept him upright. Ronan might not be able to speak, but that didn't mean he couldn't respond. Sweat-soaked hair clung to his face as he slowly lifted his head. His breaths were labored, his body one endless throb, but still he managed to bare his teeth in a feral snarl.

He'd lost count of the number of lashes he'd endured, not to mention the number of days he'd been imprisoned. Other than waking up in the cold, dank cell, he couldn't recall anything after their capture on the beach. But if Erebos thought to defeat him, he would have to try a hell of a lot harder than this.

Summoning his remaining strength, he gritted out, "Is that all you've got?"

Erebos's answering smile was cruel, his malevolent chuckle bouncing off the stone walls of his prison. "Not remotely, but I'll have to save those tricks for the day I can finally rid myself of you. For the time being, you're more valuable to me alive." Never breaking eye contact, he turned his chin to the side, calling, "Isn't that right, moonbeam?"

Shadow appeared beside him like her namesake. Gone was the woman who'd begged for his life on the beach. In her place stood the mindless murderess the High Lord created. Cold. Distant. As untouchable as the very stars themselves.

If she had any reaction to seeing him chained and bloodied, she didn't show it. There wasn't the barest flicker of emotion in her eyes. After everything else he'd endured, *that* truth was the one that flayed him wide open.

Not the torture, nor the threats, but the loss of Reyna.

He tugged at his chains, desperate to reach her. To drop to his knees before her and press his face into her thighs as he begged her to hold on to him. To the truth.

Their truth.

Because if this was how it ended, with him beaten, alone, and forgotten, then what was he fighting for? Why was he holding on for a woman who couldn't or wouldn't hold on for him?

No.

No.

He couldn't afford to let his thoughts veer down that path. Hope was all that got him through the dark years after her disappearance. It would see him through now. It had to.

Because this was not the end.

"See how he struggles? How, even when he's so clearly bested, still he resists?"

Shadow tilted her head, studying him like he was nothing more than an insect. Something that disgusted her. Something to be crushed.

"Why haven't you put him out of his misery?"

"Because he's my gift to you, Shadow mine."

"It's not my birthday."

"He's your wedding present." Much of Erebos's face was cast in darkness, but the sinister curve of his grin was unmistakable. He was eager for Ronan's reaction to his announcement.

Denial tore up his throat, but he swallowed it down, refusing to play right into his hand. This was all part of Erebos's game. Only now, instead of the whip, he wielded words.

"You spoil me, my lord."

Ronan could barely hear Shadow's soft murmur over the roar of his pulse.

It's just a game.

But even in his head, he lacked conviction.

Erebos leaned in, nuzzling into her. "It won't be long now. In fact, aren't you due for your fitting?"

Shadow hummed in assent. "You know I'm much more interested in watching you work than becoming Claudette's pincushion."

Ronan could only just make out one of Erebos's glittering eyes as he curled his arm possessively around her waist, tucking her lithe body against his as he pressed a kiss to the side of her neck. Taunting Ronan. Twisting his metaphorical dagger even deeper and waiting for him to break.

The High Lord had no idea how badly his plan was backfiring. How instead of breaking Ronan, he was igniting a fire that was bringing him back from the pain-shrouded brink. But Ronan gave nothing away, too busy keeping his attention locked on the place where Erebos touched her, tracking the subtle caresses and the ever-so-slight tightening of his fingers on her hip. He noted each and every touch. Searing them into his memory so he could repay every caress once he was free.

Because he *would* be free.

He refused to die here.

"Go on now, moonbeam. It's rude to keep your guest waiting."

Shadow's only response was a slow dip of her chin and one final fleeting look at Ronan before she disappeared out of the cell as silently as she'd entered.

Erebos's smile dropped the second she was gone, though the predatory gleam in his eye remained. He shot forward, no more than an inhuman blur as he crossed the small cell to grasp Ronan's face in one of his hands. Fingers digging into his cheeks, Erebos yanked his head up far past what was comfortable, pulling a groan from him as the muscles of his ravaged body protested the sudden jerk.

"Fight all you want, Chosen. I do so love the sound of your screams."

Ronan tried to spit out words, but he couldn't manage more than a stuttered, "S-s-she will n-never b-be yours."

Erebos's grip on his cheeks tightened. "She already is. But please, by all means, keep lying to yourself. There's nothing sweeter than robbing someone of their hope."

It was too close an echo to his earlier thoughts to be a coincidence. If the man had found a way inside his mind, not even his thoughts were safe.

"You cannot stop what is coming, Ronan. You never could."

"L-Luna—"

"Ah yes, your mother goddess. Quite the beautiful little liar, isn't she? It doesn't matter what she promised you. You. Have already. Lost."

Before Ronan could do more than suck in a breath, Erebos raised his other hand. Dark fog licked up its sides, obscuring it completely. Or perhaps his hand had become the fog? It was hard to make sense around the pain. It was taking everything he had left to follow the conversation.

Erebos moved forward until his mouth was pressed against Ronan's ear. "I know I said I wouldn't kill you, and I won't. But that doesn't mean I'm going to take it easy on you. Far from it, actually," he added with a dark chuckle. "And . . . if I get a little carried away, well, that's what the healers are for."

Without warning, the High Lord dropped Ronan's face and stepped back. "Now, where were we? Ah, yes." He drove his mist-coated hand through Ronan's chest, the extremity reforming as a fist around his heart.

Ronan gasped, unable to breathe through the agony as Erebos squeezed.

"Have you ever held a beating heart in your hand? No? It's quite the rush. Let's see how long you can—"

The words faded away as Ronan finally lost the battle to the pain.

Hours, or perhaps only minutes later, Ronan woke alone in his prison once more. His shoulders were on fire from supporting his full weight, and he was both hot and cold, probably feverish from being left to rot in Erebos's dungeon.

It was hard to know what roused him.

Everything hurt. Even breathing was an agony as it forced his chest to expand, pulling apart freshly healed welts and making them bleed anew.

Erebos hadn't been lying when he said he might get out of control. Ronan had come across roadkill that likely fared better than he had. He'd been tortured before, plenty of times, but his tormentors had been men. Not gods with a sadistic streak a mile long.

There was no end to Erebos's depravity. Or his creativity. Just the memory was enough to pull a groan from his cracked lips.

His chains rattled as he struggled to get his feet solidly beneath him once more, his breathing little more than ragged gasps as fireworks exploded behind his eyes. His leg gave way, the muscles of his thigh too abused to hold him up, and the sudden drop back down made Ronan cry out as his shoulder was torn from its socket.

If Erebos didn't hurry and send that healer he'd mentioned, nature might finish the job before he could.

"Ronan?"

He went still, not trusting that the rasped voice calling him was real. There was a long stretch of silence when all he could hear was the erratic beat of his heart before it came again.

"Ronan?"

Even strained, he recognized the lyrical lilt, and his heart, foolish creature that it was, swelled with hope. "Camille? What are you doing down here?" He had to work for every word, his lungs incapable of drawing a full breath, but he was a stubborn bastard and refused to give up. "Have you come to save me?"

Her harsh bark of laughter was followed by a rattle of chains that did not belong to him. "Not this time, I'm afraid."

His heart sank. She didn't even need to explain what happened; he could piece it together easily enough. Erebos had learned about the part she played aiding in his prior escape—if not everything she'd done to help him. Now she was paying the price for her kindness.

"I . . ." It was a full beat before he had the breath to finish. "I'm sorry."

"Don't apologize, Ronan. My choices landed me here, not yours."

"But—"

"Hush. I'll hear none of it. The Mother sends me where she wills. I could no more deny her than I could my name."

Despite the cavalier nature of the words, he could hear the undercurrent of pain in her voice. The slight bite of tension, the subtle hitch of breath. Erebos had been generous in doling out his punishments.

"Are you . . . that is, has he—"

"The High Lord hasn't touched me," she interjected firmly. Ronan had just begun to let out a thankful breath when she added, "He's reserved that pleasure for his Vulture."

If he'd had any autonomy over his body, he'd have curled his hands into fists and torn free of his shackles. As it was, he barely managed a desperate rattle. He'd never been very good at dealing with the suffering of others. Knowing that her suffering was because of him, because she'd helped him, ate away at him. Made him feel crazed and helpless in new, unbearable ways.

He wanted to say something, anything, to comfort her, but he didn't have the words. What promises could he make? What assurances could he offer that she wouldn't see for the fool's dreams they were?

But Camille didn't seem to require any. Rather, she was the one offering solace.

"Does your cell have a window? Mine does. If I hold myself just so, I can make out the moon. She's so beautiful. I'd thought her so before, but in here, where she is the only light I can see, I realize I was wrong. She's the most precious to those who have nothing else. The promise that darkness is never absolute. She is the proof that there will always be a sliver of light."

Tears burned the backs of Ronan's eyes, his throat tight with emotion. How was it this woman always seemed to know what he most needed to hear? Ronan released a shuddering breath, a lone tear burning a path down his cheek before he blinked the rest of them away.

Camille's sweet, exhausted voice reached him once more. "Do not give up on her, Ronan. She has not given up on you."

"I won't."

He didn't know which *she* Camille referred to, Luna or Reyna, but it didn't matter. Time and time again, the Mother had proven that she had not abandoned him—Camille's constant presence was evidence enough of that. She'd sent him on this journey and ensured that he had what he needed every step of the way. He would not doubt her now.

As for Reyna . . . he could no more give up on her than he could will his heart to stop beating. He'd come to Empyria vowing to free her or die trying. So far as he could tell, the only thing that had changed were the rules of the game.

I won't, he vowed, holding the promise deep in his heart and repeating it so often it became his mantra.

I will never give up.

CHAPTER 6

REYNA

Her hands were still shaking twenty minutes later when she finally arrived back at her suite. She'd known it was coming, the summons. Naively, she'd thought a lifetime of battle and bloodshed would have prepared her. But no. Nothing could have prepared her for what waited for her in that cell.

Ronan.

Her beautiful, honorable Ronan. Trussed up against the wall, arms shackled above his head, chest and legs bare, his powerful frame coated in the crimson of his own blood. From the look of it, he'd already endured more lashes than should have been possible. In far too many places, the overlapping welts left thick divots in his once smooth skin. And his tattoo, the Daejaran Jaka he'd once shown her with such pride, was little more than ribbons.

It had taken every single cell in her body to play the game and keep her expression wiped clear. She'd had to breathe through her nose to avoid heaving up the contents of her stomach then and there. But it was his life in the balance, and for him, there was nothing she wouldn't do. Case in point, this sham of a marriage.

She was no stranger to death. In fact, she'd once considered him an old friend.

Not anymore.

Not now that she knew the immortal's true face and was intimately aware of what a brutal bastard he could be.

Now he was a mark, and she an assassin biding her time.

You created me, Father, and now you must face my wrath. I will make you pay for every scratch you leave on him sevenfold. You might be a god, Erebos, but even the Lord of Death can bleed.

With the unspoken vow heavy on her tongue, Reyna swept into her room, her careful mask back in place.

"Forgive me, Claudette. I lost track of time."

She'd only met the young designer a couple of times, but as always, she was taken by her charm and style. Just like their first two meetings, she wore head-to-toe black. Though today, her simple shirt and skintight tailored pants were combined with a waist-to-floor half skirt, creating the illusion that she wore a dress from the back. Her short white hair was shaved on the sides, though the top was an artful tousle. Her brown eyes were warm and playful. Her wide lips already curving up in welcome. "No need to apologize, lady. The High Lord's intended is never late."

Reyna hoped her answering smile appeared genuine and not like the sickly grimace it felt like. She had to fight the urge to vomit every time someone mentioned her upcoming wedding. The only thing that helped her retain her calm façade was imagining all the various ways she could kill Erebos once Ronan was safely out of his clutches. It was surprisingly effective. For example, today she'd pictured driving a serrated dagger through his eye. Yesterday it had been a poison-tipped hairpin underneath his fingernail.

Just like that, she felt damn near blissful.

Eager to get this fitting over with, Reyna glanced around her chambers, expecting to see gowns of various styles or stages of design scattered across the room. Or, at the very least, swatches of fabrics in all manner of hues for her to pick from. But there was only a lone rack with a single garment bag.

"I thought we were working on the ceremony gown today?"

"Oh, we are. The High Lord has already sent me his specification."

Of course he has. My choices are no longer my own.

Reyna wasn't sure why she'd expected any differently. He'd made it clear when he'd come for her that she would be his puppet in every way. And then again when he'd tried his compulsion on her.

Only this time . . . it didn't take.

Reyna didn't know what was different. Whether it was the proximity to Ronan or the lingering effects of the oasis's pool, when he'd whispered his filthy lies into her ear, she recognized them for exactly what they were.

And then she'd acted her ass off pretending otherwise.

It was the role of a lifetime. Two lifetimes, really. Hers and Ronan's. She could not give Erebos any room to doubt his spell had taken hold. It's why she played his games. Forced herself to pretend she was the same subservient, albeit deadly, doll she'd always been.

No matter how badly it made her skin crawl.

Maybe you should string him up and leave him for the crows . . .

As it had every other time, the sinister line of thinking did the trick, and she was able to return to the conversation that Claudette had unknowingly continued without her.

" . . . made it quite easy on me, in fact. Other than some alterations, the dress should be nearly done." Claudette gestured for Reyna to spin around and undress. "I want you to have the full effect."

She mutely raised her brows but nodded.

As the High Lord's Lady, she'd be expected to wear something new daily. If not multiple times a day. In fact, the ceremony gown was only one of about seven outfits she'd be expected to wear during the multi-day celebration. Since her back was to Claudette and her shirt currently obscured her face, Reyna gave in to the urge to roll her eyes. What an exquisite waste of time.

Fashion had always been a necessary evil to her, the right outfit key to the success of her assignments, be it an assassination or a seduction. So it wasn't that she didn't appreciate a finely made garment or see the appeal of something special and new. She did. She just had about eight hundred more important things to worry about, and black leather pants and a simple black tunic almost always seemed to suit her needs.

"Arms up, my lady," Claudette said, coming up behind her in a rustle of fabric. "This one's a bit tricky, so bear with me."

It's a gown; how tricky can it be?

Ten minutes later, Reyna was forced to amend her initial disbelief.

Only loosely stitched together, each panel had to be draped over her head and then tugged into place. If not for Claudette's familiarity with the individual pieces, Reyna wouldn't have been able to make heads or tails of the garment.

Just when she thought they were done, Claudette began the process over with a second fabric, this one gauzy and a touch transparent where the other was a classic satin, both in shades of deepest black. Without the aid of a mirror, Reyna had no way of picturing the overall effect.

"Erebos came up with this?" she asked when Claudette fussed over the placement of the final fabric panel.

Removing a needle from between her lips, the dressmaker looked up from where she crouched on the floor and gave her a sheepish smile. "Well, I might have taken a few liberties. It's not every day a girl gets to dress the future Lady, let alone for her wedding."

This time Reyna didn't have to work as hard to force a smile. She may not be excited about her nuptials, but she could appreciate what this opportunity meant for Claudette.

"All right, almost ready."

"Almost?" she asked with a disbelieving laugh. "What's left? You've got me covered from throat to ankle."

"Just wait. You'll see."

The woman's excitement was palpable. Reyna had no idea what to expect, but even if she did, she wouldn't have come close to the truth.

Claudette raced around the room, throwing curtains closed and blowing out candles. When only one candle remained, she walked Reyna in front of the full-body mirror and ordered her to close her eyes. The rush of footsteps told her Claudette was dealing with the final candle.

"Okay, open them!"

Reyna did and immediately gasped. "Claudette . . . this is . . ."

She didn't have the words for it.

The dressmaker moved to stand just behind her. "He asked me for starlight. So I gave him the stars."

And she had.

Rather than sewing panels together, as Reyna assumed, she'd been stitching dozens of tiny stones to the material. Stones that glowed the palest lavender in the dark. Set on top of and within the layers of black fabric, they replicated the glitter of stars in the night sky.

It didn't take more than a subtle shift in the mirror for Reyna to understand why the job had to be done while she was wearing the gown. As she moved, so did the stones, some shifting beneath gauzy pieces, others coming into full view, creating a twinkling effect. For a people who worshipped the heavens, this dress was an ode to the night and the celestial bodies that adorned it.

"It's magic," she finally managed, unexpectedly emotional. Swept up in the moment, she forgot that her wedding was a sham and allowed herself to imagine how Ronan might react if he were the one waiting for her at the other end of the aisle. She'd never been one to care about such things, but the depth with which she longed for that reality took her breath away.

The dressmaker squealed and clapped her hands. "I'm so happy you love it. I know it's not exactly traditional, but—"

"Claudette, it's a work of art. Truly. People will be speaking about this for decades to come."

"Well, of course. Such is the nature of a royal wedding."

Reyna spun around and caught the woman's wrists in her hands. "No. Not the wedding, *you*. You are exceptionally talented. A true original that deserves recognition. Mothers and brides-to-be will be knocking on your door, begging to get one of your original creations. As they should."

"There's no need to beg when they can pay for the privilege," she said with a laugh, though Reyna could see how much her praise meant to the young designer.

She supposed that was the one good thing that came with her unwanted title—she could help those less fortunate than her. Though it was hard to feel much was fortunate about her position at the moment. The man she loved was trapped in a dungeon, being tortured by a god as a way to keep her in line while he stole both her power and her autonomy. Oh, and forced her to be his wife. A real fairy tale, that.

Reyna's smile fractured.

"My lady? Are you all right?"

"What? Oh, yes." She forced a laugh. "I just realized I haven't the faintest idea how I'm supposed to get this off."

"Well, that's your new husband's job, isn't it?" Claudette gave her a saucy wink. "But it's easier than it looks, I promise. Here, let me show you."

As the dressmaker got to work excavating Reyna from her master-piece, she continued with her endless stream of animated chatter. Which was both welcome and helpful because it hid the fact that Reyna's thoughts were centered on the man she was desperate to save.

And the future they may never have if Erebos got his way.

CHAPTER 7

REYNA

For a woman who was arguably the second most powerful person in the entire realm, she felt more prisoner than future empress. Her days were plotted out down to the second, and any deviation required express permission from the High Lord himself.

Each morning one of the staff would arrive with the day's schedule, not that one was needed. It was the same thing every day. Wake up thinking of Ronan. Eat and plot out a way to free Ronan. Bathe and worry about Ronan. Dress and find a way to pretend she wasn't thinking about Ronan. Attend Erebos. Dine with Erebos. Walk with Erebos. Visit Ronan. Try not to murder Erebos. Attend some wedding-related event with Erebos while thinking about Ronan. Fall over in her bed and fight a losing war between fury and tears because she hadn't saved Ronan until she'd eventually drift into a fitful sleep that was somehow blessedly free of dreams from which she'd wake and begin the ghastly mess all over again.

She was exhausted. And bored.

So. Fucking. Bored.

She wasn't even allowed to go on missions or train anymore, although Reyna supposed that wasn't much of a surprise. Why would her captor send her off on her own with an arsenal of weapons? He didn't even allow her to have unchaperoned visits unless her visitor was on his approved list.

Erebos had effectively cut her off from everything that had once given her days meaning. And color. Or, hell, variety.

More than once, she'd caught herself missing Shadow. At least when she hadn't known better, the invisible collar binding her to the High Lord hadn't chafed quite so much. Now it felt like the unseen shackle grew tighter every day. Choking her. Cutting off her air. Slowly killing her.

Sometimes, she wished it would. If only to escape the never-ending misery. For while Ronan might be the one in the dungeon, he wasn't the only one being tortured. The difference? Her wounds were hidden, the means of her torment of the emotional and psychological variety. In truth, there was no way to know which of them Erebos was hurting more. He'd selected their punishments well.

But the part that cut deepest? There wasn't anything she could do about it. Not yet, and it was the forced inaction that truly cut away at her. If not for the man held captive in the depths of the palace, she would have tossed Erebos over the damned balcony seven times over.

Logically, she knew defeating him wouldn't be that easy. It was the only reason she hadn't tried. He was a god. *Her* god, technically. She had no hope of defeating him on her own.

Though she wasn't without allies.

If she could free Ronan, maybe there was a way he could get ahold of Helena and the rest of the Chosen. Surely together they could find a way to defeat the Lord of Death. The Chosen had trapped him once before. It would stand to reason they should be able to do so again.

At least, that's what she kept telling herself.

Reyna stood in the early morning breeze, staring out at the sapphire sea far below as her mind raced with plans. Hopes. Prayers. They amounted to the same thing, really.

In the end, all were futile so long as Ronan was locked away. She would not leave him here to rot. Not once in five years had he abandoned his quest to save her. She owed him the same unfailing devotion.

Even if she couldn't afford to let him know it.

She wished there was some way to get a message to him. A servant who was loyal to her. But no one could be trusted. Reyna's defeated sigh was lost on the wind, and her nails scraped across the railing as her grip painfully tightened.

Except, perhaps . . .

"Careful, moonbeam. One less discerning than I might assume, wearing a frown like that, you're up to no good."

Careful to keep her body from tensing, she slowly spun to face her unwelcome guest. "Who, me?"

Erebos stood in the doorway between her bedroom and balcony, looking far too handsome to be the sadistic, manipulative god she knew him to be. While beauty had nothing to do with evil, it only seemed fair that in the case of one so vile, his outsides should match his insides. At least then, his victims might sense the trap before they walked straight into it.

He didn't rise to the bait. Instead, he closed the distance between them and brushed a stray piece of hair out of her eyes. "What's weighing on you, Shadow mine?"

To anyone else, the question would have seemed doting. But she could easily hear the undercurrent of steel in his voice. He didn't trust her, not like he used to.

"I wouldn't say anything was weighing on me," she said with a light laugh, scrambling to come up with some viable excuse.

"No? Then what were you thinking about?"

"I was trying to recall the name of a ship, actually."

His brow quirked. "A ship? Really?"

She nodded.

"Why?"

Lying to the High Lord was dangerous. She had to play this so, so carefully, which meant her lies had to be mired in truth.

"I recall hearing the tale of a famous pirate ship captained by a female. They said she was a hundred times more bloodthirsty and ruthless than her male counterparts, but for the life of me, I can't recall the name of her ship. You don't happen to know, do you?" she asked, mentally crossing her fingers.

"Can't say that I do," Erebos answered, his eyes still holding the weight of suspicion, though his voice was courteous.

She hummed, feigning disappointment. "I wonder if Glinta knows. Do you think I might be able to go down to the market today? It's going to drive me mad until I have the answer."

"I suppose I might be able to spare you for an hour. You'll take Dominic with you, though."

Sonofabitch.

"Of course."

He tipped his head, his lips quirking up in a smile she knew better than to trust. "Why are you thinking of pirates, moonbeam? Contemplating a career change?"

She laughed. "Hardly. The sea just beckoned this morning. I was thinking of those that call her home, and my thoughts wandered. Just idle silliness. You know how it is."

"Idle silliness," he repeated. "I can't say either of those are words I would use to describe the two of us."

Reyna pretended to consider. "No, I guess they aren't."

Erebos lightly brushed a finger under her chin, his smile blinding. "I suppose I should be thankful for your spontaneous bout of *silliness*. Here I was worried you were having second thoughts."

Her smile felt like it cracked at the edges, and she fought hard to keep every thought and fear off her face. Considering her opinion never once factored into his plans for her future, they would have been *first* thoughts, but any suspicion where she was concerned was problematic. For there to be any chance, she had to be above reproach. Ronan's life depended on it.

"It would seem I'm not the only one susceptible to silliness this morning."

"Hmm," he murmured, his eyes searching hers. "It's a good thing there will be no reason for such concerns after we're wed."

It felt like she swallowed one of her daggers, and at first, she couldn't manage more than a strained huff of laughter. There was no way anything she said at that moment would have sounded sincere.

Unless it was a death threat.

But since silence wasn't an option, after a beat, she asked, "Oh? Why's that?"

His grin should have been a carnal promise, but all it did was make her stomach spasm.

"Because you'll be too busy with me to leave our bed, let alone give thought to anyone else."

Why? Because you're planning on murdering me in my sleep? Well, the joke's on you, because if we make it to the wedding night, I'm taking you out first.

This time her smile was genuine. "Is that so?"

"Oh, I'll ensure it."

IN THE END, Dominic didn't accompany her to the marketplace. He was tied up with some other matter of actual importance and couldn't be spared. But that didn't mean she was allowed to walk the half dozen blocks from the palace to the town's center by herself.

Far from.

Erebos had insisted upon a full retinue. Because that's exactly what she wanted. To create a spectacle of herself and draw even more eyes her way when trying to extract and exchange sensitive—not to mention traitorous—information.

Not that she'd expected anything different. There was nowhere she could go in the city proper, nothing she could do that wouldn't get back to the High Lord by way of Dovina's network of spies. It wasn't the guards who worried her; it was the eyes she couldn't see that were the true issue.

Glinta cast a dubious glance at the contingent of armed guards and then back at her. "It's not every day I get a visit from one of the flock. Something tells me the High Lord ain't seeking a bit of the ol' salt serpent for his evenin' meal."

Reyna bit back a smile. "No. He's never been one for such delicacies."

"His Prissiness? Not one for delicacies?" Glinta scoffed. "Well, slap me arse and tickle me fanny. I wouldn't have called that one."

This time there was no holding back her laugh. Glinta was unfailingly refreshing. She hadn't had many excuses to get to know the fish merchant beyond basic pleasantries, but she was a cornerstone of the community. Everyone knew her, and she knew everyone. Which made her an excellent person to go to for information. Reyna also happened to know that she played a key role in aiding Ronan once before, which made her an ally.

"Well, if you're not here for me goods, what are you here for, luv?" Glinta's eyes went wide, and she clutched her throat. "Wait! There ain't a contract out on me, is there? I swear, no matter what that right cunt Nattie says, I didn't bewitch her man. Booker came to me of his own free will, mark my words. How was I ta know he was still fucking her on the regular? Nattie may as well put up a turnstile in place of her door for the number of menfolk that come and go all hours of the night."

"Um, I'm sure you have the right of it, but Nattie didn't send me. Or Booker, for that matter. I'm actually here for me. I have a question for you."

That shut the old bird up. "That so? I thought information was the Raven's game."

"It is. But as I said, this is for me, not the High Lord."

"Fair 'nuff. What is it you're lookin' to know?" Glinta scraped her eyes up and down Reyna's figure. "Pretty gal like you must know which end of the knob to work, so you can't be here for my sexual expertise. Which is a pity, really, 'cause they don't call me Glinta the Good for nothin'. No . . . fancy lady like you . . . you'd be after something else. The kind o' trade best done in the dark, if I had a guess."

"I'm here to ask you about a certain pirate, actually." Since that was her cover story, she couldn't forget to mention it, but she stared hard at Glinta as she said it. Willing her to pick up on the unspoken meaning behind the request.

The fishmonger didn't disappoint. "Pirates? And what would I possibly know about the scourge of the seas?" Her voice dropped, and her gaze shot back to the men standing watch a few feet away. "Dangerous game you're playing, lass."

"The most," Reyna agreed.

They shared a nod of understanding.

"So this is about him." The words were breathed, Glinta ducking her head so her lips couldn't be easily read as she started moving things about her stall to make it appear that they were discussing her wares.

"You've heard?"

"Who hasn't? There isn't a person within a day's ride that doesn't know who's fallen from his Lordship's grace."

"Then you understand . . ." Reyna swallowed and tried to code her words, "why the thought of such a vessel intrigues me."

"I do. O'course I do. Doesn't mean I can help ya."

"I have coin." She discreetly set a heavy purse on the table between them.

Glinta licked her lips, her voice pitched low. "So did he, luvvy. Didn't save him in the end. Or you, for that matter."

"Please," she begged, her lips barely moving as she breathed the word.

Reyna could only guess as to Glinta's connections, but if the woman had been able to get Ronan passage on Calypso's ship before, surely there were other contacts she could reach out to who could assist in a similar escape. Smugglers or other such folk who worked outside the strict purview of the law. People who weren't loyal to Erebos, only to the coin in their pocket.

People willing to risk the High Lord's wrath in exchange for a glorious payday.

Glinta held her gaze, shrewd eyes assessing before she gave her an 'it's your funeral' sort of shrug and palmed the coin purse.

"Captain No Beard doesn't take kindly to folks askin' after her crew, but I'll see what I can dig up. Now, you gonna buy some fish or what?"

CHAPTER 8

EREBOS

"It's as she said, my liege. She went to the fishmonger's stall and discussed pirates and purchased fish. Then she stopped by a few other stalls, though she didn't speak with or purchase anything further, before returning to the palace."

"That's it?" he asked his Raven, not sure why his disbelief was equal to his relief.

"That's everything."

He didn't believe Shadow's story about the pirate ship. Not for a second. And yet . . . he had no reason to doubt her either. She'd shown no hint of resisting his compulsion, so there was no reason for her to remember her time on the *Revenge* or the crew members she'd met. Nor would this be the first time she'd gotten a wild hair and wanted to hunt down answers. Even her dreamscape, when he walked it, had been calm. In every possible way, she'd been his perfectly obedient toy since returning.

Still, he couldn't let go of the certainty she was up to something.

Maybe he was simply reading too much into things after Luna's warning. Seeing threats where there were none. Or . . . perhaps his meddlesome wife had found a new way to interfere that he'd yet to detect.

He wasn't the only one with the ability to wield compulsion. Had Luna found a way to infect his Night Stalker? Was she the one who sent her thoughts of the lady pirate? If so, why? The bitch was dead.

Wasn't she?

"What of the pirate ship?"

"What of it, High Lord? It sank, along with most of its crew."

"And the captain?"

"No Beard has yet to be seen or heard from. She's not back in Glimmermere, if that is your concern."

"Keep an eye out for her and any of her known associates."

"Of course, my lord."

He didn't say anything further, his attention returning to his ponderings until she prompted, "Will there be anything else?"

Annoyed she'd interrupted him, he gave her a brusque, "No. Leave me."

He didn't bother to watch as Dovina left his study in a swirl of dark skirts. He was too busy trying to figure out what his errant wife was up to. It wasn't like her to play with his creations, or hers, for that matter. She preferred a hands-off approach. One that allowed her to watch from a distance, permitting her Chosen to live in the playground she'd created for them mostly undisturbed. She once told him her joy came from watching them learn and discover on their own.

What a glorious waste of time.

In news that would likely surprise no one, he was the exact opposite. He had better things to do than sit around for a couple hundred years waiting for his spawn to get with the program.

So why was she deviating now?

Because you've gotten under her skin. She's finally taking you seriously.

The thought made him smile, because it was about damned time she actually *saw* him again.

Well, do you like what you see, Luna? Do you miss me?

He glanced up at the moon, knowing it was folly to seek out her profile in the crescent, yet doing so anyway. She wasn't really there. The celestial body was named for her, not the other way around. Not to mention that this time of day, the hunk of rock was barely more than a hazy suggestion in the sky. For some reason the reminder made him feel even more disconnected from her.

His grin faded, his thoughts returning to the problem at hand. Knowing Luna's 'why' only begged another, more important, question. What did she hope to accomplish?

Erebos didn't have an answer for that one. Although knowing his darling wife, she was likely trying to teach him some kind of lesson.

Is that it, Luna? Are you trying to educate me? Well, perhaps you're the one who needs to learn a thing or two, ever think about that? Here. We'll start with an easy one. First lesson: Sometimes the student becomes the master.

Smug grin restored, he spun away from the balcony and eagerly made for his new favorite room in the palace.

Oh yes, that's right, darling. Two can play this game, and unlike you, I was never one who minded breaking someone else's toys.

RONAN

THE BODY CAN ONLY WITHSTAND SO MUCH before it shuts down, unable to process the horrors it's endured. But the mind . . . the mind is a fertile and terrible place. A breeding ground for all manner of torments. It's wild, uncontained, and, as every child quickly learns, where the monsters live.

Logic is no match for fear. For the sort of pain that cannot be contained by flesh. Once the mind has been overtaken, it doesn't matter how many times a person reminds themselves it isn't real. That it's just their imagination playing tricks on them or a nightmare from which they cannot wake up. Until it runs its course, they are lost to it. A slave to the all-consuming terror.

But what's worse, far worse, is that there's no freedom from an idea. For once the insidious fiend has taken root, it becomes immortal, lingering in the dark recesses of one's psyche, waiting to strike anew.

And *that* is where true torture begins.

Ronan knew he was hallucinating. That Erebos had begun using his magic in place of his fists, no longer satisfied with the snap of bones or his grunts of pain. The Lord of Death demanded his screams, and he was, if nothing else, a master of his craft.

But knowing did not spare Ronan from his suffering. It did nothing to counteract Erebos's depraved machinations.

The grisly images dancing through his mind could never be unseen or forgotten. The broken, mangled bodies of those he loved would forever be imprinted. Along with that damning voice—his voice—insisting that their suffering was because of him.

This is all your fault. You could have prevented it. Had you only stayed where you belonged, no harm would have ever befallen them.

But you were selfish.

Careless.

You turned your back on the ones you were supposed to protect. And now . . .

Now they will all burn.

"No," he protested. But it was a weak rasp at best. His throat was raw, his lungs barely capable of drawing in breath.

"Oh, come on, Ronan. You can do better than that. Elysia's mighty Shield? What a joke. Fight back."

He tried, his fury still a wild spark beneath his ribs, but it required more than he had to so much as lift his head.

"Pathetic," Erebos growled from his perch by the cell door.

As one might imagine, his stay in the dungeons was hardly one of luxury. Despite Erebos sending healers as promised, Ronan was far from well. Anything he was given, such as water or bread, was only out of necessity. And even that was begrudging. So he was alive, yes, but only just enough for the High Lord to continue his games.

"You are weak. Not even worth my attention. Do you know what I do to those who waste my time?"

He couldn't answer. Not even in his mind.

Erebos stalked across the cell and gripped him by the hair, yanking his head back. "I asked you a question, Shield. Do you know what I do to those who. Waste. My. Time?"

He tried to form words. Any words. But he couldn't manage more than a pained moan.

"I make them wish they'd never been born."

Erebos had called him weak. He was right.

Ronan once believed otherwise. That he was strong in both mind and body. Now he realized what a fool he'd been, for it didn't take more than the first image—that of his beautiful goddaughter, eyes foggy and unseeing—to shred through every last one of his internal defenses.

Latching onto Ronan's misery, Erebos sent image after image of Stella his way. Soon combining the pictures with her little hiccupped sobs. "Save me, Wo-Wo."

He didn't even know if the toddler was capable of stringing together such a sentence, but his mind could no longer distinguish between truth and lie.

Nor could his heart, for that matter.

"S-stop," he stuttered. "I b-beg of you."

Erebos grinned. A cruel, coldly triumphant thing that lit up his eyes like shards of glass. "No. I don't think I will. You brought this on yourself, Shield. You tried to take what is mine. Now you will pay the price. Over. And over. And over again."

More images followed the declaration, this time of Reyna. Effie. Von and Helena. Bast. One after the other. Each one in torment. Each one screaming his name. Begging him to make it stop. Asking how he could let them suffer so.

Tears mingled with the spit and blood and dirt coating him. He was one broken mess. His heart and mind now as wrecked as the rest of him.

Scream after scream was torn from him as he was forced to bear witness to their brutal deaths.

"I . . . I c-can't . . . n-no more . . ."

He was so far gone he wasn't even aware of what he was asking for. His hatred was twin only to his suffering. But right now, the grief drowned out everything else.

"Begging for mercy, are you? How adorably *mortal*. Usually, I'd be more than happy to acquiesce, but I find I quite enjoy the sound of your torment. In fact, I may never let you die. What do you think of that?" Erebos's voice turned musing and oddly gleeful. "I could leave you down here to rot. Pop in for a visit every now and then, likely still smelling of my new wife's perfect cunt while I remind you why one should never cross the Father of Dreams."

Ronan whimpered.

"You get it now, don't you?" he crooned, still holding his head up by his hair, his eyes scanning Ronan's ravaged face. "It's not the Lord of Death you should fear. Death is a kindness. The ultimate act of mercy. But the one who can walk amongst your dreams? Who can shape the very reality of your mind?" Erebos's voice dropped to a chilling whisper. "He's the one who will destroy you."

Shudder after shudder worked along Ronan's body because he knew down to the very marrow of his bones that it was true.

Lifting his other hand, Erebos patted Ronan's cheek. "Just remember that it's your actions that caused this. You alone are responsible for your suffering. If you had only left her alone, you never would have earned yourself my undivided attention. But alas, you did, so now—"

Erebos stopped with a surprised grunt, confusion washing across his face. He opened his mouth as if to speak, expression clearing as his eyes refocused on Ronan's face.

But then it happened again.

A soft grunt and a wrinkle of confusion.

Erebos took two staggering steps backward. "That's all for today."

Ronan had no idea what had just happened. Even if he'd been in his right mind, there was no explanation for the High Lord's sudden departure. He'd been well in the thick of his game, with no signs of stopping. And then he'd just . . . left.

A soft sob slipped from Ronan's lips, followed by a shuddering inhale and a tidal wave of gratitude. Not for Erebos, but for whatever invisible force had seen fit to intervene and grant Ronan the very thing he'd been so desperately begging for.

Mercy.

CHAPTER 9

KIERAN

"It's time to wake up, Dreamer. You've been asleep for far too long."

The feminine voice floated to him through the mist, tickling the edge of his awareness and caressing his senses.

"Who are you?"

He didn't speak the words so much as think them, yet they echoed with the same ethereal quality as her own.

And it wasn't just his voice; everything felt different. Insubstantial. Fleeting. He didn't feel so much as exist. He didn't see so much as sense. And he wasn't exactly awake, more like . . . sentient. Conscious for the first time in—

A frisson of anxiety shot through him, disturbing the mist.

"Wh-where am I?"

"Shh, Dreamer. Give yourself a moment to adjust."

"Why can't I move? What's wrong with my body?"

"You're trapped."

A bolt of panic followed the declaration, the mist rippling away from him like water before flowing back and returning to its original state.

"What do you mean, trapped?"

"Exactly that. Your body has been taken over, your mind a hostage."

"B-but how? By who? When?"

The ripples were full-on waves now, his fear and panic battering him from every side.

"Think of it like a siege. It happened slowly over time. Brick by brick. Or perhaps more accurately, dream by dream."

"My dreams?"

Kieran's mind raced. Or he thought it was his mind. Everything was such a blur. The last thing he remembered was saying goodbye to Cyril so he could find the girl from his dreams. She had a name, but it felt so distant now. A whole other lifetime ago.

There was a hesitant, apologetic quality to the voice when it next came. "I'm sorry, Kieran. You've been used terribly. Manipulated by forces beyond your control. Made to do . . . terrible things."

"I . . . I would never."

But then the images came. One after the other. Each memory blossoming like a firework and fading just as quickly, only to be replaced by the next.

Leaving home. Joining the Keepers. Meeting Effie. Her rejection. His awful plan to win her back. Finding the prophecy and staging the markers. The attack on the citadel.

Elders above, the citadel.

So many innocent people dead.

Because of him.

"No. No! I-I wouldn't. It was just a dream. Only a dream."

"Your dreams were sent to deceive you. To send you down this path. You've been lied to for longer than you can imagine."

He didn't even know what to do with that information.

"Maybe that's true, but I didn't actually *do* those things."

"You did."

"No! You've got the wrong person."

"You *did*, Kieran. Not wholly by choice, true. But it was the weaknesses of your heart that allowed Erebos to exploit you. He provoked your jealousy, heightened your desperation, all so you'd become susceptible to the ideas he planted in your mind. He needed you to free him. Every task you completed helped turn you into his perfect vessel. And with every step down that dark path, you opened yourself up more fully to his assault, ceded more control, until inevitably, your defenses were destroyed, and he walked right in. As if he'd been invited."

Kieran felt like he was going to be sick. Or he *would* be sick if he had a body. The same instincts and sensations were there. The shortness of breath. The roll of his stomach. The tightness of his throat. And yet . . . he had none of those things.

All of this was in his mind.

"No," he moaned. "This isn't real. None of this is real."

"It is, Dreamer. It is the most honest and true thing you've experienced in a very long time."

"How? How are you able to reach me now?"

"Don't worry about that. Our time grows short, and there's one very important message I have left to impart."

He was reeling, barely able to comprehend all that she'd already told him, but it didn't matter. She wasn't finished with him yet.

"You need to fight, Dreamer."

"Fight? How? You said yourself I'm trapped. A hostage."

"Be that as it may, it's time for you to break free and reclaim what was stolen from you. Fight, Kieran. If not for yourself, for all of those who can no longer fight for themselves because of you."

It was a low blow, but fuck if it wasn't effective.

Now that he knew the truth, that none of it had been a dream and every single one of those terrible things had actually happened, he couldn't turn a blind eye to what he'd done. People had suffered—died—because of him. There was no ignoring that, no matter how desperately he wished he could. He might be a selfish, arrogant prick, but he wasn't a monster. He never would have done any of those things without Erebos's influence.

This he knew.

This was the truth he clung to.

"That's it. *Fight.* Take back what is yours."

Her voice was fading now.

"No. Wait! Don't leave me here. Please. I don't want to be alone."

"This part you must do by yourself. You want to atone for your sins?"

"Yes, more than anything."

"Then fight."

"How?"

There was no answer.

"How, damn you?" he screamed, the mist around him exploding outward.

His breath caught when what appeared to be a flicker of light filled the space vacated by the mist. As the echo of his shout died down, the mist returned.

Curious, Kieran let out a wordless bellow. Once again, the mist reacted, and when the sound ceased, it reclaimed the emptiness.

Not at all sure what he was doing, but feeling he was onto something, Kieran released the floodgates, pouring everything he had into the scream. His fear. His regret. His fury. All of it. And as his emotions boiled over, the mist retreated further and further away, that distant light coming more into focus.

He screamed for longer than should have been possible if the sound had been fueled by the oxygen in his lungs. But he didn't stop, knowing this may be the only shot he had to break through.

So he dug deeper. He found long-forgotten pain and poured it into what he now realized was a war cry. And with the pain went his grief and guilt. Grief for what would never be, the family he'd lost, the love he'd never know. Guilt for being weak in the first place. For being a target for the predator who had turned him into someone he didn't even recognize.

And finally, just when it felt like he'd transferred every last drop of himself into that ear-splitting shout, he added his truth.

I am here.

I am here, and I will never allow you to send me away again. You fooled me once, Master of Lies, Manipulator of Dreams, but I know the truth now.

You may call me the Dreamer, but my name is Kieran. I am a prince of

Eatos. My father's unwanted son. My mother's noble sacrifice. My sister's failed protector.

You cannot trick me, Deceiver. I know my heart. I know who I am.

And I will never again be your willing vessel.

With those words, the light exploded outward like thousands of glittering shards of glass. And as the shards fell away, the light was replaced with a new image. One so repugnant, Kieran tried to draw away.

Nothing happened.

That's when he realized that despite the weight of his body settling around him, he had no control over it. He was frozen in place, threats pouring from his lips in a voice he didn't recognize. His mind had broken free, but his body was still the prisoner of another.

So Kieran did the only thing he could. He kept shouting.

He couldn't stop.

He wouldn't.

Because as he stared out at the red-haired man chained to the wall, one thing was crystal clear. The fight to reclaim his life had only just begun.

CHAPTER 10

BAST

"*L*and ho!"

"At last," he groaned, pushing himself up on trembling legs at the sound of the first mate's cry.

Sebastian had never been so happy to see dry land in his life. To be fair, he'd never much considered it one way or the other, but the storm that had chased them back to Glimmermere made for rough waters.

More than once, he'd been certain the gale would overtake the *Lorelei* and capsize it, but despite the merciless wind, pelting rain, and rolling waves, the true brunt of the tempest never quite caught up. He had his suspicions as to why, but since he'd spent the better part of the voyage with his head buried in a bucket, he never got around to confirming whether Bronn's steady presence on the deck had anything to do with it. There was more to Calypso's crew than they let on, but he hadn't been in any state to ferret out their secrets.

"Drop anchor!" Iggy shouted. No one balked at the first mate giving orders. The captain had rarely left his quarters after being outsmarted by Calypso. Not that Bast blamed the man. His pride had taken quite a spanking. And not the fun kind.

Then Iggy's words penetrated the cloud of his relief, sending panic

67

blasting straight through it. *Wait, what? Drop anchor? Here? But we are still leagues away from the dock, and even more important, precious land.*

Scrambling forward, he gripped Bronn's shirt in his fist and gave the quartermaster a desperate shake. "What does he mean, drop anchor?"

"I would think it quite obvious," the pirate said, grinning as he slapped a hand on Bast's shoulder. "He means . . . drop anchor." The slowly emphasized words made those nearest laugh, but Sebastian was uncomfortably familiar with being the butt of every joke, so their laughter hardly fazed him.

"Here? But land is still ho." He pointed dramatically. "I have to get off this damned ship. I'll die if I have to stay aboard another minute."

"One can only hope," Jagger muttered, the boson not having warmed to him any further despite their journey together. Sebastian didn't take it personally; the man didn't seem to care for anyone save his bird and his captain.

"If you haven't died yet, Bast, what with the way your stomach has been attempting to crawl out your throat, I think it's safe to assume you're going to make it," Bronn said.

Releasing the quartermaster, Bast spun around and pinned Calypso with his gaze. "He's joking. Tell me he's joking."

She offered him a sympathetic smile, though her eye—a deep sea green today—shimmered with amusement. "Sorry, friend. Keeper's orders. No one sets foot off the ship until the rest of her guests arrive."

"*Merde.*"

If Effie made the request, that was it. Drake and Calypso might bear the title of captain, but the little firecracker was the undisputed person in charge. If anyone tried to protest one of her 'suggestions,' it didn't take more than her Guardian's dark scowl to get them back in line.

He hadn't seen much of her since they'd gotten underway. Last he'd heard, she'd taken to her cabin after a particularly nasty vision.

"What guests?" he sputtered after a second. "No one tells me anything."

"How could we when you've been puking your guts out?" the

pretty captain challenged. "Besides, we can't very well waltz into town and announce ourselves, now can we? This is a stealth rescue mission, Bast. Need I remind you?"

No, you needn't remind me. It's my Ronan . . . err, my friend we're saving.

"What about this"—he waved his arms around to indicate the massive warship—"says stealth to you."

Caly mocked his flamboyant arm wave, gesturing to the dozen or so other boats bobbing nearby. "I don't know, Sebastian. Maybe the twenty other ships arriving every day to celebrate the High Lord's wedding. Ever heard of hiding in plain sight?"

He put his hands on his hips, tossing her a mulish glare. "It must be so boring being right all the time."

"Hasn't happened yet," she said with a smug grin. "But I'll let you know if that ever changes."

Bronn snickered appreciatively, the sound nearly drowned out by that of the anchor giving way.

"Who are these guests anyway? How will they know where we are if we're hiding?" he asked, feeling logically superior for one fleeting second.

"Lucian's already left to get them."

Sebastian huffed and then spun around to face Effie. "So nice of you to join us," he grumbled.

Her eyes twinkled with mirth. "Glad to see you're feeling better."

"Is it? You all seem to get such a laugh out of my misery."

"Aw, don't be like that, Bast. Someone has to be the jester," Bronn cajoled.

He was two seconds away from kicking the smug bastard in the shin. "You would know all about that, wouldn't you? Seeing as how you've held the title for the last few years."

The resulting cheers gave Sebastian a bit of a jolt. He hadn't realized their antics had gathered a small crowd. Though, he was nothing if not a showman.

Bronn's eyes tightened, and his usual easygoing smile appeared forced. "Jester or not, I serve a purpose. Unlike you, who doesn't seem to know how to do anything other than make a mess of himself. Admit it. If not for Ronan, you'd still be hanging in that cage, pissing yourself and begging not to be eaten. You are nothing more than a waste of space, Sebastian. Your only value is in the entertainment you provide. So I'd tread carefully, because the day that ceases to be true is the day I toss you overboard."

Bast knew it was true, but it didn't make it any easier to hear. He'd spent the better part of the past decade creating this caricature of himself. He shouldn't be so upset people believed it was real, that he was nothing more than a simpering fuckboy with absolutely no redeeming skills. It simply meant he'd done his job. Yet, in that moment, it felt so profoundly unfair.

But he couldn't say any of that, so he settled for a fuming, "If Ronan were here, you wouldn't dare to speak to me like that."

"If Ronan were here, he'd be leading the charge."

"Take that back!"

"What are you going to do? Puke on me?"

Bast flung himself at Bronn, only to come up short by a hand in the collar of his shirt.

"That's quite enough of that, puppy."

He didn't recognize the smooth, cultured drawl, but he certainly recognized the sharp ring of authority. Unfortunately, he was too far gone to heed it. Spinning around, he kicked out, not caring who was on the receiving end of the blow.

"Unhand me, you miserable swine!"

"Excuse me?" The question mimicked the quiet rumble of thunder that preceded a storm.

Bast blinked up into a pair of smoky gray eyes, and all his bravado fled. This man practically oozed danger. And sex. But mostly danger.

"Von, let him go. Clearly you interrupted a heated moment. He didn't mean any harm."

Bast didn't recognize that voice either, but he appreciated the aqua-eyed woman coming to his rescue. Distantly he realized these must be the guests that Calypso referred to. Apparently they, along with a few others, arrived while he'd been in the thick of it with

Bronn. And now he was making an arse of himself in front of yet another group of powerful people. *Can this day get any fucking better?*

Despite the woman's request, Von didn't release him, so Effie chimed in. "It's true. Sebastian wouldn't hurt a fly."

"That's not what it looked like," Von murmured, his eyes still assessing.

"My quartermaster goaded him. He was provoked, I assure you."

"Whose side are you on?" Bronn grumbled, casting Caly a dark glare.

Bast wasn't surprised the women came to his defense. They always did. Women loved him. He was surprised, however, when Lucian did.

"Hands off, brother. That one still has an important part to play. Can't have you damaging the goods just yet."

Von made a soft, considering sound deep in his throat. "Oh, I don't know. Helena can heal him."

Sebastian gulped.

"Mate," the aqua-eyed woman snapped, although now her hair floated on the breeze and her eyes flickered with iridescence. Her husky voice was multilayered, terrifying, and crackling with power. "You've had your fun."

The dark-haired man dropped him, and Sebastian staggered backward. Humiliation and anger pulsed through him. He straightened with a glare, brushing both hands down his stained doublet. "Just wait until Ronan hears about this. He'll put all of you in your place."

Von arched a dark brow. "Oh? And what is it you think you know about Ronan, puppy?"

Bast defiantly raised his chin, refusing to be cowed by the curl of violence in the man's question. "He's my best friend and the most bloodthirsty warrior this realm has ever seen. He won't stand for anyone to disrespect me."

"And who do you think taught him everything he knows? Don't presume to tell me about my blade brother. I've known him since we were barely out of nappies."

It was the possessiveness that got to him. Ronan was *his* friend, the only one he had who he'd blindly follow to hell and back. They may not have known each other long, but after what they've been through together, they had the kind of bond that not even death could sever.

"And yet he's never mentioned you."

Von took a threatening step forward, but Effie's voice cut through the simmering tension, halting him.

"Ronan is going to die laughing when he learns that two grown men nearly came to blows while in the midst of a pissing contest over which one loves him more."

"What do you think Reyna's daggers will have to say about them trying to stake claim on her mate?" Helena added conversationally.

"Quite a lot, I'm willing to bet," Calypso said with a frightening grin. "She told me herself she's not one for sharing."

"All right, enough," Lucian said, huffing out a laugh. "That goes for you as well, ladies. Mother's tits, it should be illegal for the three of you to be on the same continent together."

"Just wait 'til we get Reyna back. Then you'll really be in for it," Effie taunted.

The newcomers chuckled, though it was tinged with melancholy at the reminder that their friend was in harm's reach.

"And as for you two," Lucian continued, shifting his attention back to Von and Sebastian, "You're no better than a pack of feral beasts. We're here to do a job and get our friends home alive. Now, put your cocks away so we can get on with it."

"Oi, don't stop them now. They were just getting to the good part," a bald man who looked like a miniature mountain said with a wide grin.

"Kragen, you're not helping," an older man chided, shaking his head.

"Oh, come on, Tims. You were thinking it too."

The older man gave an offended sniff. "Be that as it may, I was wise enough not to say so."

Realizing just how many people had been watching what had effectively been a meltdown, Sebastian stepped back and took a deep breath, reminding himself for the thousandth time why he could not afford to give in to his emotions. Between the seasickness, lack of sleep, and worry for Ronan, he was spiraling, and it was harder than ever to hold on to his nonthreatening persona. Especially when all he really wanted to do was start throwing punches. Or in Bronn's case, a swift kick to the dick.

You haven't come this far to fall apart now. Stay the course, Sebastian.

He focused on his breathing, tuning out the murmur of conversation, the indistinct shouts of the pirates as they went about their business, and the steady crash of the waves against the *Lorelei*.

Once he felt in control of himself again, he snapped his head up and asked, "Well? Now that the gang's all here, how much longer do we have to leave Ronan rotting in that prison?"

He didn't even care that he might have just interrupted their discussion. Nor did they, for that matter, because everyone turned to Effie for the answer.

She cocked her head to the side, as if listening for something none of the rest of them could hear. And then, almost as if on cue, they could.

Bells.

Her lips twisted up in something too dangerous to be a smile. "We make our move tonight, as soon as the sun slips beneath the horizon."

"Then we better get on with the planning. We don't have much time," Von said, earning nods from his mate and the others.

Refusing to let him have the last word, Bast added, "And we aren't going to get a second shot at this."

CHAPTER 11

REYNA

*T*his was it. The end of the line. No amount of denial or fervent wishes could make it otherwise, because neither would change the truth.

Today was her wedding day.

It couldn't be more different from the one she once contemplated as a young girl picturing a distant future. Instead of celebrating with family and friends, she was alone with only her thoughts. Instead of greeting the dawn surrounded by the Forest of Whispers' most ancient sentinels to receive their blessing, she was locked in her room while the sun slipped into the sea, welcoming the night. But worse, far worse, was that instead of pledging to cherish and safeguard a man she loved and respected, she'd been coerced into giving her vows to one who made her skin crawl.

She could always try to run, but it would be Ronan who suffered, and her heart simply could not endure another second of his torture. He'd given so much for her; she wouldn't repay his sacrifice with selfishness. The least she could do was endure this for him.

Her eyes moved to the black gown hanging beside her mirror, waiting for her.

At least she'd get to wear Claudette's stunning creation while facing off against a literal nightmare. For what else was the Father of Dreams if not the King of Nightmares?

Unbidden, a long-forgotten memory slipped into her mind.

~

REYNA WAS SEATED at her mother's vanity, her youthful face twisted in a grimace as Regina ran a brush through her hair.

"I don't see why I have to wear this stupid dress," she sulked.

"Because you can't very well wear your dusty leathers to a wedding, young blood," her mother scolded with a laugh.

"Ryder doesn't have to wear a dress," she muttered with as much bitterness as she could muster, kicking her leg out and making the vanity jerk.

Her mother gave her hair a warning tug. "Why is it you compare yourself to Ryder every time you come up against something you don't like?"

"Because we're the same age, and it's not fair. Boys and girls should be treated the same. It's not right that there's one set of rules for him and another for me. I can do everything he can do, better even. Just ask Master Grey! Yesterday I beat Ryder to the top of the Nest, and I—"

Her mother interrupted what was sure to be a full-blown rant with a softly uttered, "You're right, Reyna."

It was so rare her mother agreed with her that the declaration shut her up.

"Boys and girls *should* be treated the same."

"Then why—"

Her mother continued speaking, holding her gaze in the mirror. "But future *queens* are held to higher standards. And as the Night Stalker's leader and her heir, it would be a massive insult to Pippa and Hilde if we were to show up to their special day wearing clothes better suited to fighting than celebrating. Think about the message that would send to everybody else. Do you want to disrespect two of our most highly decorated scouts after everything they've done to keep us safe?"

"No," she mumbled. She loved Pip and Hilde; she didn't want to do anything that might make them think otherwise. Especially since Pip was teaching her how to hit a bullseye from way up high, and Hilde snuck her sweets. It was the stupid dress she objected to.

She hugged herself, her lower lip trembling. "I don't want to be queen, mama. Queens are never allowed to have any fun. I want to run and fight, like Ryder and papa."

Her mother set down the silver and pearl enameled brush and let out a heavy sigh, crouching down to face her.

Reyna straightened, sensing one of her mother's special lessons was coming.

"You don't think queens fight, young blood?"

She considered it and slowly shook her head. This felt like a trick question, because fighting was fun, and a queen's work was boring, so . . . "No?"

"My sweet girl, all we do is fight. It may not seem like it on the surface because our wars are waged with words and wiles. And our battles are not for ourselves, but for those we love. When we lose, countless suffer. It's why we train so hard and so long never to do so."

Reyna gulped, and her mother brushed her knuckles over her cheek. "You are going to grow up to be a fine and strong queen, Reyna. Just like the women in our family who came before you. It's in your blood, daughter. We do not have it in us to fail."

The words felt important, and they made her nose feel funny, and her eyes get hot like she was about to sneeze. Or cry. And she *never* cried. Not since the time Ryder called her a crybaby.

Uncomfortable, she squirmed in her seat again. "What if words and w-wilds don't work?"

Her mother's eyes flashed. "Wiles. And in those cases, we use our dagger."

Reyna nodded, finally feeling like her mother was speaking sense.

But then another issue swam up in her mind. "But how am I supposed to wear my dagger in this dress, mama?" She plucked at the tulle skirt in disgust. "Seems like a silly thing for a queen to do if she might need her blade."

Her mother laughed. "A dress does not prevent me from wearing a blade, young blood. It gives me more room to hide them." Standing and picking up the brush, she met Reyna's eyes in the mirror. "And anyone foolish enough to believe a woman isn't a deadlier threat than a man deserves everything that's coming to them. Let them underestimate you, Reyna, but then you teach them the error of their ways. Do you understand?"

She didn't, but it was obvious her mother expected a different answer, so she nodded. "Yes, mama."

"Good, now sit up straight. We don't want to be late."

A KNOCK at the door interrupted the memory, and Reyna blinked, snapping back to the present as a soft ache settled beneath her ribs. Just like it always did whenever she thought of her mother.

"Lady Shadow?" Claudette's apologetic voice called. "I gave you as much time as I could, but we really must get you dressed if we're going to make it to the ceremony on time."

She blew out a heavy breath, about to invite the dressmaker in, when Claudette playfully added, "And I'm not the only one who's come by for a visit. It looks as though someone left you a gift."

Glinta.

She'd been waiting for the merchant to contact her, but so far it had been crickets. Instead of waiting for the dressmaker to open the door, she rushed across the room and yanked it open, surprising a laugh out of the young woman.

"I thought that might entice you," she said, holding out a thick gray envelope.

"Come on in," Reyna said distractedly, tearing it open and spinning around to greedily read the contents.

Only there wasn't a letter, just a small iron key. As she dropped it into her palm, she realized her mistake. This wasn't from the fishmonger. It was from Erebos.

Claudette peered over her shoulder, swooning. "Oh, how romantic. The High Lord sent you the key to his heart!"

But it wasn't. Not even close.

If anything, it was the key to *hers*, because it belonged to one of Ronan's shackles.

Reyna didn't need a letter to tell her what it symbolized. Just like she didn't need a key to get to Ronan. She could pick the prison's locks with her eyes closed and one hand tied behind her back, and she could have slit the throat of any guard keeping watch a thousand times over by now. But it wouldn't do any good because they'd never make it out of the palace alive.

No, this wasn't a gesture of love. It was a warning.

One toe out of line today, and he would pay.

Message received, High Lord. Loud and clear.

"Here," Claudette said, reaching out and taking the key from her. "You'll want to keep that somewhere safe while we get you ready."

Feel free to toss it off the balcony.

"My, you're quiet today. Nerves getting to you?" Claudette asked, keeping up her usual steady stream of chatter as she set the key down on the bedside table and pulled the gown free of its hanger.

"Must be," Reyna said with a tight smile.

"Well, it was supposed to be a surprise, but why don't you open that box I brought with me while I pull this down?"

"Oh, you didn't have to do—"

"Hush, I won't hear a word of it."

Curious and a little trepidatious, Reyna moved to the box Claudette had set at the foot of her bed. Brides were given all sorts of gifts on their wedding day. It could be literally anything, and she really didn't want to have to feign excitement over something meant to seduce her future husband.

Please don't be something naughty. Please don't be something—

"Oh!" Reyna breathed, reaching into the box and pulling out a harness of sorts.

Claudette wore a pleased smile as she continued prepping the dress. "I know it's not a traditional bride's gift, but since we already had your undergarments taken care of to work with the dress, I thought you might appreciate something special for one of your daggers."

Reyna raised a brow because it was *exactly* the sort of thing she would have selected for herself. She hadn't gone anywhere without her blades since the day she'd first received one.

"Claudette, this is gorgeous craftsmanship. Did you make this yourself?"

The dressmaker shrugged. "Leather isn't my chosen medium, but it seemed a fitting gift for the High Lord's Shadow, and I already had your measurements, so . . ." She looked embarrassed as she trailed off with a shrug. "Not that you'll need your dagger today—"

Darling girl, you could not be more wrong.

"—but perhaps if you have something familiar to touch when you get a bout of the nerves it might help settle you."

"That is unbelievably kind of you. Thank you, Claudette."

She made a happy humming sound. "Go ahead and put it on. I'll have to fasten the dress around it. And if you have a special dagger in mind, you can grab that as well."

Reyna knew exactly which blade she'd wear today. It was the one Dominic had stolen from Ronan. One of her mother's blades. She hadn't realized Ronan had carried it all this time, but this way, she'd carry a piece of each of them with her today. As she turned away from the box, something blue caught her eye. Narrowing her gaze, she located the cerulean wax with its three swimming fish tucked against the side of the box.

This was from Glinta.

The merchant must have hidden it here knowing Claudette would be seeing her and anything coming from her wouldn't be inspected too closely. Risking a glance to make sure Claudette wasn't paying attention, Reyna pulled the hidden message free. It was coded, but familiar with more than a dozen common ciphers and having created more than a few herself, it didn't take any effort for Reyna to decipher it.

N.B. and crew wearing Xs.
Sea's run dry. Infestation.

ON ITS OWN, the decoded message might appear little more than gibberish, but Reyna was well-versed in smuggler's lingo. Wearing Xs referred to being Xed out or killed. Infestation meant the city was crawling with spies, that it was a dangerous time to send messages or meet with contacts. The sea running dry had two meanings. The first was that information's dried up—likely due to the infestation—but also that she'd find no escape route by way of the ocean.

Put all together, Glinta was telling her No Beard and her crew were presumed dead, so she wasn't going to find succor on the sea. No one had details on the pirates or their whereabouts, and further information wouldn't be forthcoming because it was too dangerous. Or taken another way, Reyna needed to be careful if she tried to dig any deeper. Enemies were everywhere.

"Lady Shadow?" Claudette prompted.

Crumpling the note in her hand, she cleared her throat and grumbled, "Sorry, my mind ran away with me."

"It's to be expected on a day like today."

Reyna hummed in agreement and hurried to grab her dagger from its sheath and strap on the harness Claudette had fashioned for her. It belted over her hips and individually over each of her thighs, sort of like a leather version of a garter belt. She did all of this mechanically, her mind still reeling from the merchant's missive.

It took everything in her to swallow down her scream of absolute fury. Glinta had been her last hope. Her only hope, really, for she walked a razor's edge in this game of hers, pretending to be Erebos's perfect, obedient pet. All of her moves had to be made in secret, and even then, he had eyes everywhere, which further handicapped her progress.

She'd done everything she could think of to prevent the inevitable, but in the end, none of it mattered. She was no closer to freeing Ronan today than she'd been since returning to Glimmermere. Given more time, maybe she would have been successful, but the last grains of sand had just slipped through the hourglass.

Time was up.

With nothing left to do but see this farce through, Reyna woodenly obeyed the dressmaker's instructions, lifting her arms and twisting as directed. After setting a diadem made of glittering onyx, a few of Claudette's glowing stones, and flawless pearls on Reyna's brow, the dressmaker stepped back and clapped her hands.

"All right, Lady Shadow. All done."

Reyna lifted her eyes to the mirror and took in the sight of herself in her wedding dress. Claudette's creation was somehow even more stunning than the first time she'd seen herself in it, but there was no sense of wonder today. Only icy dread and bone-deep resolve.

The dressmaker's wide grin faded, a crease forming between her brows. "Forgive me for saying so, my lady, but you don't look very happy."

Under the crushing weight of lost hope, she didn't suppose she did. Reyna forced a smile and gave Claudette a half-truth. "I find I'm missing my mother today."

The girl's expression filled with sympathy. "Of course you are. It's only natural. It's hard to be separated from family in times such as these."

"Too true. Would you mind waiting outside for me? I have something I'd like to do before we go down and join the others."

"Of course, my lady. I'll send word and let them know we'll be coming shortly."

"Thank you, Claudette."

The second she was alone, the fake smile she'd plastered on her face vanished, and she rushed over to her desk. Knowing she had minutes at best, Reyna dipped her quill in ink and started writing.

She might be out of time, but that didn't mean she was out of options. The wedding would go forward as planned . . . but no one said she had to keep up with this charade *after*. If she had to end the day a wife, she would greet the dawn a widow. And if she failed . . . well, at least she was leaving this world on her terms.

Reyna continued her furious scribbling as her mother's words returned to her once more.

"Let them underestimate you, Reyna, but then you teach them the error of their ways."

"I will," she vowed, setting her quill down and pouring a thin sprinkling of sand over the ink to help it dry. Sealing her letter, Reyna stood and swept through the room, finding Claudette waiting for her as promised.

"Deliver this for me, will you?" she asked, holding out the folded parchment.

Claudette's eyes went wide as she skimmed the name Reyna had scrawled across the surface, but she nodded without hesitation. "Of course, my lady."

"Now," she said when the dressmaker made no move to leave.

"Oh, right. Okay."

She scurried off, and Reyna pressed her hands to her stomach, sucking in a deep breath and trying to control the frantic beat of her heart.

There was no turning back now. The die had been cast.

Taking another deep breath, she dropped her arms, the fingers of her right hand brushing against her mother's dagger. As Claudette suspected, the reminder of its presence soothed her. For the first time that day, her lips lifted in a genuine smile as another of Regina's lessons echoed in her mind.

"All we do is fight . . . our battles are not for ourselves, but those we love."

"What if words and w-wilds don't work?"

"We use our dagger."

"Blade it is, then," she whispered.

There wasn't a hint of nerves as she strode down the hall and made her way to the ceremony below. She was sure in her steps and confident in her purpose. She no longer feared what came next, because for the first time since her memories returned, Reyna truly allowed herself to embrace what the forces in her life had forged her into.

She'd been born from chaos and blessed by darkness, a forsaken heir whose birthright was blood. Tonight, in this court of death and dreams, the shadow queen's reign would finally begin.

CHAPTER 12

EREBOS

It was a peculiar thing, being mortal. Well, not *being* exactly. Even walking among them while bound to one of their bodies, he was more god than man. And generally, Erebos found their limitations more of a nuisance than anything. But on very rare occasions, their muted senses were a relief. It was a nice break not to *feel* everything all the time.

Mortal emotions were mere echoes of the gods'. Fear. Anger. Jealousy. Love. Nothing they felt came close to what a god was capable of experiencing. After spending the last few years in his vessel, he'd almost forgotten how intense it could be. But with each Night Stalker he reclaimed, his power swelled, and he became closer to his true self.

With the return of his power also came his heightened, well, everything. He blamed that for the near-overwhelming anticipation surging through him. He couldn't remember the last time he'd been this . . . what even was the word for what he was feeling? Euphoric? Giddy? Either way, he supposed it made sense. After tonight, centuries of plotting would finally come to fruition.

There was no disguising it either. Everyone who looked at him could tell how keyed up he was. The humans of his court assumed he was simply an eager bridegroom, though he couldn't care less about taking a second wife. His first marriage was enough of a disappointment to dissuade him of the entire notion.

No, it was what came *after* that truly mattered.

Once he and his bride suffered through the requisite festivities, he would take Shadow to their marriage bed, where he would harvest her power and complete his transformation.

He'd be the first god to walk the mortal realm in his true form without forfeiting any of his power. A feat the mother goddess herself hadn't accomplished. Which would make Erebos, in more ways than one, her superior. And not even Luna, in all her smug pomposity, would be able to deny it.

After millennia spent ignoring him, she would be forced to come crawling back. To admit the grievous error of her ways. Because when all these filthy Chosen of hers bore witness to his ascension, they would fall to their knees in worship of *him*.

He would be the one true god, and the Mother would be forgotten. A false idol. She would become as irrelevant as she'd once made him. Forsaken by the very children she put above all else.

How will you feel then, darling Luna? Learning that you turned your back on me for nothing. That the ones you spent your immortal life serving don't give two shits about you. That you are replaceable, as utterly meaningless and inconsequential as a single speck of dirt.

You will fade away, your name little more than a distant memory, whereas mine will transcend time. I will live forever, my rule eternal. And I will do all of this without you, just as you once tried to exist without me.

Let's see how much you like it once the proverbial shoe is on the other foot, wife.

He couldn't have picked a better night for his ascension. In order to fully sever Shadow's access to his magic—instead of just depleting her reserve as he'd been doing—he required a celestial event to give his vessel the power boost it needed. Any celestial event would do—a full moon, the rise of a new constellation, a meteor shower, but he didn't want to settle for something common and underwhelming.

No.

He'd been waiting for something special, with the magnitude befitting the occasion. Something that would be the perfect 'fuck you' to Luna. What better event could there be than a lunar eclipse? It might be petty, but he secretly loved that he was about to usurp her reign as supreme being borrowing power from a celestial occurrence involving her icon.

So far everything had gone to plan. Well, almost everything, but a few blips were to be expected. And those were out of the way. Shadow was well in hand, and her pathetic lover was little more than a lump of whimpering flesh.

Erebos made a mental note to send the healer down once the ceremony was over. He couldn't very well place the blame for his wife's untimely murder at the man's feet when he couldn't even stand on them.

"She's arrived, High Lord," the Arch Cleric said, his voice respectfully lowered.

Erebos blinked, realizing he'd been lost to his thoughts for far longer than he'd suspected. Full night had fallen, and the only light in the Night Temple came from the stars above and the lanterns lining the aisle. It was more than enough to see by, and the flickering glow created a mystical and intimate air in the otherwise auspicious space.

The temple was set on the edge of the eastern cliffs, overlooking the sea. The roof and most of the eastern wall were made of glass, bringing the outside in while protecting worshippers from the worst of the weather. So as not to compete with the view, the rest of the temple was sparsely decorated. Other than the rows of pews and an obsidian hardwood altar inlaid with a pearl mosaic of the night sky, which was also mimicked along the back wall and center aisle, the domed room was bare.

Or it would have been bare if not for the couple hundred people currently crammed into it.

"Are you ready to begin?" the Arch Cleric inquired when Erebos had yet to acknowledge him.

Clearing his throat, he gave a sharp nod. "Let's get on with it."

"Eager to see your bride, I see," the older man said, a merry twinkle in his eye.

Erebos didn't have to force his grin. "You have no idea."

The cleric gestured to someone off to the right, and a ripple of awareness shot through the crowd as they realized the main event was about to start. Erebos let his eyes trail over the room, picking out familiar faces, happy to see that Dominic had placed soldiers discreetly throughout without needing to be asked. His Vulture was still stationed below, with strict orders to keep his eyes on their prisoner. Dovina and Dmitri were seated in the front pew, along with a dozen other prominent courtiers. There wasn't time for him to take in more than that before the temple doors opened and the soft strains of instrumental music swelled.

Their wedding might be a means to an end, but when Shadow appeared, Erebos was far from immune to her. She looked so much like his Luna in that moment, her starlight-colored hair a waterfall of loose waves, her skin luminous and expression serene, eyes demurely lowered, a bouquet of night-blooming flowers clasped between her hands. Then she stepped forward, and he saw she adorned herself in the colors of the night sky—*his* colors—and he yearned for Luna with a ferocity he hadn't felt since her betrayal.

For a single heartbeat, he allowed himself to imagine that it *was* her. That this was real, and they were the ones making vows to love, honor, and cherish one another. That the night would not end in bloodshed, but with them losing themselves in the sort of frenzied lovemaking only two soulmates could ever truly experience. The kind where it was no longer possible to tell where one of them ended and the other began because the answer was the same regardless: each other. It was the most perfect union, a rare moment of total bliss, and once experienced, anything else was a pale imitation. He would know; he'd endured centuries without it.

Just as her name was about to leave his lips on a ragged groan, Shadow looked up, and irises the color of jade, gold, and emerald met his instead of Luna's iridescent orbs. The fantasy withered, leaving him painfully aroused and furiously aware of why they were here.

Every diabolical thing he'd done since he woke had been with a single focus. Every lie, every manipulation, every death by his hand or in his name, served a greater purpose—his only purpose. To punish *her*.

To remind her who he was and how far he'd go to have her.

All of this was for her. Because one did not experience perfect bliss to survive its absence. Not without going mad and risking everything to know it again.

Sweet Luna, you will return to your rightful place at my side. One way or another, you will be mine.

The crowd gasped, pulling his attention back to the present in time to watch Shadow make her way down the aisle in her twinkling gown. She kept her eyes locked on his, her procession equal parts regal and defiant. He might have feared her intent if not for the fact that he'd been monitoring her dreams and liberally topping up her daily compulsions. He'd taken every precaution to ensure his Shadow remained his. There was no doubt she belonged to him. He was seeing things that weren't there, worrying over nothing now that the finish line was in sight. She'd always hated the spectacle of his station and had fought against these sorts of public displays since the very first. This was nothing new, just her typical impertinence.

Still, he couldn't help but offer her a silent warning. *Careful, Shadow mine. Your willing participation is useful but not necessary. I can take what I need from you either way.*

It wasn't the marriage itself he required. It was the sympathy and renewed support he'd receive from the realm after her untimely demise. Thanks to the Butcher's very public demand for Shadow as his boon, none would doubt that his obsession with the assassin led him to murder her rather than see her with another. A brilliant bit of luck, really. Saved Erebos the hassle of framing another *and* gave him the excuse he needed to declare war on Elysia.

That would be the ideal outcome, the easy way forward.

But it wasn't the only one.

Once his power was fully restored, there would be no stopping what was coming.

Holding that thought in mind, he smiled, playing up his role as doting groom. Her answering grin was as enigmatic as the woman herself.

"Perfect, High Lord. You chose your Lady well," the cleric uttered softly.

He grunted his assent, still pondering the meaning behind her fucking smirk when she reached him. Aware of the eyes on them, he offered his hand to her. Before she could accept it, an infernal scratching started on the inside of his skull, the same as it had the other night in the dungeon.

A shudder worked its way down his spine, and he had to clench his jaw against the unsettling sensation. It was over as quickly as it began, lasting no more than a second, perhaps two, but it was enough to draw a quirked brow from Shadow, who could feel the tremor through their joined hands.

"Your beauty undoes me," he lied through gritted teeth.

"So it would seem," she murmured, moving into place beside him.

Once they were positioned, the Arch Cleric lifted his hands, signaling the crowd to be seated as he intoned, "Marriage . . ."

Erebos immediately tuned him out, too inwardly focused to remotely care about a bunch of meaningless words. He had no explanation for that insistent tickle in the back of his mind, but he had little doubt Luna was somehow involved.

When the scratching started up a second time, he knew he needed to hurry things along. If Luna had somehow found a way to break through, to interfere with his vessel, then time was running out.

" . . . it is the culmination of love, true love . . ."

"Get on with it," he growled.

The cleric blinked at him, then smiled and stage whispered, "I'd be eager too, High Lord, but there is a certain order to these things."

"If you do not hurry, you're about to become intimately familiar with the taste of your own arsehole."

Shadow snickered beside him.

No longer smiling, the Arch Cleric cleared his throat. "Do you have the rings?"

CHAPTER 13

RONAN

"Pssst, Butcher! Are you still alive?"

The urgent whispers permeated the fog in his mind, pulling him out of the dreamless sleep he'd been lost in.

"Ronan!" Camille's voice came again, still pitched low. "Answer me."

He struggled to lift his head, his body weaker than a newborn babe's in the wake of Erebos's ministrations. "Unfortunately," he rasped.

"You don't mean that," she chided.

Don't be so sure.

He hurt in a way he hadn't known it was possible to hurt. It went far beyond abused muscles and broken bones. If it was possible for one's soul to ache, that's what this must be. There was no relief from the agony. Erebos's cruelty chased him from consciousness to dreaming, ensuring he had no peace from the tormented screams of his loved ones.

More than once it felt as though he'd been on the brink of madness, his mind fracturing under the relentless assault but never shattering completely. In those moments, it was nearly impossible to distinguish reality from the hallucinations. Each time Camille brought him back, her lyrical voice a lifeline in the darkness. It was humbling to admit, but he didn't think he'd have lasted this long without her.

"I have a letter for you."

A letter? Was she serious? Since when were prisoners allowed post? Who would even care he was down here? Besides Reyna . . . were she in her right mind.

The shredded remains of his heart gave a painful lurch, as they did every time he thought about her. He hated knowing Reyna was every bit as trapped as him, even if her shackles were of a different making. She never should have traded her freedom for his. It was far too high a price to pay, especially when Erebos had no intention of honoring his deal.

Ronan couldn't be too upset with her. Even knowing where he'd end up, he'd have done the same. There was very little he wouldn't do for her. Including rot away in a madman's dungeon. The futility of his situation weighed on him, and he had to force the unhelpful thoughts away, not wanting the wave of despair to drag him back down.

It didn't matter who the letter was from; it wasn't like he could read it anyway. He could barely open his eyes. The right was swollen shut, and the few times he'd succeeded in peeling open the left, the room swam so badly he immediately closed it.

"Not sure what I'm supposed to do with it," he finally grumbled, wincing when he tried to relieve some of the pressure on his dislocated shoulders. He shouldn't have bothered. There was no escape from the pain.

"You could try reading it." Cami's deceptively sweet voice was almost enough to make him smile.

"How? There some secret passageway between our cells you know about?" His voice grew stronger with use, though he couldn't seem to shake its hoarse rasp. "Even if you managed to get it to me"—he rattled his chains for good measure—"I'm not exactly going anywhere any time soon."

Camille muttered something he couldn't quite make out, though he was sure it had to do with him being a stubborn arsehole. It was a familiar refrain amongst those closest to him and more than deserved, if he was being honest.

"I could read it for you," she haltingly offered.

He understood her hesitance. There was no knowing what information that letter contained. It might not be something he'd want getting out, and there was always the risk of them being overheard.

"Is it safe?" he asked, knowing she was much better at keeping track of the guards' movements than he was. She didn't suffer from long bouts of unconsciousness, for one thing.

"If it wasn't, do you think I would have suggested it?" When he didn't answer, she sighed, adding, "There's something happening today. The bells have been ringing nonstop, and most of the guards haven't shown up for their usual shifts. Can't be anything too serious, the Vulture is here, but he's off doing rounds since there are fewer eyes."

No wonder Dovina recruited her. Even trapped as she was, Camille still collected a wealth of information. She didn't hoard it, either, but shared what she knew freely. Probably because it was all she could do to keep him lucid. He couldn't imagine she'd be so generous under different circumstances.

Thanks to her, he now knew the dungeon was a series of serpentine tunnels deep beneath the palace. The labyrinthian layout was enough of an escape deterrent that it required fewer guards to stand watch. Anyone who managed to get out of their cell could easily waste away without ever reaching an exit. Or be caught before they made it very far.

Unless, of course, they knew what to look for. Having not seen it herself, Camille could only explain the maze markers as fingerprint-sized etchings near the top of the walls. Their presence identified the routes needed to find one of the two doors. Either the main exit, which led back up into the heart of the capital, or the second, lesser-known one, which was rumored to connect to the docks. Supposedly it was an old escape route, should the High Lord ever find himself in a position where he needed to flee the palace.

Given all she'd learned, he supposed the prison guards' watch schedule was child's play, but still he had to ask, "How can you possibly know all that?"

"I listen," she said simply. "Now, do you want me to read this to you or not?"

"Fine," he grunted. What other choice did he really have? Someone went to the trouble to make sure he got the message. It would be rude not to at least hear what they had to say.

There was a beat of silence, likely so she could open the letter, but Ronan didn't hear anything through the wall that separated them. He couldn't even hear those bells she mentioned, although he could make out the soft scuttle of a rodent on the other side of his cell.

His stomach bottomed out when Camille's whisper-soft "Oh," reached him.

"What? What is it?"

"It's from Reyna."

How the hell does Camille know who Rey— Before Ronan could complete the thought, his pulse began to race. Reyna. She'd said *Reyna,* not Shadow. But that meant—

"Read it," he growled, unable to say anything else over the sudden thundering of his heart.

Camille cleared her throat and began. He knew she was the one speaking, but all he heard was Reyna's voice as she relayed her words.

Ronan –

Today is not exactly what I pictured when I imagined my wedding day. To be honest, I hardly thought of it at all.

Until you.

I still remember that night at the Kiri's palace when you spoke to me of mates, and I told you I didn't believe there was only one person in all the world who could make us happy. Imagine my surprise when I learned you were right.

I know, it's a shock. You're never right.

I didn't know what it was to be complete until you. I've been in love with you longer than I care to admit. Probably since you kissed me on that battlefield. The way you looked at me as if I was the reason for the very air in your lungs, it was like I finally understood what the bards were always going on about.

Love isn't a foreign concept. I love my people, my daggers, the forest. But what I feel for you, Ronan. I don't think there's a word for it. What I do know is that I made a promise to myself, then and there, that I would never again settle for anything less than everything.

Which is to say: you.

You're it for me. My everything. My air.

I knew you weren't ready to hear it then, that your heart was still so freshly broken. So I bided my time, thinking we had forever. But then forever was stolen from us.

Learning what you did, how you fought for me when I couldn't fight for you—or even myself. How you never gave up though many in your place understandably would have. It just proved once again that this thing between us transcends words.

We do the best we can to give it a name. Love. Fate. Soulmates. In the end, the words don't matter, just the truth. In all the universe, there is only one person meant for me.

You.

You should be the one I walk toward today. The one who gets my vows. Since you cannot be there to hear them, and since neither of us may survive long enough to find our forever, I wanted to give them to you now. Because I cannot leave this world—or you—without knowing you have my truth. So if you trust nothing else, trust this. When I speak my vows today, they are for you. Only you, Ronan.

You are mine.

The Night Stalkers have a legend. I'm running out of time, so I'll have to paraphrase, but the important bit is this. From darkness came light. From chaos, order. They may seem to be polar opposites, but the truth is they are perfect counterpoints. Harmonious. Made for each other. As I was made for you. Without each other, they do not make sense. They are diminished. Without purpose. For what is the point of the dark if there isn't light?

I thought I knew what it was to have a purpose. But it wasn't until you looked at me and I saw myself reflected in your gaze that I truly understood what it meant to be whole.

You are my light. My flame in the dark. The order to my unending chaos. The only person who makes me make sense.

I will do whatever I must to find my way back to you. In this life or the next.

But if it must be the next, Ronan, know that with my very last breath, I am loving you. Burning for you. Fighting for you.

Because this is my truth: there is no me without you.

Ever yours,
Reyna

RONAN DIDN'T KNOW which of them had started crying first, Camille or him, but her sniffles punctuated the words, echoing his own. He felt raw, ripped open and exposed, but not in the way Erebos's visits left him. Instead of wanting to roll over and die, in the wake of Reyna's words, all he wanted to do was fucking live.

There's no way I'd let you give me all that, kitten, and not expect you to make good on your promises.

He knew what she was doing, what the purpose of that letter really was. She was saying goodbye in case they didn't make it out alive. Which meant she was preparing to make her final stand.

Tonight.

The hell I'll let you have all the fun on your own.

Not caring that he was hardly in any state to fight, that he probably wouldn't even make it through the cell door, Ronan tipped his head back and roared. He poured everything he could into it, finding strength in the booming shout.

And as the sound of his battle cry drowned out everything else,

Ronan did the only other thing he could. He fisted his hands around his chains and pulled.

CHAPTER 14

EFFIE

"Anyone else feel like this has been a bit too easy?" To his credit, Bast didn't cower under the weight of the half-dozen glares aimed his way.

"Wandering around a damned maze for over an hour is your idea of easy?" Von asked incredulously.

Kael pinched the bridge of his nose, the Guardian's usual smirk replaced with a pained grimace. "Can someone remind me why he was allowed to come with our group?"

"I swear it's like you haven't learned a fucking thing," Bronn said, smacking Bast upside his head. "We. Do. Not. Tempt. Fate."

The tips of Bast's ears reddened, but he didn't back down. Rather, he gestured at the empty tunnels in front of and behind them. "I'm just saying, don't you think there should be guards or, I don't know, traps or something down here?"

"No," Von snarled dangerously.

"*Non?* Well, I suppose you would be the expert."

"On rescues? Without a doubt."

Helena and Effie exchanged loaded glances. "Am I remembering it wrong, or weren't you the one who rescued him?" Effie murmured.

"Definitely the one who rescued him," Helena confirmed.

Oblivious to their whispered commentary, Bast gave Von a cheeky grin and shot back, "On prisons."

Instead of being insulted, Von laughed. "Well, that's to be expected with the kinds of exploits Ronan and I used to get into."

Bast's smile wilted. He despised any insinuation that he wasn't Ronan's dearest friend.

Much to Effie's amusement—and exasperation—the rivalry that had begun on the *Lorelei* only escalated in the subsequent hours. It didn't matter what Bast said or did; it always seemed to rub Von the exact wrong way. Their bickering had gotten so ridiculous during their strategy session that Helena had threatened to let Starshine eat them both at one point. The great winged Talyrian hadn't come with them, but that was easily remedied with three portal-creating Guardians in the ranks, which was probably why the threat was so effective.

"You would think they might take some precaution for one such as him. Stars, we practically waltzed right in. What even was the point of the disguises?" Bast plucked at the thick black robe he was wearing as if it personally offended him.

Von snorted. "What were you expecting to find down here, an entire army? Who in their right mind attempts to break *into* a dungeon? The real fight will come when we try to get back out."

Realizing this would likely continue indefinitely, Effie stepped forward with a sigh. "Bast, I already explained the need for disguises. Once we get back above ground, we'll need to blend in."

"Who ever heard of such a ridiculous tradition? Guests wearing potato sacks to a wedding instead of their finery."

"Hmm, I thought it quite lovely," Helena said. "Not only is it a way for the people to honor their beliefs, but also the couple they're celebrating."

"How do you figure?"

"The humble attire ensures the focus remains where it belongs: on the couple."

Bast sniffed. "I suppose, when you put it that way, there's a certain *je ne sais quoi* about it."

"Mother's tits," Von groaned, "I have no intention of dying of old age down here, so can we please get on with it? Or do I need to throw *you* in one of these cells?"

"With our luck, he'd probably enjoy it," Bronn muttered.

Kael chuckled. "Threatening him with a gag might be more effective."

Bronn gave Bast a dubious once over. "I wouldn't be so sure about that."

Bast proved him right by lifting one shoulder in a blasé shrug. "Wouldn't be the first time someone tried to shut me up by shoving something in my mouth. Won't be the last."

Helena couldn't quite contain her sputtering laughter. "Can we keep him?"

"Absolutely not," Von said, tossing a smoldering silver glare her way. "I know you love collecting strays, *Mira*, but this one's beyond saving."

"Please?"

"It's him or me."

Helena pretended to pout, but her eyes flashed with merriment.

Effie stood at the back of the group, watching their antics with a soft smile. Helena had once told her laughter was a symptom of hope. It was one of the truest things she'd ever heard, which was why she cherished these rare moments of levity. They made a dark situation that would otherwise be oppressive or terrifying, bearable. During the Corruptor's war, she'd learned how important it was to indulge in them. Almost like pausing to take a deep breath and reset one's mind before beginning the next stage of an arduous task.

She hadn't said so to anyone else, but that was the real reason she'd insisted Bast come with their group. He, more than the others, was gifted at being a source of light. His soul was every bit as burdened as theirs, arguably more so, and yet . . . he shone.

Lucian peeled away from the others, coming to stand beside her. Once he was close enough, he curled his hand around her nape and gave it a gentle squeeze. *"How are we doing on time?"*

The familiar weight of her mate's voice in her mind soothed her.

He knew just how on edge she was despite the calm front she'd been projecting since arriving in Empyria. He was also the only one who knew the full extent of her visions.

"We have time. Not much, but enough."

"Enough for this?" His eyes flicked to a pouting Bast and scowling Von.

Effie dipped her chin in a nod. *"Believe it or not, they're bonding. And it's those bonds that will see us through the worst of this storm."*

He made a soft humming sound that sent little tingles down her spine as their group resumed the search for Ronan's cell.

"Do you think they're ready?"

"They have to be."

His thumb caressed the side of her throat. *"And you?"*

She knew the question wasn't an idle one. They were rapidly approaching the end of what her visions had shown her.

Six years ago, she'd inherited her grandmother's gift of prophecy, and almost every day since, she'd resented it. At first it was because the visions were obscure, disorienting, and oftentimes physically debilitating. Just when she'd started to make sense of them, they changed. The warnings no longer coming in flickers of possibility, but directly from the Mother herself. Effie hadn't realized how reliant she'd become on that direct line of communication until it had been taken from her. And she resented *that* most of all.

For months she'd received daily visits filled with dire warnings of what was coming, of what would be required, only for them to just . . . cease. All her visions consisted of now were echoes. Fragmented pieces of past conversations with Luna and one terrible image. It was always the same, day after day. But nothing beyond that frozen moment in the temple. Nothing that came *after.*

Part of Effie feared it was because there might not *be* an after.

She supposed she was about to find out because she was down to her last two glimpses of the future. Everything else she'd Seen had come to pass exactly as she'd been told it would. Which meant these final pieces would too, and her heart was no more prepared for them now than the first time the Mother showed them to her. Not even

Lucian's arms had been enough to stave off the resulting panic. Then or now.

"This is not the time to lose hope, fledgling."

"All I have left is hope, Lucian."

"Not all. Not even close. Look around you. Could you ever imagine a more unlikely group of heroes? A Kiri and her Circle, the Vessel and the Voice, Guardians, hell, even pirates . . . and whatever Bast is."

"I've already told you, Lucian, he is the light . . ."

"My point is, we are all here, in this time and place, because of you."

"No, not me. Ronan. We're all here for him."

"We might be here to save him, but the fact that any of us were able to make it this far is because of you."

Effie's lower lip quivered, and her throat was tight as she swallowed past a sudden ball of emotion. *"What if he never forgives me? What if Reyna—"*

"You can't worry about the what ifs, sweetheart. If you let the doubts consume you, you'll never do what needs to be done. You must absolutely believe you will succeed. Luna led you here. She gave you every clue she could to help you. You know how prophecy works, the risks of revealing too much. She's shown you what you needed to See. The rest is up to you. Up to all of us."

She lifted misty eyes up to his, but before she could say anything further, a ripple along her consciousness had her eyes darting to the left. She was familiar enough with the sensation by now to recognize it for what it was. A vision was coming to pass.

"Here we go," she murmured.

She had no way of knowing if the others heard her, because not even a second later, as the guards Bast had been so worried about rounded the corner, an ear-splitting cry shattered the relative peace of the dungeon. It was the signal they'd been waiting for, her second to last warning.

"You know what to do," Effie said, her eyes locked on the first guard just as he twisted his head their way.

"Hey! You there! What do you think you're doing?"

"Kael, Lucian, with me. The rest of you follow the sound of

Ronan's voice. Get him out and wait for us beside the temple. Do *not* go in without us."

Several more shouts rang out, joining Ronan's enraged bellow. Lucian and Kael had already drawn their weapons and were sprinting forward to deal with the group of guards.

"Helena!" she shouted as the others took off at a dead run.

The Kiri spun back around, her aqua eyes transitioning into shimmering pools of iridescence as she summoned her power.

"Conserve your strength! The fight's just getting started."

CHAPTER 15

RONAN

*H*is throat was raw, on fire from dehydration and the additional abuse he'd put it through. He shook from his failed attempt to pull his chains free of the stone. If he'd had access to his Earth magic, he would have been out of here the second he opened his eyes. As it was, his body was so ravaged he wasn't entirely sure even magic would have made a difference.

It was hard to hear anything over the roar of blood in his ears, but he just made out Camille's frantic, "I hear shouting. Someone's coming."

Let them.

He may not have much left in the way of strength or stamina, but he'd be damned if he died chained to this wall like a trussed-up goose.

No. Not good enough, Ronan. You're not dying here, period. You're titled three times over, your name whispered about across entire realms. You are better than this. But more than that, your woman needs you, so sack the fuck up and figure something out.

As far as pep talks went, it might not be his most eloquent, but it did the trick. He willed his heart to slow, focused on making his ragged breaths even, and then listened hard to see what he could learn about his visitor.

Make that visitors.

The rushed scrape of boots over stone definitely belonged to more than one person. It was hard to pick out the exact number, but he heard at least three distinct treads, possibly four. Usually Erebos came alone, but he didn't always. Sometimes he would bring Shadow, other times the rest of his flock. Ronan couldn't dismiss the possibility the bastard wanted everyone here to witness his latest game.

More people meant more bodies between him and the exit.

You never were one to take the easy route, Daejaran. Life dealt you a cruel hand from the first, and you made a right beauty out of it. So, let's do the same with your death. Blaze of glory, yeah?

He was aware that he was officially fucking mental, but something had happened to him after hearing Reyna's letter. He didn't know if it was newfound desperation or perhaps renewed hope, but whatever the reason, he refused to passively wait for death to claim him.

If this was the end, so be it. But he'd meet it on his terms, fighting tooth and nail to the last like the warrior he was. His name alone had made grown men piss themselves in fear. He would not roll over and meekly die now.

He was Ronan of Daejara, the Kiri's Shield, the bloody Butcher, and the High Lord's fucking Champion.

So let them come.

If he was going out, he was taking every last miserable piece of shit with him. And they'd better pray he didn't get free of these shackles because if he did, he wasn't just going to make them pay. He'd make them burn.

There we go. Much better. Now you're getting into it.

There was a scuffle outside the door, followed by something that sounded like a grunt of pain or surprise, and then the lock rattled.

Ronan kept his eyes trained on that handle, breaths regulated, his internal dialogue growing even more bloodthirsty and violent. The words themselves were irrelevant. It was the intent behind them that mattered because it helped him stay focused. With the flames of his rage stoked until they all but consumed him, there wasn't room for anything else. It provided much-needed relief from the pain, offering him the briefest respite. Ravaged as he was, he knew it wouldn't last, but he'd cling to it with everything he had.

When the door blasted from its hinges instead of swinging open, Ronan had to blink a few times, no longer sure he could trust his vision, for standing there struggling to squeeze through the narrow passage was not Erebos as he'd originally expected, but two men. One fair-haired, the other dark, both as welcome a sight as they were unexpected.

"Bout fucking time," he rasped, still not convinced he wasn't hallucinating.

"Now is that any way to greet your oldest friend?" Von asked in his silky drawl, elbowing Bast in the stomach and eliciting another soft *Oof* as he pushed himself forward.

Bast glared at Von's back and moved so that he was standing not beside but *just* in front of him. "Yeah, is that any way to greet me, *mon ami*? When I went to such lengths to rescue you?"

Ronan snickered, but it hurt, so his laugh turned into more of a wheezing cough. "I'm fresh outta crumpets . . . so you'll . . . just have . . . to make do."

A familiar feminine snort preceded Helena's entrance into the room, her derision quickly morphing into panic when her gaze swept over him. "Mother's tits, Ronan. Is there any part of you that's not currently black and blue?"

"Doubtful."

She stepped further into the room, and he thought there might be someone else hovering behind her, but his vision was starting to swim, so he couldn't be sure. Helena began bossing the others around like she'd been born to do, which, come to think of it, she had.

"Quick, we need to get him down. He's not going anywhere in that condition. Wait, on second thought, let me check the extent of his injuries first. We might do more harm than good if we move him."

She pushed past the others until she stood directly in front of him, smelling like the sea and home. She cupped his cheek in her hand, her eyes roving over his face. "Oh, Ronan. What have they done to you?"

He didn't want to burden anyone else with those nightmares, so instead he quipped, "Leave me a scar or two this time, yeah, Hellion?"

Helena laughed, but it was watery. "I think you and I have more than enough scars on the inside."

She had him there. He'd bear the invisible reminders of Erebos's attention for the rest of his life. In fact, it was because of that attention he couldn't be sure any of this was real.

His one good eye searched hers, and he dropped his voice, not wanting the others to overhear his moment of vulnerability. "Am I dreaming? No . . . can't be. My dreams are shit. Hallucinating, then. Are you all going to make me think I'm saved and then up and disappear? Or will it be the screams again?" He shuddered. "Please, anything but the screams."

Helena sucked in a gasp, her eyes bright with unshed tears. "No, Ronan. You're not dreaming. We're really here, and we aren't going anywhere without you. We're going to get you healed up and then go find Reyna and all go home together, okay?"

"This is all sounding too good to be true. I'd be more inclined to believe you if it hurt."

"I'd pinch you, but you've suffered enough, Shield."

"I can take it."

"You always were as stubborn as you were loyal," she muttered, sweeping her thumb under his busted eye and drawing a hiss of pain from him.

"You really are here," he breathed, his gaze lifting over her shoulder to find Von and Bast staring back, both wearing twin expressions of worry. The two men could not be more different, but for the moment, they seemed united in their concern for him.

Ronan wasn't sure what *his* face was doing, but he assumed his eyebrows were somewhere near his hairline and perhaps there was some kind of manic smile about his lips.

"Did you really think we'd leave you?" Helena asked, shaking her head. "After everything we've been through together, of course we came for you." She pressed her palm lightly over his chest, pushing a little of her healing magic into him to counteract any pain the touch might cause. Then she pushed it further, her magic flowing over him like warm water, washing away the pain and leaving him lightheaded in its sudden absence.

"You shouldn't have come. It's too dangerous."

"So what? We thrive on danger."

"But—"

"You know, Ronan, for someone so smart, you can be incredibly stupid. Don't you get it? We let you leave on your own because it's what you needed to do. But we were never going to let you go for good. You're the heart of our family. We need you. We will *always* come for you."

Her fierce words shouldn't hurt, especially when her touch was so gentle, but they did. After what he'd done, who he'd become to deal with his grief, and then how he'd pushed them all away, he didn't feel worthy of such devotion.

"Hellion, I . . ."

He couldn't manage more than that, but she understood. Of course she did. She was the sister of his soul. "I know."

"Can you ever forgive me?"

"There's nothing to forgive."

He squeezed his eyes shut, finding it hard to breathe even as she repaired the extensive damage to his lungs and ribs.

"I, uh, hate to break up this tender moment, but we need to get a move on," a familiar voice called out from the doorway.

So there had been a fourth, he thought a beat before his mind registered who the voice belonged to. *Bronn.*

Even the quartermaster was here to rescue him.

They'd come. The Circle. The pirates. Bast. All of them.

After everything he'd done, they'd still come for him.

He and Reyna were going home. Together.

Finally.

And then, whether from blood loss, the realization that he was truly safe, or perhaps simply from shock, Ronan blacked out.

CHAPTER 16

BAST

*R*onan slumped forward in his restraints, his powerful frame going boneless as he fainted. *Perhaps that's for the best. The story painted on his skin . . .* Bast winced. It was the kind that could make grown men weep.

"Can you heal him?" he asked, afraid the damage might be too extensive.

"Can she . . . Mother's tits, do you have any idea who you're talking to?" the current bane of his existence spat.

"No, actually. We've never met before today, and as I said, Ronan never mentioned any of you." Returning his attention to Helena, he asked, "So, can you?"

Helena risked a single glance over her shoulder. "Yes, I can heal him, but his injuries are—" She paled, and a muscle feathered in her jaw. "I'll do what I can, but I'm going to need more time than I can spare right now. I fear he'll still be in considerable pain for a while yet." A crease appeared between her brows as she frowned back at Ronan.

"What is it?" Von asked, his voice considerably gentler when he spoke to his mate.

"The bones and skin are easy enough to repair. But the organ damage and blood loss . . . that's delicate work that requires significant power."

"And Effie told you to be conservative," he finished for her.

The mention of the Keeper's name was all it took for Bast to understand the predicament. A seer's warning was not something to ignore lightly. If she made a point to give the order, it was because the night's outcome might hang in the balance.

Helena bit her bottom lip and nodded. "But it's Ronan. How can I not—"

Von's silver eyes flared a molten gold. "Take what you need, love."

"Take what you need?" Bast looked between them, losing the thread of the conversation. "Are we donating something? Can I help?" If there was something he could do, however small, he'd like to try.

Helena gave Bast a gentle smile, the kind one might offer a child who'd said something sweet but entirely unhelpful. "Von is referring to his power. As his Mate, I can tap into his source and use it to amplify my own."

"Oh, I see." Bast flushed, realizing his misstep. He had no power to share. Having only just learned of the Chosen and their gifts a few hours prior, he knew the oversight could be forgiven, but he hated seeming an even bigger imbecile than usual. He also hated that Von's offer made him soften toward the silver-eyed devil. By helping Helena provide the more intricate healing Ronan needed, Von would ultimately weaken himself. It was hard to think badly of a man who would do such a selfless thing.

The bastard. One-upping me in a way I can't match. Ugh. Handsome and kind. How insufferable.

When Bast risked a glance his way, Von was staring at him, brows furrowed, as if he was trying to puzzle something out. With a slight shake of his head, he returned his attention to Helena.

"Do not let him suffer if it can be avoided. Besides, the more you can do for him now, the bigger an asset he'll be in the fight to come."

The look they shared was charged, and Bast would have sworn they were communicating without words.

After a beat of silence, Helena nodded. "All right. Help me lay Ronan on the floor and then take my hand and kneel beside me. The link is always strongest when we're touching."

"Whatever you're doing, make it fast, Kiri. I hear footsteps coming," Bronn said, eyes trained outside the cell.

Von's eyes blazed gold as he held his palm above the metal shackle holding Ronan's left hand in place. In less than a heartbeat, the cuff snapped free. Helena repeated the same on the other side, calling over her shoulder, "Can you buy us some time?"

Bast pointed to himself. "*Moi?*"

Helena nodded distractedly as she and her Mate carefully caught Ronan's weight and lowered him to the floor.

"By myself?"

Flicking her eyes up to him, she knelt beside Ronan's shoulder and brushed sweat and blood-matted hair off his forehead. "Well, yes. We need Bronn to guard the door and keep anyone from getting in while we work, which leaves you," she said, as if it was the most obvious maths in the world.

Which it was. He just didn't love the idea of wandering off in this maze alone.

"Oh, come on, Sebastian. Why so hesitant? This should be an easy task for you. You were born to be a distraction." Von's teasing words didn't hold the edge they had earlier. Something Bast had said or done since they set foot in this cell must have made him reevaluate his low opinion.

"All right, fine. But if I die—"

"No one is dying down here, Bast. You have my word." This time her voice was changed, resonant and harmonious, as if an entire celestial choir spoke through her. Bast didn't doubt her words, not when they were delivered in *that* voice.

Reaching down, he tapped the side of his leg, ensuring the weapon he'd strapped on before leaving the ship was still in place. Then he checked the hidden pocket in his robe for the flask he stashed there just because. If one tool didn't work, the other certainly would. That done, he tossed a final glance at Ronan, who'd since been magically cleaned of all blood and dirt, and left the cell confident his friend was in good hands.

Bronn caught his eye, jutting his chin toward the footsteps. Their source had yet to round the corner, but they were close. And there were two of them from the sound of it.

He was a bit rusty, but he should be able to handle two guards on his own. The old Sebastian—back when he'd been known throughout Colvers as Bash the Dash due to a particularly clever move of his—wouldn't have batted an eye. But it had been a while since he'd had any chance to train. Revealing his skill was too risky and hard to explain. Much easier to let everyone believe he was nothing more than a worthless philanderer until it was time to strike.

To that end, it was a fair bit of luck he'd been tasked with distracting rather than guard duty.

Pulling out the flask, Bast took a healthy sip.

"Really? I enjoy a tipple as much as the next bloke, but this is hardly the time—"

Bast raised a brow at Bronn as he wordlessly splashed the rest of the contents down the front of his robe.

Bronn grinned and gave Bast a little two-fingered salute. "My mistake. Carry on, matey."

With a wink, Bast turned away and began a slow, staggering lurch down the hall. Playing drunk was easy. Most tended to overdo it with overexaggerated gestures and raised voices—which definitely worked —but he learned early on that the key to believability was in the subtle details. A soft slur combined with a periodic thousand-yard stare, a combination of fluidity and clumsiness, which often resulted in an overcorrection of balance, and an intense focus on simple tasks due to a loss of basic motor skills, to name a few.

His favorite drunken trait, however, was laying on the charm. Lower inhibitions meant things like personal boundaries and recognition of social cues went out the window. It was an excellent way to catch someone—say, a prison guard or a pickpocket's mark —unaware.

Bast began to softly hum a popular bawdy tune, off-key and interspersed with the occasional hiccup. His gaze was trained on the ground, giving the impression that he was carefully watching where he was going, although he continued to weave haphazardly instead of in a straight line. Once the footsteps sounded only a dozen or so feet away, he added a couple of off-beat snaps and a few mumbled lyrics to the mix.

"Something something honey . . . flashes a bit of her cunny . . ." He hummed a little louder, waving his hands like he was conducting an entire pub in song. "Ride you so hard . . . make you see stars . . . tip of your prick turns blue!" At the final word, he clapped his hands and did a little flourish, throwing his body off balance just as the guards came into view.

"Oi! You there! How in the blazing hells you get down here?" a feminine voice heavily laced with suspicion called out.

He used his bent-over position to steal a peek at his opponents, quickly assessing them while they tried to make sense of his unexpected presence. He was glad to see only one of them was female. He didn't love fighting women, not because he felt them weaker or inferior or anything remotely in that vein. He just much preferred fucking them. They were so sweet-smelling and soft, their breasts and gently rounded bellies making perfect pillows. Who wouldn't rather roll around in bed with one? Or two, as the case might be.

Bast straightened, eyes half-closed as he continued his little one-man show. In another life, he would have made a brilliant bard. This was a top-notch act right here.

"He's off his tits," her companion muttered, though it was harder to tell if it was disgust or jealousy coloring his tone.

"Not another one," the female groaned. "Everyone's enjoying the High Lord's wedding 'cept us."

"Barney's already promised to save us each a pint. Just another couple turns on the old watchtower, and we'll be right there in the thick of it."

She let out a heavy sigh at her partner's words. "In the meantime, let's help this sorry shite find somewhere safer to sleep it off."

They were making their way toward him, not sensing any threat as he began the second verse of Voluptuous Vilma. Once again, he snapped and twirled, performing an uncoordinated jig that allowed him to spin away from the guards and reach into his robe unseen.

By the time they reached him, he still wasn't sure whether he was going to debilitate them or kill them outright. It seemed a shame to opt straight for murder, but Ronan's life was on the line. Reyna's too. They could ill afford either of these two waking back up and sounding the alarm.

What would Shadow do?

His dagger was out and embedded in the first guard's gut before he finished asking himself the question.

Murder. Obviously.

She blinked surprisingly lovely dove gray eyes at him. Her sooty lashes tangled together as she opened and closed them.

"Ah, *mon chéri*. It's not personal, well, not for me. But Ronan saved my life, you see. More than once. It's only fair I repay the gods for the souls they were denied."

As she slackened in his arms, he pulled her shortsword free, twisting and bashing her partner on the temple as she fell to the floor, then sticking him in the gut for good measure.

They were both dead or dying before he finished speaking.

He pulled both blades free, wiping the blood on his robe as he surveyed his work. "Not bad, Sebastian. Not bad at all."

Distracted as he was by his scuffle, Bast didn't hear the third set of footsteps until it was too late.

"You will die for that," a familiar voice growled.

The shock of it, here and now, had a chill running down his spine and his blood boiling in his veins. Bast slowly lifted his head, taking in the dark-haired man as his heart galloped beneath his ribs.

There was no way out of this. No faking drunk to gain the element of surprise. He'd been caught red-handed by the one man he'd been trying to get alone for years.

This is it, he realized, *the moment Effie promised me.*

"Vulture," he greeted with a sneer, eyes lingering on the scar along the other man's cheek. "When a man takes an innocent's life, he should be prepared to die." The taunt was unmistakable, as was the threat.

Dominic raised a brow, his eyes nearly black as they assessed him. "I couldn't have said it better myself."

"Few rarely can. I have a way with words." Bast took a few test swipes with the woman's borrowed sword, familiarizing himself with its weight. The shortsword wasn't his weapon of choice. He preferred something with a bit more panache, like a saber, but beggars and all that.

Never breaking the Vulture's penetrating stare, Sebastian slid into a defensive stance. He allowed the mask he'd worn for so long to drop, revealing the depth of his loathing for this man.

Dominic flinched. "I don't believe we've met."

"No. We haven't. But your reputation precedes you."

He smirked as he raised his own weapon. "It always does for one such as me."

"One such as you? But there are so many titles that fit. Which are you referring to? That of murderer? Or rapist?"

Dominic's smug smile curdled, the skin around his scar pulling tight as the muscles in his jaw clenched. "You must have me confused with somebody else."

Bast spat at his feet. "*Non.* You are exactly the monster I believe you to be. You killed my father. And my mother. And my sister. Leaving them all to rot in a river of their own blood."

"That does sound like me." The Vulture's lips twitched. "Which would make you the prodigal son. Pity you were away. At school, was it? They were always away at school. Or recently enlisted. Funny that the protectors were never at home where they belonged. Perhaps if you were, you could have joined them and saved yourself all this needless anger."

"Were I home, you wouldn't have laid a hand on any of them. But especially not her."

"How can you be so sure?"

The arrogant curl of the bastard's upper lip had Bast's fingers twitching around the hilt of his sword. "Because I would have cut your hands off right after I rid you of your shriveled dick. It might be too late to save them, but not to ensure that you will never harm another."

"You certainly think highly of yourself . . ."—the Vulture sniffed, regarding Bast with a smug smile—"I'm sorry, I seem to have forgotten your name."

Rage churned in his belly, but Sebastian battled it down. For this, he needed absolute calm. "My name doesn't matter, but hers was Marguerite Villehardouin, and she was practically a child, you fucking monster."

Dominic's eyes flashed, and he grinned, entirely unrepentant. "Ah, yes. I remember now. The Flower of the South, isn't that what they called her? Such delicate features, that one. And ripe little curves. What a breakable doll she turned out to be."

Bast's control snapped, and he shot forward, unleashing a flurry of blows that Dominic just barely managed to deflect.

"Oh, ho ho, he's angry!" the Vulture laughed, eyes glittering manically. "I love it when they're angry. She was, too, you know." Dominic pointed at the scar marring his cheek. "She gave me this. I couldn't let her live after that. Otherwise, I would have kept her for myself. A sweet piece like that? I would have ridden her hard and put her away wet. Nightly."

Bast saw red. He was only distantly aware of the flash of steel against steel, his limbs moving faster and with more precision than ever. He'd waited years to avenge his family, and he was not about to waste the opportunity.

Dominic's smile soon faltered, and he was panting heavily as he fended off Sebastian's relentless strikes. The Vulture was not without skill. He landed several glancing blows of his own, many of which drew blood, but Sebastian was fueled by his fury, and he felt nothing but the need to destroy.

At some point they'd gotten turned around, and Dominic tripped over the boot of one of his fallen soldiers. Seeing his opportunity, Bast spun, kicking his leg out and knocking the man backward. Dominic tried to catch himself but had already been off balance and ended up sprawled on his back on top of the corpses.

Bast threw himself on the Vulture, not hesitating in the slightest as he pressed the tip of his borrowed blade to the other man's groin.

"Anything you want, it's yours," Dominic panted, trying to shy away from the weapon.

Sebastian held the man's stare, pretending to consider the offer.

"Money, titles, name it. Whatever you want, you can have it."

Baring his teeth in a feral snarl, Bast drove the blade in to the hilt. "All I want is my family back, *toi fils de pute.*"

There was a wet gasp as the body beneath him twitched, the Vulture's dark eyes wide with pain. Bast twisted the blade, making good on his earlier promises. After pulling the weapon free, he stood and left the bastard who'd starred in his nightmares for far too long to bleed out. Just as he'd done to them.

It's over, ma chère soeur. *Finally, you may rest in peace.*

Something that might have been relief tore through him, but there was no time to bask in it. He was needed elsewhere.

Bast jumped over the pile of bodies and raced back to the others.

"What the bleeding hell happened to you?" Bronn asked, wide-eyed.

Bast glanced down, taking in his blood-soaked appearance. "You told me to distract them. I did what I was asked."

Helena was still kneeling beside Ronan, though he was awake and moving now.

"Almost done?" Sebastian asked.

"Finishing up now," she confirmed without looking up.

A light scratching had Bast reaching for his weapon, but before he had a chance to raise it, a soft voice rang out from the cell beside Ronan's.

"Please, take me with you."

Camille.

He'd only met the woman a handful of times, but he had a fondness for the courtesan. She reminded him of home, which was why he'd always made a point to avoid her. There'd been a chance, though small, that she might recognize him or piece together who he really was, and he didn't want her to accidentally out him.

I guess it doesn't matter anymore.

The realization was bittersweet.

He made for the lock, intending to pick it, but Von stopped him.

"Allow me," he said, holding out his hand and sending a bolt of energy at the lock, just as he had the other.

Bast wasn't prepared for the sight of her. Camille's merry eyes were weighed down with the ghost of her torments, her skin bruised and waxy. Ronan wasn't the only one who'd been brutalized.

"Helena," Bast called. "We have another one for you."

"No," Camille insisted, tucking what appeared to be a letter into the tattered remains of her dress. "There isn't time. We must go."

"But you—"

"She's right," Ronan said, surprising them both. "We have to stop the wedding."

Bast could have wept at the sound of his voice, strong and clear once more, though he looked as ridiculous as the rest of them wearing the black robe Effie insisted they bring for him.

Camille nodded in agreement, accepting Bast's outstretched arm with a slight wince. "The bells. I should have realized, but I didn't put it together until Rey . . ." She trailed off, shooting Ronan an apologetic glance.

"It's all right," he said, his voice gentle as he came closer. "You've done more than enough. Can you walk?"

Instead of answering, Camille reached for Ronan's cheek. "It's good to see you looking well, handsome. She's going to need your strength."

"What about you?"

She waved him away. "I have a part yet to play. Worry not."

"If you're sure . . ."

She nodded again. "Reyna needs us. It's time to put an end to this, Ronan."

Bast wasn't sure how it was possible, but Ronan appeared to swell in size, the kindness he'd shown Camille fading away and replaced with the bloodthirsty Butcher Bast had first met in the tavern.

Just when he thought Ronan would take off without another word, he paused and looked at Bast. "Thank you, *mon ami.*"

Sebastian's throat grew tight with unexpected emotion at Ronan's use of his native tongue. "For what?"

Ronan's gaze scraped along his body. "From the looks of it, a whole hell of a lot." He reached out and squeezed Sebastian's shoulder, gesturing to Camille. "Keep her close, hear me? Protect her with your life."

Bast straightened, touched that Ronan thought him capable of it. Since no one yet knew about Dominic or the guards, he had no reason to believe so, just faith. Given the persona he'd created and the way he'd been treated because of it, the show of support meant a lot. Especially since it was the first time anyone outside his family had ever deemed him worthy of such a task.

"You have my word, Ronan."

Ronan gave him a tight nod and then started down the hall, his voice pitched low as he strategized with the others.

Camille made to follow, her leg giving out as she tried to put weight on it. Without missing a beat, Sebastian swept her up in his arms and started walking.

She squeezed his arm, offering him a shy grin. "My hero."

"Not yet, but maybe soon."

Cami lifted her thumb and wiped some of the blood off his cheek. "If this belongs to who I think it does, then you've done more for me than you could ever know."

Bast shuddered, his smile dimming as he pieced together everything she didn't say. "He will never lay a finger on you or anyone else ever again, *mon ange*, I swear it."

"Like I said, Sebastian. My hero."

He knew it was impossible, that she was long gone, but for a second, he would have sworn it was Marguerite looking up and thanking him. Throat suddenly tight, Bast couldn't do more than brush his lips over her forehead.

Tucking her head into the space between his neck and shoulder, Camille held on tight as he carried her out of the dungeon. And even though her tears dampened his skin, and his dripped down onto her head, neither of them mentioned it.

CHAPTER 17

RONAN

After existing in near-constant agony for who knows how long, the sudden and absolute lack of discomfort was surreal. It had been a while since he'd had need of one of Helena's healings. He'd forgotten about the . . . side effects.

When the Kiri healed someone, she didn't stop at just their physical wounds. It was as if a massive burden was just gone. One he'd carried for so long he'd didn't remember a time he hadn't borne its weight. His heart felt lighter, his mind sharper, and the sheer amount of energy surging through him . . . he may as well be a whole new person.

He'd say it was a miracle, but when it came to Helena and what she and her magic were capable of, this barely scratched the surface. He'd witnessed her do things that defied explanation; he shouldn't be surprised by the miraculous nature of what she labeled a 'basic' healing. But he was.

Likely because he and he alone could appreciate the gift she'd given him.

Thanks to Camille's information, it didn't take long for them to identify the markings etched into the walls and navigate their way out of the dungeon. And thanks to Luna, or whatever other forces continued to watch over them, they didn't run into any other guards either.

Now it was simply a matter of waiting for Effie and the rest of the party to join them. Easy in theory, but Ronan was slowly losing his mind with the need to get to Reyna.

"Peace, Ro. They'll be here soon."

"I know."

"Effie was very clear. She specifically said not to go in without her," Helena repeated for the fifth or sixth time.

"I *know*," he gritted out, his eyes trained on the temple doors where he could only make out a sea of black-robed figures.

Effie's visions meant they were all similarly attired. Except for Camille, who they hadn't known to account for, but Bast was keeping her well hidden. The man hadn't left her side since they freed her. Ronan didn't know if that was due to the order he gave or Bast's personal feelings, but he wasn't complaining. After all she'd done for him, Camille deserved an attentive protector. Who knew the flamboyant Bast would have the makings of a real hero?

You did. Otherwise, you never would have entrusted him with the assignment.

Ronan glanced over to the couple, tucked away behind a stone half-wall across the way from his own perch. He could just make out their profiles. Bast was once again free of gore thanks to Helena's magic, and Camille seemed uncharacteristically shy as he tucked some of her hair behind her ear. Bronn was with them, trying hard to pretend he wasn't intruding on what was so obviously an intimate moment.

"What's the story with him?" Von asked softly, following the line of his gaze.

"Who? Bast?"

Von nodded.

Ronan considered the question, knowing his friend was trying to distract him and willingly taking the bait. Before he could land on any sort of answer, cheers and laughter rang out from the partially open doors.

Ronan tensed. They were running out of time. If they were going to go put a stop to this wedding, they needed to go *now.*

He straightened, leaving the protective covering of the wall to take one step toward the temple.

Von snatched his arm and held him fast. "Ronan. She said to wait."

Desperation clawed at him, and Ronan knew it showed because his friend's fierce expression softened. Sensing an opening, he pressed the advantage. "What if it was Helena? Would you willingly stand idle knowing she was *right* there?"

"Effie wouldn't have given the order if it wasn't important."

He knew Helena had a point, but he kept his eyes locked on Von, knowing he was the one to convince. "You once asked me to break into a palace with you knowing it could have gotten us both killed. A temple is a paltry thing in comparison. Are you really going to make me do this alone? Because I *am* doing this, brother. With or without you."

The look Von tossed him was so patently *him*—brotherly exasperation and haughty superiority combined with a warrior's love of the fight—that Ronan almost laughed. It was the same look he'd earned countless times over the years.

"I didn't come all this way just to let you have all the fun."

"Good, then get off that soft arse of yours and let's go get my woman back." Now that battle was assured, it was easier to joke.

"Soft?" Von asked with an insulted curl of his lip.

"Yeah, from all that sitting you do."

"I don't think you were looking closely enough, Shield. My arse is as perfect as it's always been."

"Sure it is, brother. I'll leave it to your mate to make the call on that one, shall I?" Ronan asked, creeping toward the temple doors.

Helena seemed to realize she'd already lost the fight to stay put because she didn't bother saying anything further; she just gestured to the others that it was time to move.

"Probably for the best," Von said as he pulled his weapon free. "Wouldn't want you getting jealous."

"The day I'm jealous of another man's arse . . ." Ronan started with a shake of his head, but he never finished his sentence.

As he'd moved into position, his line of sight through the double doors shifted, and his line of sight was no longer limited by a sea of black robes. From this vantage point, he had a perfect view of the couple standing in the middle of the altar. The cleric's attention was on Reyna as he asked, "And you, Lady Shadow, do you take the High Lord as your husband?"

Her eyes lifted at that exact moment, inexplicably finding Ronan's at the other end of the long aisle. As soon as they did, her lips curled in the barest hint of a smile.

"No."

~

REYNA

IT WAS the predatory celebration in Erebos's deep green gaze that had tension coiling her muscles. She'd already guessed whatever he'd had planned would happen tonight, but it was that unspoken *'gotcha'* that made her want to hike up her skirt and run away.

Far away.

Reyna wasn't one to flee from a fight, but anything that made the Lord of Death smile like that was nothing she had any interest in sticking around for. At least not by herself. She was skilled. Incredible, really, but not 'facing off against a god who was already assured of his win' incredible.

Her only hope was taking him unaware. But based on the self-satisfied smirk that hadn't left his lips since the cleric started yammering on, he was onto her. A caebris ready to strike, the shadow cat's prey in sight with absolutely no idea of the looming danger. And she was very much the prey.

Thus far, very little about this ceremony had to do with her. Which registered as odd only because she was the one whose life was about to irrevocably change; one would think she'd be a bit more of a participant. But then, this wasn't really about her, she supposed. This was Erebos's spectacle, and she a mere prop. She knew her moment had finally come when the cleric subtly shifted her way.

"Lady Shadow . . ."

She was only distantly listening to what he asked her because, for whatever reason, instead of looking up at him, her gaze was drawn in the other direction, like a magnet helpless to deny the pull to its counterpart.

Ronan.

He was here.

He'd escaped.

There was a hint of movement behind him, and she immediately recognized the dark hair of Helena's mate, meaning he'd brought reinforcements.

A slight smile ghosted her lips as she realized she wasn't alone. She never had been, not really. For as long as Ronan's heart beat, he would always find his way back to her. Hadn't he proven it more than once?

And if she wasn't alone, there was no reason to flee.

No, quite the opposite. It was time to stay and fight.

"No," she said, answering the cleric's prompt and echoing her mental epiphany. Tearing her gaze from Ronan's, she glanced at the holy man. "I'd say sorry for this, but I'm not." In a seamless move, she pulled out her dagger and stabbed him in the throat. "Wedding's off," she shouted, a savage smile blooming across her face as she pulled her weapon free, the cleric's blood spraying across her hand and face as he dropped to the ground.

And then . . . all hell broke loose.

So many people jumped into action it was impossible to track everything. Reyna reveled in the resulting chaos, knowing this momentary confusion could only aid her and her allies.

Ronan and the other Chosen rushed in, taking out the guards closest to them. The crowd broke into shouts of shock and horror, some cowering, others trying to flee and trampling each other in their haste. Those with weapons unsheathed them but didn't seem to know which threat to deal with. Her or the newcomers.

"What are you waiting for? Kill them!" Erebos shouted. As his guards rushed to obey, his pitch-black gaze returned to her. "Have you forgotten who you serve, Shadow mine?"

"The only person I serve is myself. Whether you intended to or not, you made me a queen, Erebos, which means I am no man's puppet. And certainly not yours." She lunged forward, her dagger aimed at his heart.

Despite her expert aim, his godly reflexes were faster, and he knocked her arm wide, the blade barely grazing his chest.

"You dare?" he drawled dangerously.

Twirling her dagger in her hand, she smirked, "I more than dare."

She attempted another slash, but a clawed hand made of dark mist raked down the side of her face and curled around her throat. It cut off her air as effectively as a solid one, causing her to gasp and tears to prick her eyes.

"Reyna!"

Ronan's shout boomed through the temple, but she couldn't see her red-headed warrior through the spots dancing in her periphery.

"It could have been your wedding. Instead it will be your funeral."

"It was . . . always . . . going to be . . . a funeral," she choked out.

Erebos shocked her by grinning, seeming almost giddy as he leaned in and whispered, "You're right. You were never going to survive long enough to see the sunrise." He glanced out the window, his eyes scanning the sky and the eclipse that was nearly complete. "Close enough," he muttered before his eyes returned to hers. The same mist that choked her now swirled in the once white orbs. Even more of it started to peel away from his body, coalescing into a half dozen thick black tentacles that seemed to be attached to his back. "You have something that doesn't belong to you. I want it back."

As one, all six of the tentacles snapped forward and pierced her flesh, stabbing her as easily as a blade, but not actually cutting through her skin. There was no blood. Not even any pain, really. Just a weird detaching of self as her consciousness splintered. Unable to support its weight, her head tipped back, and her arms fell uselessly to her sides. She thought she fell to her knees, but when she was able to focus, she realized she was floating, the tendrils holding her aloft as Erebos leached away the power that lived inside her.

Her last thought as Ronan's roar of her name reached her through the sound of raging battle was that maybe there'd never really been a chance, but at least she would die free.

And, as she promised, loving him.

CHAPTER 18

RONAN

*R*ushing into a fight with only half of their numbers was arguably not the greatest battle strategy. Even if Helena *did* count for the better part of an army entirely on her own. Then again, he wasn't exactly given a choice when Reyna pulled out her dagger and stabbed the cleric.

There wasn't even time to confer with Von and the others. As he rushed in with his weapon drawn, he had to trust that they'd have his back, as they had so many times before. His only true goal as he started mowing through the guards rushing him was to get to his woman. The rest would sort itself after.

It was tempting to light his blade, but with so many innocents around, it was too dangerous. He knew Von and Helena had reached the same conclusion because he'd yet to see a single ball of Fire arc through the air.

Ronan bit back a curse as guards number five and six raced toward him. He hadn't expected an easy fight by any means, but he'd hoped for a few less-trained warriors. Things would go so much faster if they could all focus on Erebos, and every person that came between him and his ultimate foe only heightened his impatience.

That was the only excuse he had for allowing his attention to drift.

He wasn't usually one to make novice mistakes, such as looking away from the men he was currently fighting, but when Reyna's strangled gasp reached him through the fray, he couldn't help but check on her.

He barely registered the slash of the blade through his arm. He was too focused on the midnight-colored mist collaring Reyna's throat. Ronan immediately recognized Erebos's favorite trick. He'd been on the receiving end of it more than once and was intimately familiar with how effective it was and how powerless he'd been against it.

"Reyna!" he shouted, desperation clawing at him. His attacks grew harried, and it was more brute force than actual skill that was responsible for the dead men at his feet.

Using his foot to kick the guard still skewered by his sword off his weapon, Ronan charged ahead, jumping over the bodies of the fallen in his haste to reach Reyna. He watched in horror as little wisps of the mist peeled away from Erebos's body only to hover around him like some mystical shroud. Then, as if he'd given the mist some kind of command, the dense cloud wiggled into a new form, this one not immediately clear until one of the six cylindrical shapes snapped forward like a whip.

Tentacle.

"Reyna!" he bellowed, the shout equal parts warning, disbelief, and abject terror.

He barely made it another two charged steps before each one of the misty tendrils shot toward her, hoisting her up until she hung suspended in the center of the altar. Dangling as she was, she appeared for all the world like a fallen star with the ripple of her pale hair and the twinkle of her gown set against the apocalyptic night sky. The overall effect was haunting and sinister, especially combined with the full moon and its eerie orange glow.

There was very little room for sanity of thought in the wake of that. The only thing that mattered was her. Getting to her.

Saving her.

Fuck it. This entire gods-cursed temple can burn. I refuse to let her die here like a damned pagan sacrifice.

"Ronan, no!"

He ignored Helena's plea as he summoned his Fire and unleashed the unholy inferno straight at Erebos. The Fire spiraled out from the center of his palm, bolstered by his Air as it turned into a swirling funnel, easily double the size of a grown man as it consumed everything in its path, including—he hoped—the bastard god himself.

Focused as he was on whatever he was doing to Reyna, Erebos didn't immediately see the firestorm coming for him. Ronan held his breath, fervently praying that the High Lord was about to go up in flame.

Luna must not have been the one to hear his prayers, because Erebos's head snapped his way, the orange and red of the fire dancing over his outraged face. He jumped aside seconds before the fiery cyclone made contact, the swirling flames crashing through the six smoky tentacles instead of flesh. It wasn't the result Ronan aimed for, but he wasn't about to complain when the blast severed Erebos's connection to Reyna.

He was already running as she began to drop to the ground—and he wasn't the only one. Erebos and several guards were also on the move, but Ronan couldn't spare a second of attention for anything but her. Not the wall of flame he ran headlong toward. Or how with every step he cut himself off from the rest of the party.

None of it mattered.

The only thought on his mind was reaching her before she hit the ground.

EFFIE

"Oʜ, for the love of—why do I even bother warning people if they aren't going to listen?"

"Fledgling . . . Effie, wait!"

Lucian's exasperated shout reached her just as she crested the hill the Night Temple sat atop. It hadn't taken more than a cursory glance to see that the others had disregarded her warning and gone ahead. To be fair, the screams from within the temple had been a pretty big clue long before that.

Effie surged forward, heart in her throat as she braced herself for what was coming. She'd Seen this part so many times. Dreaded it almost as much as she had the very worst of her visions. They didn't always deal in specifics, but these ones had been crystal clear, and they featured those she held dear. There was nothing more terror-inducing than that.

Before she could run inside, Lucian's hand wrapped around her wrist, pulling her up short.

"Lucian, what are you doing? They need us."

"I'm stopping you from running into a burning building without me."

"It's not burn—" Smoke hit her nose, and a panicked cry escaped her lips. "Mother, no. We're too late. Reyna! Lucian, we have to get to her. We *have* to. He will never forgive me if—"

"Shh, I know." He met her stricken gaze with infuriating calm. As always, he was her port in the storm. "I know, sweetheart. And we will."

He didn't release her until she gave him a nod to show that she not only heard him, but she believed him. She had to believe. Otherwise all was already lost.

Black plumes of smoke wafted out of the doors, along with a wave of terrified wedding guests. There were so many people crowding the doorway, everyone trying to flee at once, that they'd bottlenecked the exit and effectively prevented anyone from getting out.

Or, in their case, *in*.

"Everybody move!" Kael bellowed, pointing toward the gate to indicate the path he wanted them to go. The crack of his voice seemed to do what simple logic had not, and the first person popped free, followed by a second, then a steady trickle of panicked Empyreans.

Effie waited only long enough to verify no one else was trying to escape before she darted in.

"Dammit, Effie," Lucian growled as he raced in after her.

She skidded to a stop almost immediately, her blood turning to ice as the vision that haunted her nightmares for months became her reality. Fire climbed the walls, eating away what little furniture existed as it ravaged everything it touched. The fiery glow a reflection of the eclipsed moon hanging swollen in the night sky. Reyna falling, snaking tendrils of inky mist wriggling like worms from her torso, her graceful figure limp and lifeless. Erebos's hand outstretched, more of that deadly fog curling out of his fingers as he attempted to reestablish his connection to the Forsaken queen. Ronan close, but still too far away due to the wall of flame between them. Cut off from his love and the rest of his allies. Enemies converging on him.

"Luc—"

"I'm on it. Get the others," he said, eyes already glowing bronze as he tapped into his Guardian's power to reshape the fire. "Kael, once we're done here, you're going to need to go back for Calypso and the rest of her party. We'll meet you on the *Lorelei*."

Kael nodded, attention only half on Lucian as he sucker punched the guard running for him so hard the man went airborne before falling onto his back completely unconscious.

Knowing Lucian would clear the way for her and that Kael would ensure the rest of their friends made it to safety, Effie focused on gathering the others.

A quick glance to the right showed Helena weaving Water and Air to bank the flames encroaching ever closer while her Mate and Bronn engaged in battle with what appeared to be nearly twenty armed guards.

Terrible odds—for the guards.

The pirate was not without his own gifts. He had some ties to the Air branch, if Effie had to guess based on the way his swords flew around and attacked unaided. Another orbited his hips, swinging around to slash anyone who dared get close to him. There wasn't time for her to see more than that as he continued to pick off enemies from one side while Von did the same beside him. Effie had seen the famed mercenary in action often enough to know that his combination of lightning-quick moves and burning sword would make short work of anyone stupid enough to go for him.

As for Bast, he wisely stayed close to Helena, using his body to shield a clearly injured Camille. Tucked away as they were near the back corner of the temple, he kept his gaze focused on the fight in front of him. Meaning he didn't see the guard creeping up from the side.

"Sebastian, look out!" Effie screeched.

He spun just in time, bodily shoving Camille out of the way and toward Effie's outstretched arms as he intercepted the blow intended for her. He let out a pained grunt, his weapon falling uselessly from his hand as the guard's blade slashed clean through his shoulder muscles.

"Bast!" Camille cried, her panic a twin of Effie's.

She didn't need her gift to know his wound was a bad one. The sheer amount of spurting blood told her everything she needed to know. As did the barely attached limb. He was going to lose the arm if they didn't get him out of here and taken care of.

Hearing Camille's scream, Helena spun around, creating a spear of Earth and Fire and launching it straight through the attacker's head, pinning his corpse to the temple's back wall. Camille struggled in Effie's hold, desperate to reach her protector.

"Bast!"

Since the immediate threat had been handled, Effie gave the terrified courtesan a shake. "Camille, we have to go."

"But, Sebastian. The High Lord . . . the fight isn't over," she protested.

"It is for us. We cannot win divided as we are. We need to regroup."

Camille shook her head, not in denial but in despair. "All of this . . . it cannot have been for nothing. We cannot let the High Lord win."

"If we stay, he will," Effie said, a hollow certainty settling in her stomach.

It had been a losing battle the second Ronan set foot inside that temple without the rest of them. With a consolidated effort, they might have stood a chance. And even then, the outcome wasn't up to her. She'd never had any say in that. But the one thing she *could* control was getting her friends out of a losing fight before they lost more than a limb.

Camille gave a resigned nod, her body relaxing against Effie's. "What about Sebastian?"

"He's coming with us. No one is getting left behind," Effie promised. Then, making good on it, she shouted, "Helena!"

The Kiri tossed one look over her shoulder, caught Effie's eye, and then placed a hand on both Bronn's and her Mate's shoulders, blinking—a magical feat that allowed her to travel short distances instantly—all three of them to Bast's huddled form. As soon as they appeared beside him, Von wrapped his arm around Helena's waist so she could grasp Sebastian with her free hand and blink the four of them over to where Effie and Camille stood.

They could have just as easily made a run for it, but running would have required they continue to fend off attacks. Blinking bought them all much-needed seconds.

"We have to get to Ronan and then back on the ship," Effie said as soon as Helena appeared.

The Kiri's expression was grim as she took in the still raging fire. Lucian had done what he could, but it was spreading faster than he could bank it. There were also about a dozen guards remaining between them and their friends.

Bast sagged in her hold, the blood loss taking its toll. Helena's eyes glittered as she tapped into her power and helped knit his flesh back together. "I'll have to heal it properly once we're safely away."

"Cami . . . where is . . . she," he panted, his eyes swimming in and out of focus as he searched for her.

"I'm here. I'm right here, Bast," she murmured, rushing to his side and helping support him. "You saved me. You were so brave."

He lifted blood-stained fingers to cup her cheek, a winsome—if not outright delirious—smile tilting his lips. "Now . . . I'm a . . . hero."

"You always have been, Bast," she said, lifting up to press her lips against his.

In a surprising show of strength, Bast lifted his good arm and wove his fingers through Camille's hair, anchoring her more firmly against him as he dipped her down and kissed her back. Effie rated it among the most romantic kisses she'd ever witnessed, though she'd wager those she'd participated in still eked them out for the top spot.

"Sure, have a bit of a cuddle," Von muttered, "not like we're in the thick of it or anything."

"We could die any minute. I'm making the most of the time I have," Bast shot back, pulling away from a flushed and besotted Camille.

"No one is dying," Effie gritted out. "Helena, when I say go, you deal with the fire. Lucian," she continued as he rushed over to join them, "you see to the portal. The rest of you, start running and do not stop until you are through that portal and safely on the deck of the *Lorelei*. Do you hear me?"

"What about him?" Lucian asked, jutting his chin to Erebos.

While they'd gathered, the High Lord had successfully reestablished his connection to Reyna, meaning she once again hovered in midair. Now that he had her secured, he could split his focus between her and Ronan, who was distracted by guards and didn't notice the misty figure Erebos was creating right behind him. Effie knew they didn't want to still be here by the time he finished.

"We can't worry about him right now. If we try to fight, we all die. Ready?"

Everyone nodded.

"Go!"

They took off running, trusting Helena to do what she did best. Within only a few steps, all the fire in the room snuffed out as simply as if someone had snapped their fingers. But it wasn't gone; it had been reclaimed.

Tossing a look over her shoulder, Effie watched as Helena created a massive fireball in the air above her head. Then with an outward flick of her wrists, the miniature sun exploded into smaller balls that flew straight at every remaining enemy in the temple.

The men and women fell with soundless screams, dead instantly.

Even Erebos wasn't spared, though Effie knew it would take far more than that to kill him for good. Still, he had to deal with the flames lest he wanted his vessel to burn, which gave them the precious seconds they needed for Lucian to finish the portal. Already Bronn, Bast, and Camille had ducked through.

As an added bonus, Helena's trick with the fire once again severed Erebos's connection to Reyna.

Without any guards or fire to restrain him, Ronan raced up the shallow steps to the altar, catching her falling body and pulling her into him. "I've got you," he whispered, eyes closed as a shudder raced down his spine. "I'm never letting you go again."

"Is that a promise?" Reyna's thready whisper had tears blurring Effie's vision.

Ronan's eyes snapped open, the icy orbs blazing. "It's a vow."

"How touching," Erebos sneered, his long hair singed and uneven. His clothes were still smoking and revealed more than a little charred skin.

"Ronan, go!" Effie shouted, her thighs burning as she raced the last few inches for the portal.

Helena shot through, Von on her heels. Lucian stood beside the shimmering oval, the pirate ship undulating on its surface, his hand ready to grab her and pull her through.

Erebos lashed out with one of his misty tendrils just as Ronan jumped through the displaced air. Effie was right behind him, meaning the attack intended for him hit her instead. She gasped as the unexpectedly solid weight of it crashed into her, knocking her off balance but pushing her through the portal.

Effie landed on her hands and knees on the deck of the *Lorelei*, her body seizing up as a feeling like the skittering of a thousand icy spiders crawled beneath her skin. She fell onto her back, a sudden weight crushing her lungs and her eyes rolling into her head as an unexpected parting gift from the High Lord caught her in its web.

Lucian dropped to his knees beside her, the familiar feel of his hand in hers registered as distantly as his voice in her mind. *"Effie? Can you hear me, love?"*

There were no words she could give him, so she simply gripped his hand tighter and gave him the only thing she had to offer.

A vision.

CHAPTER 19

EFFIE

If she'd learned anything about visions in these last half dozen years, it was to expect the unexpected. Sometimes they were riddles hidden within a chaotic flash of seemingly unrelated pictures. Other times a scene acted itself out in her mind. And on very rare occasions, it was a literal visit from Luna herself.

What she experienced now was similar to those only in the sense that it had taken her completely by surprise. But that's where the similarities ended. Likely because this was not an extension of the power gifted to her by the Mother. This vision had been triggered by coming into contact with Erebos's magic, meaning it had been sent by him—or perhaps stolen from was more apt. Effie found it hard to believe he'd willingly give her any inside information.

This vision did not consume her mind. There was no rapid assault of images. Instead, she found herself wandering around in a place leached of all color. It wasn't quite a landscape in the traditional sense. There were no trees or sky, but even so, it had the feel of a place waiting to be given purpose. Almost like an empty room, or a . . .

Sandbox.

The word came unbidden, but that's exactly what it felt like. A place where a child could create all manner of delights, if only given the opportunity to let their imagination run wild. This was a blank canvas in search of someone to define it and give it form. No, that wasn't quite right. Intention maybe?

No.

This place was waiting for a dream.

A dreamer.

As soon as the thought struck her, a figure appeared in the distance. A man by the look of it, but he was turned away from her, so she couldn't make out any details aside from the regal cut of his garments. This was no peasant. A courtier?

She took a step that felt like ten with the way the world rippled around her and pulled her closer to her target. That's when she realized she wasn't actually walking but willing herself forward.

One more 'step' propelled her all the way to her goal, bringing her a mere foot away from what she could only describe as a glass case. *Prison*, that same mental certainty corrected.

From this vantage, she could easily spot the crown resting atop his head. So, not a courtier, but royalty. The crown was modest, meaning it wasn't a king. A prince, perhaps?

Ex-prince, she decided, her gaze zeroing in on the crack in the golden band. Whoever he was, he used to be a royal, but no longer.

Niggling suspicion wormed its way through the back of her mind, but she refused to acknowledge it, wanting to see as much as she could before the vision ended. She stepped around the cage, once again finding intention alone was enough to move her.

A soft gasp left her as a very handsome, very familiar face came into view. But recognizing him did not fill her with comfort. If anything, it only made her more cautious. Thankfully, the man's eyes were closed, so he hadn't noticed her. The fact that he couldn't sense her emboldened Effie enough that she continued with her inspection.

A pulse fluttered lightly in his neck. Not dead then, just in stasis. No. He was asleep, but not peacefully. He appeared tormented, trapped within the very worst sort of nightmare.

The thought made her heart ache.

He was the dreamer of this fertile but untouched land, yet completely cut off from it by . . . what? The glass prison?

While studying him, she noticed a tiny fissure in the clear pane. One so small she may never have noticed it if she hadn't tilted her head *just* so. Reaching out, her fingers brushed that nearly invisible crack. As they did, the glass shattered, and the man sucked in a gasping breath as his eyes snapped open. Familiar green eyes bore into hers.

"Effie."

"Kieran," she whispered, his voice answering a question his face had not. For more than one man wore it, and only now could she tell which of them was trapped.

"Help me."

"How?"

He reached for her, desperation softening the haughty lines of his face. "Set me free."

As soon as he touched her, she was ripped from the vision, her eyes snapping open to find her mate's concerned face hovering over hers.

"Did you See?" she panted, feeling as though she'd just sprinted for miles.

Lucian nodded.

"You know what this means, don't you?"

"Aye," he said softly, helping her up to a seated position, wincing in sympathy at her soft groan. "Kieran's soul is trapped."

"We have to help him."

Lucian looked conflicted.

Effie glanced around the deck. It was a mad dash of people rushing everywhere to follow shouted orders. In the resulting chaos of their unexpected arrival, no one seemed to be paying the two Guardians any attention. "How long was I out?"

"Not long, seconds. The others didn't even notice."

She might have been offended if not for the fact that Bast had a major injury in need of Helena's attention and Ronan and Reyna were lost in each other. Of course, their focus was elsewhere.

"We have to help him," she said again, more firmly this time. "I know Kieran did terrible things. But there's no way we can know which of his sins are his own. Not if Erebos has been manipulating him for longer than we can ever know."

"I know," Lucian said with a resigned sigh. "But after what happened to you . . ."

"Hey, look at me."

Turbulent umber eyes met hers.

"I'm right here with you. Where I belong. Everything happened the way it was supposed to, so you and I could be . . . you and I. If Kieran hadn't foolishly triggered an ancient prophecy he didn't remotely understand and, in doing so, accidentally kick off the Shadow years —" Her eyes snapped to Reyna as an epiphany exploded through her mind. "It was always about her," she whispered. "Reyna . . . Shadow, she's the heart of all of it."

Lucian's expression mirrored her own shock and awe. "If Erebos is allowed to finish what he started . . . to harvest her power . . ."

"It's lights out for us," Effie finished. "We can't let that happen. It's all connected. Kieran. Shadow. All of it. Erebos needs both of them to fulfill whatever diabolic plan he intends to unleash—just like Luna needed Helena and me. We're all vessels, just in different ways. Kieran gave Erebos a body, and I gave Luna a voice."

"And Helena and Shadow both contain vast amounts of their godly magics," Lucian concluded, following her train of thought. "Together you four are their most powerful weapons."

"Exactly. If we can keep Erebos away from Reyna while we free Kieran, we take away everything he needs to remain on this realm. We find a way to do that, we defeat him." She let out a disbelieving laugh. "We can do it, Lucian. Together, all of us, we can defeat a god."

Lucian rested his forehead against hers. "When did you get so wise, fledgling?"

"It was bound to happen sometime. I have a very good tutor."

"I'll be sure to let Smoke know you think so," he said with a soft chuckle, though he almost immediately sobered. "We need to tell the others."

"We will," she agreed, her gaze once again wandering over the deck. "Soon, but not yet. I think they've earned a moment of peace. Don't you?"

"Give them the night to recover," he agreed. "The morning is soon enough to let them know the war is far from over."

"True, but at least now we know it's a war that can be won."

<h1 style="text-align:center">CHAPTER 20</h1>

<h2 style="text-align:center">RONAN</h2>

The second his feet touched down on the sturdy wood of the *Lorelei's* deck, Ronan's hold on the woman in his arms shifted. Instead of carrying her, he allowed her to slide slowly down the front of his body, keeping her steady with one hand on her hip, the other cradling her cheek.

The evidence of her ordeal was written on her face. In the purple smudges beneath her eyes. The pallor of her skin. The gaunt cast of her cheeks. And yet . . . she was still the most beautiful creature he'd ever seen. If anything, she was more precious to him because of it. Because of how close he'd been to losing her.

For good this time.

"Ronan?" she whispered, luminous eyes searching his.

"Reyna," he groaned, lips swooping down to steal hers. He kissed her with a reverence bordering on worship, his need for her greater than any he'd ever known.

She clung to him, her fingers weaving through his hair as she met his fervor with her own.

The rest of the world fell away as an undeniable truth rocked through him. This woman was . . . everything. And he'd almost lost her. Again.

First to another man.

Then to death.

It was an endless cycle of her being torn away from him, and it had to stop. He could not go on another second without staking his claim to her in every possible way. Here beneath the stars, under the ever-watchful eye of the heavens above, and surrounded by the people who mattered most to him on this earth.

With effort, he pulled away, his forehead dropping to rest on hers as he took her face between his hands. When her eyes fluttered open, he took a deep breath, his voice breaking around his whispered demand.

"Marry me."

"W-what?" The question came on a tremulous laugh.

Swallowing, trying to ease some of the tightness in his throat, he repeated, "Marry me. Tonight. Right now."

"Ronan. You can't be serious."

"I have never been more serious about anything in my life."

"But—"

He cut off whatever protest she'd been about to utter with his mouth. This time he pulled away just enough for his lips to feather over hers. "Marry me."

"Get a room!" Bast called from somewhere behind him.

Ronan released Reyna only long enough to give him the finger, but Reyna laughed, color suffusing her cheeks as she pulled herself free from his embrace.

"Sebastian, hush," Helena whispered, though sound seemed to carry out here, meaning her words easily reached them. "You're ruining it."

Ronan sighed and looked their way, finding Bast in the middle of a one-shouldered shrug, his other arm freshly healed but bound to his torso, likely to give the traumatized muscles time to rest. "I'm helping. She clearly needs some convincing. What better way than between the sheets, hm?"

Ronan bit back a curse while Reyna peeked up at him beneath her lashes. "He's not wrong. I do find you the most convincing when you're naked."

"That can be arranged."

Before he could set about making good on the promise, Helena's voice carried to them once more.

"How about you focus on not undoing my hard work and leave the proposing to him," she said, pushing Bast back down onto the crate he'd been using as a stool.

"I don't know," Bast said, biting his lip. "He's not very good at these things, *ma petite.* I'd hate for him to ruin it. He might need a little coaching. Some words of encouragement, perhaps."

Von burst out laughing, as did everyone else within range, meaning there were a good twenty or so people—strangers and friends alike—currently laughing at him. As happy as he was to see them all alive and well, he did not appreciate being the butt of the joke during his big moment.

"I mean it," Bast continued. "He's terrible. Have you ever heard him in action? He'd have better luck seducing a cactus."

"Oh, for fuck's sake," Ronan growled, grabbing Reyna's hand and tugging her toward the ship's bow, and more importantly, *away* from everyone else.

The giggles that pulled from her were enough to blunt the edge of any true temper. He loved the sound of her laugh, even if it was at his expense.

Once they reached the bow, he glanced around to ensure they were alone. Then he placed her at the helm and took two steps back. "There."

She raised a brow, a small smile playing about her lips. "Can't help but notice this isn't a bedroom."

"I wanted to ensure I have your undivided attention. We get anywhere near a bed and your focus will stray."

"Oh, I don't know. If you do it right, I'm pretty sure I'd be wholly focused on you."

"On my cock, you mean."

"And what's it's doing. I'm also a fan of your tongue," she added with a little wag of her brows. "Oh, and that thing you do with your fingers right before I—"

"Reyna," he groaned, the images she painted torturing him almost as much as the husky cadence of her voice. "Mother's tits, can you please just let me propose properly?"

She sobered. "Stars, Ronan, you're trembling. This is really important to you, isn't it?"

He hadn't realized his hands were shaking until she mentioned it. He'd been so focused on her, on what he wanted—no, needed—to say to her. It took two tries before he could speak around the ball of emotion lodged in his throat.

"Today I received a letter, or rather, a letter was read to me . . ."

Even in the moonlight, he could see the blush staining her cheeks.

"Did you mean them? The things you said?" he whispered, suddenly afraid she'd written them in the heat of the moment and might have second thoughts now that they weren't both on the verge of annihilation. The silence stretched, and he feared his heart would cease beating until she reached out and gripped his hand.

"Every single one."

He sank down until he was on his knees. Tradition dictated one, but Reyna deserved absolute surrender. She already possessed his heart, but he wanted her to know every last piece of him was hers. His love, obviously. But also his pride. His protection. His name. For however long he had left in this world, all that he was, was hers.

"Then marry me, kitten. Be my wife."

She blinked away tears and tried to pull him back up. When he didn't budge, she knelt down in front of him, uncomfortable with his show of submission. "Ronan, I know you're worried. The last few weeks have been . . . a lot. But I'm not going anywhere. We don't have to rush into this."

"You don't know that."

"I do. No one's coming between us again. I love you. Nothing is going to change that. Not a ceremony. Not some piece of paper. I promise you, there's no rush."

"There is. Today proved that none of us can know how much time we have. I don't want to go another second without knowing that you are bound to me in every possible way. I need this, Reyna. You gave me your vows, and it meant more to me—" He had to break off to breathe around the constriction of his throat. "Please, sweetheart. Allow me the opportunity to give mine to you. I know it's not going to be a fancy ceremony. Just you, me, a few friends, and the stars and sea—"

"That's all I need."

"Then say yes. Say you'll be mine."

"I've always been yours."

He could have kissed her then, but she still hadn't given him what he needed. "There's only been one person in my entire life that calms the restless beast that is my heart. Only one who makes me want to stand still and just be after a lifetime of wandering. I watched you at that altar tonight with another man knowing it should have been me. You're mine, Reyna. My forever. My home. So please, stand still with me. *Marry me.*"

Her lip wobbled, but her voice was filled with amusement. "Okay."

His hand gripped hers, and he blinked a few times, unsure he'd heard her correctly. "Okay?"

She nodded, tears spilling free as she laughed. "Let's get married and stand still, or run, or swim, or fight. Whatever you want, so long as we love."

"No one will love you more," he promised, pulling her to him so he could kiss her. But he cut it short, needing to hear her say it one more time. "We're really doing this? We're getting married?"

Her laugh was breathless against his lips. "I mean, I'm already wearing this dress. It would be a shame to waste it."

He knew his smile was pure sin as he leaned back down to reclaim her lips. "As gorgeous as it looks on you, kitten, I'm looking forward to the part where I get to peel it off."

"That makes two of us."

"Best we get this over with then, isn't it? That way we can get on to more private celebrations."

"We're alone right now. Seems pretty private to me."

He reached around and gave her arse a squeeze, drawing a low moan from her. "So we are. But the next time I fuck a woman, kitten, she's going to be my wife." Reyna let out a soft whimper as he nipped her lower lip and stood, pulling her up with him. "What do you say, you ready to go get married?"

She snuggled into his side, her palm resting lightly over his heart. "You know, for the first time today, I think I am." Then she let out a tinkling laugh.

"Why's that funny?"

"It's not. It just occurred to me that Bast was wrong. You *can* be convincing with your clothes on."

Ronan joined in her laughter. "Well, to be fair, Bast is almost *always* wrong. But in this particular case, I did find myself exquisitely motivated. I wasn't going to settle for anything other than a yes."

"As much as I appreciate your commitment to the cause, there was never any doubt of my answer, Ronan. You heard my letter. You know my heart."

"I do, but now it's time for you to hear the words written on mine."

CHAPTER 21

REYNA

"I mean, I suppose I should ask Drake, but I *am* a captain, and the *Lorelei* is technically my ship, so I don't see any reason why I couldn't officiate a wedding."

Reyna opened her mouth, but Helena beat her to a response, glancing over at Caly while still holding on to her hand for the health check she was currently performing. "I'd be happy to do it. Surely not even Drake can argue that the Mother's Chosen Vessel trumps captain when it comes to any sort of pecking order."

Effie shot her an amused glance, her voice pitched low. "I don't know if I've ever been so glad Lucian and I never officially married."

"You didn't?" Reyna asked, surprised that the Guardian wouldn't have demanded it. It struck her as the sort of thing he would insist on, much in the same way Ronan had.

She shook her head, a soft contented smile playing about her lips as her gaze shifted to her mate, who stood across the ship with Ronan and the other males. "He merged our souls. Not sure a wedding's really necessary after that."

Reyna sputtered out a laugh. "No, I guess it would be a little redundant."

Effie's eyes widened, and her cheeks went bright pink. "Not that weddings aren't beautiful and the height of romance—"

"Peace, Effie. I took no offense."

The Keeper pressed a hand to her forehead, looking mortified. "You would think with as much talking as I do these days, I'd be better at it. Why the Mother selected *me* as her Voice, I'll never know."

Reyna reached out and gave her arm a squeeze. "I think your honesty is refreshing and your words inspired. Actually, I was hoping you would be the one to officiate for us. If you wouldn't mind, and you two wouldn't be upset—" She glanced at Caly and Helena, who'd fallen silent to listen to their side conversation.

"I think it's a brilliant idea," Caly said, her smile huge as she looked to Effie.

"Aye. It will be as though the Mother herself is blessing the union," Helena agreed.

Relieved her request hadn't offended the other women, Reyna looked at Effie, who'd yet to speak.

"M-me?" she stuttered, remnants of the shy girl she'd once been peering out.

"Yes, *you.*" She took Effie's hand between her own. "It's because of you Ronan and I found our way back to each other. *Both* times, from what I've been told. This wedding wouldn't even be possible without you. And I know he thinks of you as a sister. I can't imagine there's anyone more suited for the role."

"I . . . I . . ." Effie blinked rapidly and cleared her throat.

As if he could sense her approaching tears, Lucian's head snapped toward his mate, a small crease between his brows. After a beat, his expression cleared, and a smile flitted across his handsome face. It was then Reyna recalled that Guardians could communicate telepathically. Given the sheer adoration shining in his gaze, he must have asked her what was wrong, only to find out there was no cause for alarm.

Likely bolstered by his support, Effie sucked in a watery breath and beamed. "I would be happy to officiate for you, if that's what you and Ronan really want."

"It is," Reyna said with an emphatic nod.

"Well then, I suppose I should go figure out what in the Mother's name I'm going to say," she said with a nervous laugh, rushing off to the area the crew had cleared away for the ceremony—which, truth be told, was really just the middle of the deck.

"I've got her," Helena said with a wink before patting the back of Reyna's hand. "As for you, everything looks fine. Despite Erebos's best efforts, you and the babe weren't harmed at all. You might be a little more fatigued than usual because of the magic drain, but nothing a couple days' rest won't take care of."

"I-I'm sorry. I'm going to need you to repeat that. I thought I just heard you say babe, but I . . . I can't . . . I'm not able to . . ."

"You didn't know." Realizing she'd just given Reyna shocking news, the Kiri's eyes widened. Then she shook her head. "Of course you didn't. It's still very early. Only a few weeks at most."

Their night spent at that oasis. It had to have happened then; it was the only time they'd been together.

Spots danced in her vision, and Reyna struggled to catch her breath. "But I can't have children," she mumbled, her voice sounding as if it came from a far distance.

"Shit, I think she's going to faint!" Caly swooped in, wrapping an arm beneath Reyna's shoulders and catching her just as her knees gave out.

Helena reached for her face, brushing some hair off her brow while offering her a welcome burst of soothing energy and confirming what she also suspected. "I think whatever it was in that water that healed Ronan's injuries and freed your mind from Erebos's influence might have healed a few other things as well."

A place of power, Jagger had called it. Seems like he'd been correct.

Reyna's hand dropped to her belly, protectively curling over the flat surface. "You really mean it? I'm . . . we're . . ." She flicked a worried gaze to the men and dropped her voice. "Pregnant?"

Helena's answering smile was filled with a mother's compassion. "You're pregnant. Congratulations, mama."

Reyna burst into tears.

"I take it that's not good news?" Caly ventured, her arm tightening supportively. "Because nothing has to be decided right now. You have options—"

"No, it's not that . . . I just . . ." She furiously wiped at her face and fought hard to slow her breathing. A second wave of Helena's calming magic helped. "The last few years, the life I led . . . there was no place for a child in that world. I told myself I was unfit, that my damaged womb was karma for the life I'd chosen. I'd made peace with it, was relieved even.

"But before Erebos, when I was just Reyna, a child would have been a blessing." She shook her head, another tear spilling free. "And a child with Ronan? One that was borne of our love. Our own tiny miracle? I . . ." She shook her head, a laugh escaping. "I didn't know how badly I wanted it until I thought it wasn't possible. If ever there was a man who was made to be a father . . ."

The thought of them going through it together, her thick with his child, him even more overprotective and doting than he already was. She didn't think her heart could grow any fuller without bursting.

"Do you think this is something he wants?" she asked, her voice whisper thin. They'd never gotten around to talking about starting a family. It was sort of a moot point when you might not live long enough to see the morning. What if he was the one who didn't want children?

"Are you kidding me? He's going to be over the moon, Reyna. That man loves you beyond reason." Helena's expression grew distant, but her voice was filled with fond remembrance. "Ronan once gave me his sigil. Traditionally during the Jaka ceremony, the one who marks you hides their symbol within the design. Do you know what his symbol means?"

Reyna shook her head.

"Loyalty. Ronan is the most unfailingly loyal man you will ever know. He will be by your side through all of life's adventures. The good and the scary. But in case you have a single doubt in your heart, banish it here and now because any child of yours will know nothing but love. He's going to spoil them endlessly, teach them things you probably rather he wouldn't, and protect all of you with his dying breath. You could not ask for a better or more devoted partner."

"I know." She sniffled, feeling foolish for crying in front of these women but unable to stop herself.

Helena took Reyna's face in her hands and then leaned up to press a kiss to her forehead. "You don't have to tell him about the babe tonight if you don't want to. Enjoy just being the two of you for a little while. You'll know when the time is right."

She released her and stepped back, but Reyna reached out, brushing her fingers against her hand. "Helena?"

"Yes?"

"Thank you."

"For what?"

For giving me this gift. For freeing Ronan from his vow. For healing him and being by his side when I could not.

But that was too much to say, and far too revealing, so instead she shrugged and offered a heartfelt, "Everything."

"You deserve it."

Reyna wasn't sure about that, but she wasn't going to argue with the Kiri over it either. Thankfully, she was saved from having to say anything by the sound of a throat being cleared.

"Uh, I hope I'm not interrupting anything?"

Reyna was surprised to hear Bronn's voice, but after another quick wipe of her face, she spun around and pasted on a bright smile. "No. Not at all."

It was clear by his pained expression she hadn't done a very good job disguising the fact she'd just been in the midst of a life-changing and emotional moment. "I, uh, just wanted to come over here to give you this." He held out a familiar silver dagger. She must have dropped it during the scuffle with Erebos, and he, not even knowing what it meant to her, had the wherewithal to grab it before darting through the portal.

The sight of her mother's weapon, on this day, in *this* moment, was enough to set off a fresh round of waterworks. "Stars, I'm a mess."

"You're not a mess. You're just happy," Caly said, rubbing her hand up and down Reyna's spine.

"This is happy?" Bronn asked with a dubious lift of his brow.

"I think we've got it from here," the captain said, scowling at him. "Why don't you tell the others to get in their places?"

"Aye, cap'n," he said, giving her a little salute and doing nothing to disguise his relief at having an excuse to flee the leaking bride. As he spun and raced off, his whistle cut through the night, drawing the attention of everyone on deck. "Get over here and grab a bit o'plank, ye mangy curs."

"I guess this is the part where we sit down," Helena said. "Are you going to be all right by yourself?"

Dagger safely tucked back in its sheath and hands resting lightly on her belly, she smiled. "I'm not by myself."

My mother and my little miracle are with me.

Before Helena made it a single step, the sound of raised voices had them both spinning toward the makeshift 'altar' where Effie waited with her hand pressed to her lips, her shoulders quaking with laughter. It only took a second to see why.

Bast and Von were facing off, glaring at each other as they each tried to stand in the place of honor beside Ronan. For his part, the groom seemed uninclined to settle the argument by choosing between them. He simply raised his hands and shook his head, a wide grin lighting up his face as he watched their antics play out.

Her heart gave a happy leap in response to Ronan's joy. This is where he belonged. Not on a ship, necessarily, but surrounded by the people he loved. He'd spent much of the last few years pulling away and isolating himself from the people he needed most, and his soul had suffered for it. Like a tree denied sunlight, it had begun to wither and die. Only now, basking in the warmth of their companionship, was he able to thrive once more.

"Stand aside. Your place is beside your lady wife," Bast said.

"My place is beside the brother of my soul, as it has been since we were children," Von snapped back, his silver eyes flashing.

"You've known him longer, big deal. I've saved his life."

"As have I."

Bast flushed for a second, then grinned triumphantly. "Well, *I* taught him the proper way to seduce a woman. Which I think we can both agree is more relevant to the night's festivities."

"Hey now—" Ronan started, but Von spoke over him.

"As did I."

"Well, he wasn't very good at it before I showed up, so you must have been a shit teacher."

Von's expression darkened, the vein pulsing in his throat visible even from here.

"I'd be jealous of how territorial he's acting if I didn't know how much he loves me," Helena grumbled, shaking her head in exasperation at her Mate's antics. "I've never seen him like this."

"Like what?"

"Like a schoolboy fighting over his first love."

Reyna snickered. "He *has* known Ronan longer. I can understand his reluctance to stand aside for another who wants to claim his place."

"Be that as it may, there's no need for anyone's place to be taken. Why does it have to be either or?"

"Pride?" Reyna ventured with a shrug, not about to pretend to understand the minds of men.

Helena sighed. "You're probably right."

They fell silent just in time for Bast's huffed, "Well, if you won't move willingly, then I'll have to make you."

"Oh, I would love to see you try," Von said with a quiet laugh that rolled around the deck like thunder.

The *Lorelei's* crew had been maintaining a respectful distance until now, lending an illusion of privacy to their . . . if not welcome guests exactly, tolerated passengers at the very least. But at the hint of a proper scrap, they let out approving cheers and inched in closer.

Looking around at the crowd they'd gathered, Bast's face flushed. As if he just realized he was going to have to make good on his threat. With a determined set to his shoulders, Bast pushed up his shirt sleeve on his unbound arm as best he could and then gamely shoved Von as hard as he could.

Von didn't so much as rock back on his heels. Instead he laughed and then repeated Bast's move, sending Bast flying backward into the row of chairs that had been set out for wedding attendees who might prefer to sit.

Sebastian managed to retain his balance, but only just. Reyna could see him preparing to tackle Von and released an aggrieved sigh. If she didn't intervene now, this would go on until someone—likely Bast— got seriously hurt.

Suddenly inspired, she called out his name. "Sebastian!"

He glanced over his shoulder, clearly surprised by her summons.

A little embarrassed she was about to shout her half-formed request in front of what had to be about a hundred people, she cleared her throat. "Do you have a moment?"

He looked at Von and then back to her. "I'm sort of in the middle of something."

Realizing she wasn't getting off easily, Reyna blurted, "I was hoping you might give me away. I have no family here, and well, after all we've been through, you are one of the closest things I have left."

Bast's mouth dropped open, and it took several heartbeats before he recovered his usual roguish swagger. He straightened, tugging on his shirt and tossing a smug look at Von. "It would seem I've been given a grander assignment."

Ronan caught her eye, laughter curling his lips. "Thank you," he mouthed.

She nodded, feeling his words like a caress along her skin. Honestly, she didn't much care about the details of the wedding. She just wanted to get to the part where she and Ronan were declared man and wife. Anything that helped speed that ending along was a win in her book.

As Bast made his way over to her, Reyna noticed Camille's gaze trailing him. There was a wistful expression in the courtesan's eyes she couldn't recall seeing before. Cami was a gifted spy, one of Dovina's best, yet she'd risked everything to help them. The woman didn't do anything for free, so there had to be something in it for her, but for the life of her, Reyna couldn't puzzle out just what that was.

"You seem to be collecting admirers," she teased Bast as he reached her.

"I've been known to leave a trail of broken hearts in my wake, *mon ange.* That is nothing new."

"Something tells me you don't intend to break this one."

Bast followed her line of sight, his expression transforming as he spotted Camille. Instead of playful, it was tender. And curious, as if he was still trying to figure things out himself. "Perhaps not."

"Does this mean Loren is out of the picture?"

"I . . . don't know. I suppose I'd have to find him first."

"Is that something you want? To find him?"

"But of course. It is the least I can do."

"So maybe you figure it out then. Sometimes what seems like love burns hot and fast and is good for only the course of a single night. Other times, it is slow to catch fire and burns eternal. It is not always easy to tell the difference between the flames at the start."

"And sometimes love is a sandwich."

Reyna froze, the words so unexpected and seemingly off-topic that she could only laugh. "I'm sorry, what?"

"A sandwich," he repeated, a small furrow forming between his brows. "Is that not the word for it? When there are two pieces of bread and a delicious slice of meat in between. I could have sworn that's what the shopkeeper called it."

"I'm familiar with what a sandwich is, Bast. But why do you believe love is like one?" She struggled to keep her expression as serious as his, but laughter threaded her inquiry.

"Because bread is delicious, and two slices are better than one. Obviously."

"Obviously," she repeated, pressing her lips together to keep the giggle climbing up her throat from escaping. "And I take it Loren and Camille are the metaphorical bread in this scenario? Is that your way of saying you want them both?"

Bast shrugged. "Maybe. I guess we shall see. But why can't a heart love more than one person at once? I am an excellent lover. It stands to reason I would have more love to give than the average male."

She reached up and tucked a stray strand of hair behind his ear, smiling into his guileless gray eyes. "There is nothing average about you, Sebastian. Follow your heart. It will lead you to your perfect . . . sandwich." She was going to say mate, but in honor of his metaphor, she'd changed her mind.

"I wasn't sure I'd live long enough to experience true love's sting, but then I met Ronan and saw the way he looked at you. He proved to me it was out there, if one was only willing to fight for it."

Reyna's heart performed a series of backflips beneath her ribs. Hearing Ronan loved her shouldn't have affected her so. He'd declared it openly many times over by now, but Bast's admission that he'd recognized it as true love long before she did just hit differently.

She pressed a soft kiss on his cheek. "Thank you, Bast."

"That's enough of that. You're a soon-to-be married woman!" Ronan shouted, rousing more teasing cheers from the crowd of onlookers.

Bast wove her arm through his and gave her husband to be a cheeky grin. "Maybe I decided I would like to keep her."

"And maybe I'll throw you overboard and let you test your luck with the Lusca."

Sebastian blanched. "On second thought . . . perhaps you should keep her."

"Oh, I intend to." Ronan grinned, his eyes flashing with blue fire as they caught and held hers. The heat of his gaze seared her, turning her insides molten. Despite the cool sea breeze sweeping over her, a bead of sweat rolled down her spine, and she discreetly tried to fan her face.

"On that note, why don't we get started? Is everyone ready?" Effie asked, looking far more composed now that she'd had a chance to gather her thoughts and think on what she wanted to say.

A chorus of 'ayes' rang out as the last few people rushed to take their seats. The Guardians filed in first, followed by the Kiri and the other members of her Circle, who claimed what chairs were left. Caly and her crew stood behind them while Effie stood up with Ronan and Von beside her. The Keeper stared intently at Reyna, waiting for her confirmation.

With Ronan's promises and Helena's life-changing news floating through her mind, Reyna was smiling so hard her cheeks hurt. "Aye," she said, her voice soft.

She may as well have just said 'I do' with the way Ronan's expression twisted. He looked halfway ready to storm over and sweep her off her feet. Reyna knew only his desire to formally speak his vows held him in place.

"Ronan?" Effie prompted when he still hadn't given her his go-ahead. "What do you say?"

"I say it's about damned time."

CHAPTER 22

RONAN

"This won't do at all," Effie muttered, her lips twisting down as she stared hard at the ceremony space.

"What do you mean?" he asked, ready to get the fuck on with it already. There was a beautiful woman in a fancy dress standing *right there* who'd just agreed to become his wife after he spent years fighting tooth and nail to get back to her. Every passing second was an opportunity for her to change her mind—or worse—for fate to snatch her from him again.

"A few smelly crates and borrowed chairs scattered between some cannons doesn't exactly scream wedding. We can do better than this."

A protest was ready on his lips, but then he looked at Reyna, and he couldn't deny Effie's assertion. Even if his bride claimed to not care about the details, she deserved more than this. It may be last minute, but that didn't mean they had to cut corners. After tonight, she would be his forever. He could wait a few more minutes to ensure it was memorable and that when they looked back on the night, neither of them had a single regret.

"Do it."

Effie's eyes gleamed, and she waved Helena and the Guardians over. They exchanged concerned looks, wondering why Effie went from insisting it was time to begin to calling them up. But as soon as she explained what she wanted, they all mirrored her excitement.

"Here's what I'm picturing. Do you think you can handle that?" Effie asked, using her Guardian power to project the thought to them.

"I love it," Helena said, iridescent irises sweeping over the deck. "I can take care of the decorations if you three want to deal with attire."

"Ronan does love my haircuts," Lucian said, rubbing his hands together with a chuckle.

Recalling the time the bastard cut off his braid to make a bit of cloth, Ronan scowled.

"Just be quick about it," he grumbled.

He'd seen his friends use their gifts countless times, but it never got old. In less than a minute, Helena and the Guardians transformed the deck of the ship from plain and utilitarian to something inviting and, dare he say, romantic. Orbs of soft flickering light hovered playfully in the air. White flower petals created the illusion of an aisle. The crates and mismatched chairs were now proper seats with wildflowers and lanterns hanging from the arms. There were also large fragrant floral arrangements on either side of him, and more behind the guests.

Ronan was sure there were other details, but his attention snagged on the breeze rushing over the back of his neck. His hair had been down, meaning he shouldn't have felt the wind, and for one stomach-dropping second, he feared Lucian had done something drastic like shave his head, but a quick check had him huffing out a laugh.

The Guardians must have taken Helena's instruction about attire to heart, because Ronan's outfit had been upgraded from the smooth knot at the top of his head down to the tip of his polished boots. There wasn't a mirror for him to look in, but the finely made garments were far more appropriate for a groom than the prisoner's rags he'd been wearing prior.

And he wasn't the only one. All the guest's battle-stained garb and borrowed black robes had been replaced with clothing more appropriate for a celebration. If Bast's excited exclamation and the reverent way he ran his hand over his fresh silk shirt were any indication, everyone approved of the enhancements.

"Better?" Effie asked with a knowing grin.

"Much." He curled an arm around her neck and reeled her in for a bear hug. "Thank you, Efs."

She wound her arms around his waist, giving him a tight squeeze. "I couldn't let the man who taught me—"

"The proper way to skewer someone?" he offered, remembering the first lesson she'd attended with him.

Laughing, she pulled away. "I was going to say see my own worth."

"I didn't do that."

"You did."

"When?"

"Every time you stayed up late with me to help me master a new skill. Every time you reminded me not to give up on myself, that I was just as capable as anyone else, and the only one standing in the way of my potential was me.

"I don't know if I ever told you this, but besides my grandmother, no one had ever included me in anything like that—until you. And it's because of what you taught me that I'm standing here. Your lessons helped me not only face some of the most terrifying moments of my life but overcome them. I might be the Mother's Voice, Ronan, but you helped me find my own."

"Effie, I—" He blinked hard, his vision swimming in light of her confession. Heart-to-hearts weren't exactly his forte, but it seemed it was the day for them. He was feeling too many things, most of them impossible to name, but the one emotion he had no trouble identifying was pride. "I'm so fucking proud of you and the woman you've become. I always knew you were destined for greatness. You might be a tiny scrap of a thing, but you were always fierce. I'm honored I was able to help you see it too."

She stood on her tiptoes to cup his face and press a soft kiss to his cheek. "I've missed you. I've missed that man, Ro. The one who looked at me and saw what I could be if only I allowed myself to do so. There is little I wouldn't give to have him—*you*—back. In the end, all it required was helping you find her. Hardly a steep cost at all. There was no way I'd diminish this gift the Mother has given us. It would be a crime not to celebrate the return of those we hold most dear. You, the return of the one who makes your soul complete. Us, the return of our beloved friend. Not to mention your union to each other."

Ronan stared at her, at a total loss for words.

Not seeming to require any sort of response, Effie gave his shoulder a squeeze and pulled away. "You are loved, Ronan. So much more than you know."

Ronan wiped at his nose and cleared his throat, struggling to work past the overwhelming emotion lodged there. Wordlessly, his eyes sought out Reyna. Joy shone on her face, a wondering laugh escaping her as she took in the deck's transformation. As if she could feel his attention on her, her gaze found his, and the soft sheen of tears in her beloved jewel-bright eyes told him everything he needed to know. She was the happiest he'd ever seen her.

"Now we can begin," Effie said softly, having witnessed their silent exchange.

From the corner of his eye—for he found himself unable to look away from Reyna—he saw Effie give someone a little nod.

Immediately, a haunting yet undeniably beautiful melody sounded as a few members of Caly's crew began to sing. He vaguely recalled being told about the cook's gift, but it in no way prepared him for the reality of hearing it.

What would have been an unremarkable tune about a shipwrecked sailor following the sound of his lady love's song back home became something far greater when slowed and expertly performed in Cookie's resonant bass. The song was elevated further when little Willie joined in with his sweet tenor. Shivers broke out along the back of Ronan's neck and arms as their voices merged and swelled, floating out into the night like an offering. Though the goosebumps might have also been the result of Reyna's procession toward him.

Ronan forgot how to breathe as he watched, his body drawn tight as a bowstring as he fought the urge to run to her. The smile playing about her lips told him she knew it, too. She moved with the same sensual grace as always, every step sure and even. As if she were both certain of her destination and eager to get there. The knowledge that said destination was at his side had Ronan standing taller with masculine pride. This woman without equal, this queen, had chosen him.

It felt like forever before she reached him, and Ronan barely had eyes for Bast as he carefully untangled their arms and placed Reyna's hand in his.

"What happened to just our friends, the sea, and the stars?" she asked as her palm slid against his.

"I was told that wasn't good enough."

Her soft laughter cradled his heart, and he found himself simultaneously blinking away tears and grinning like a madman.

"You clean up nicely," she murmured, drinking him in.

"I look even better naked."

Effie and Von overheard his whispered words, and both choked on laughs. Reyna's eyes glittered with a hunger he recognized as she purred, "That you do."

"Your beauty outshines Luna herself, kitten."

She leaned in, her lips at his ear. "I look better naked too."

He hummed in agreement. "Why do you think I'm marrying you?"

The air grew charged between them, but Effie's not-so-subtle cough pulled them apart as the pirates' song ended.

Tossing the crowd a conspiratorial grin, she said, "I've been informed that Captain Lawless has agreed to open several casks of his reserve in honor of the occasion." Every pirate on deck let out a heartfelt cheer. "So, with that in mind, I'll endeavor to keep this short and sweet." The cheers grew even louder until she had to interrupt. "All right, all right, settle down. This may be my only chance to officiate one of these things. I want to do it right."

A few soft chuckles met her declaration, Ronan and Reyna's included. There was no doubt in his mind she would excel at this task as she had every other set before her. Her next words proved it.

"I was once told that mortals mistakenly believe love is the strongest bond they can form on this earth. That their short lifespans preclude them from forming deeper, more meaningful connections. I stand here today knowing that isn't true."

Her eyes darted toward her own mate, whose lips were twitching with exasperated laughter. Clearly, she must be disputing something *he'd* told her.

"Death offers a clarity immortality cannot. When you know your life is finite, your days numbered, you learn to appreciate each and every one. And when you find someone to fill those hours with joy instead of sorrow, you cherish them even more for the gift they are to you.

"Sometimes these people are not just a gift, but a blessing. And these people do not just fill our days with light, they are the other half of our soul. Soulmates are not unique to immortals, though they are rare and even more precious because of it. The moment anyone, mortal or otherwise, finds the person who makes their soul cry out with recognition is monumental. Life changing. Worthy of celebration. And it is such an occasion that brings us here today."

Ronan glanced down at Reyna, noting the trickle of a tear down her cheek. He reached over, brushing it away and earning himself a tender smile.

"These bonds are sacred, a gift from the Mother herself, and they should be treasured, for this blessing is not given lightly. Oftentimes soulmates must fight for the privilege of being whole. It is for this reason I can say with utter certainty that you, Ronan and Reyna, are one such pair. Very few who walk this earth have ever fought harder to be together, and it is your endless devotion to each other that proves you both worthy recipients of the gift you've been given."

Reyna's hand tightened on his, her breath hitching in response to Effie's speech. Ronan was no less affected. The words were powerful on their own, but coming from her—the Mother's Voice—was akin to hearing them from the goddess herself. The affirmation went a long way to soothing the years of heartache. If that was the price the Mother demanded in order for him to spend the rest of his life with his soulmate, he would pay it again many times over.

"And so it is with absolute joy that I find myself standing here with you to recognize the culmination of two such souls reuniting at last. Ronan, Reyna, would you like to offer your mate your vows?"

Reyna turned to face him, still holding his hand, her eyes bright but steady as they met his. "I seem to recall some rather rambling vows I already offered you today."

Ronan's answering laugh was a husky rumble.

"Forgive me if I plagiarize or repeat myself, but I believe the important part went something like this: You are my flame in the dark. The order to my unending chaos. The only person who makes *me* make sense. Whatever obstacles we face in this life, or as many forces try to keep us apart, I will do whatever I must to find my way back to you. In this life or the next. But if it must be the next, know that with my very last breath, I am loving you. Burning for you. Fighting for you. Because there is no me, my love, without you."

It was true; the promises were similar to those in her letter, but hearing them directly from her lips, combined with the depth of her emotion, made them brand new.

He reached for her, intent on kissing her, on expressing to her how much her vows meant, but the wave of laughter from the crowd checked his movement. As he went to straighten, Reyna's free hand swept up and pulled him back down, sealing his lips to hers.

"You are the Butcher, and I, Empyria's assassin," she whispered fiercely, kissing him a second time. "We make our own rules."

The resulting cheers were deafening.

"Your turn, Ronan," Effie said, her eyes shining with mirth when they finally pulled free of each other.

He cleared his throat, uncomfortably aware of the stares aimed his way. But as he took a steadying breath, he found his footing in the safety of his mate's loving gaze. Everyone else fell away, leaving only the two of them as he began.

"I'm not a man used to making long-winded speeches. In my life, there's been no need for me to learn flowery words of poetry—"

"It shows," Bast shouted, earning his own wave of approving chuckles.

Ronan ignored him, mentally promising to pay him back for that later.

"Instead, I will do as I've always done and make do with the truth as it is written in my heart." He lifted her hand and pressed it against his chest, holding it there beneath his. "My heart beats for you. It's belonged to you from the very first. When you left, you took it with you, and I was adrift. I became little more than a shell of a man, for as we know, a man cannot exist without his heart. And certainly not without his soul, and you, my beautiful Reyna, are both.

"So here is my promise, my vow to the woman whose love not only mended a broken heart but whose presence in my life taught it how to beat anew. I will love you. Eternally. In this life and every one hereafter. No matter how many times we are reborn, my soul will seek yours, and I will find you, for without you, I am lost. A hopeless wanderer in search of home. *You* are my home. And no matter how long and far I must search, I will *always* find you, and with every beat of this heart, I will love you."

"Ronan," she whispered, his name tight with emotion.

"I love you, kitten. I always have. I fought for years to find you. And I will spend the rest fighting at your side. My heart, my sword, my life, they are yours to do with what you will."

"All I want is you."

"I am yours."

Effie had to speak around her tears as she asked, "Do you have rings or some other tokens to act as the physical representations of the promises you've made to each other?"

Ronan and Reyna exchanged bemused glances, both at a loss.

Shrugging, Reyna said, "All I have is my mother's dagger."

Effie gave her a considering look. "Is it something you'd be willing to part with?"

For a second, Reyna seemed unsure, but then she pulled the blade free and handed it over to Effie. A little jolt went through him at the sight of the blade he'd safeguarded for her. He'd thought it lost, but seeing it now, realizing the part it was about to play in their future after the one it had played in their past, filled him with a sense of absolute rightness. It was a blade they'd both held, loved, used in their battle to be reunited. What better source for the rings that would represent their vows to each other?

Dagger in hand, Effie's eyes flared a blinding sapphire as she tapped into her Guardian power and transformed Reyna's beloved dagger. When she opened her hand, the weapon was gone, replaced by two stunning silver rings. The design that had once wrapped around the hilt was etched into the metal. They were exact replicas of each other, with one exception. The words inscribed on the inside were different. In Reyna's was the echo of Ronan's vow: 'I will love you' and in his, the echo of hers: 'In this life, and the next.'

"Effie, they're perfect," Reyna murmured.

"I was inspired," she said with a watery laugh.

Taking the rings, Ronan and Reyna placed them on each other's fingers and then looked at Effie expectantly.

"What?" she asked, then her eyes widened with understanding. "Oh! I pronounce you man and wife. You may kiss—"

There was no need for her to finish. Ronan wrapped his arms around Reyna's waist and lifted her up as she slid her hands into his hair and fit her lips against his. This time, Ronan barely heard the raucous cheers of the pirates.

He was too busy kissing—and loving—his wife.

CHAPTER 23

RONAN

It was easier than one might think to slip away on a pirate ship. Despite the close quarters, the night's revelries were well underway—and the other passengers well in their cups—meaning no one noticed when the guests of honor ran off in search of a room.

Well, almost no one.

"Where do you think you're going?"

The unfamiliar voice drew them up short.

Ronan tried his best to be charming, though what he really wanted was to lay the fucker out. His patience only stretched so far, and waiting to get Reyna alone this past hour had taken all of it. "Just seeking out our cabin for the evening."

The pirate, a greasy-haired man Ronan couldn't remember meeting before, leered at Reyna appreciatively. "I bet you was."

"Careful, now. I don't take kindly to other men eye fucking my wife," he said, curling his arm protectively around her hips. Ronan let his hand drift down to ghost over her arse. The material of her skirt was deceptively thin. He could feel the heat of her beneath his palm as he flexed his fingers into her taut flesh. "That's my job."

The pirate gulped, but Reyna just laughed. "Can you point us in the direction of the guest rooms? We seem to have gotten a bit turned around."

The man glanced between them, his lip hooking upward. If he hadn't been so distracted by the feel of Reyna and all the things he wanted to do to her, he might have paid a bit more attention when the pirate jerked his thumb to the left. "Sure thing, lovey. Got a honeymoon suite all done up for you. First door on the left, can't miss it."

"Thank you," she said graciously, grabbing Ronan's hand before it could continue its journey and tugging him unceremoniously down the hall.

As soon as they reached the door, he tossed a glance over his shoulder to ensure they were alone and then pushed her up against it.

"Ronan, what—"

He cut off whatever she was about to say as he claimed her mouth, his tongue delving in for a quick taste before he growled, "I need to get inside you. Right. The fuck. Now."

Her hand groped blindly for the doorknob beside them, and Ronan pulled back with a low chuckle as he gave it a quick twist, sending her toppling back as the door swung inward.

"That wasn't very nice," she said, her voice equal parts hungry and breathless.

Ronan kicked the door closed. "I'm done playing nice, wife. I want you, have spent *years* wanting you. Now I intend to spend what's left of this night taking you in all the ways I've dreamt of. By the time I'm through with you, there won't be a single part of you I haven't memorized. Kissed. Tasted. *Fucked.*"

Reyna's eyes glazed, and her tongue darted out to wet her lips. "That's a whole lot of talk for a man with such an ambitious—oh!"

Ronan lunged forward, grabbing Reyna and spinning them both around until she was pressed against the door once more, this time with her hands pinned above her head with one of his shackling her wrists and the other cupping her center. "You were saying?"

She arched her back, rolling her pelvis down and into his curled fingers. "Get on with it."

He could tell by the flare of her eyes that she realized her mistake as soon as his low chuckle rumbled out of him. "Get on with it? Oh, kitten. Now I'm going to make you beg."

He brushed his lips against hers, sipping on her mouth as if he had all the time in the world. If she thought his need for her meant he was about to rush his way through this, she was about to learn one hell of a lesson.

Her hips moved against his hand, demanding more friction, and a whimper left her when he pulled it away. He let his gaze rake over her, taking in the rapid rise and fall of her breasts, the flush of her face, the siren's call of her body.

"Tell me how to get this dress off you."

"She sewed me into it."

Ronan's fingers tightened around her wrists. "Do. Not. Move." He waited a beat to ensure that she was paying attention before he pulled away and finally glanced around the room.

For a ship, the lodgings were sumptuous. Everywhere he looked, shades of ruby, gold, and onyx glinted back. Thick furs blanketed the floor and rested atop a four-poster bed, and multiple pillows were scattered along the silk and velvet bedding. A decanter of wine sat on a small table beside it, along with a single goblet. There was also a chest at the foot of the bed, filled with all manner of scarves and scattered treasures.

Ronan knew what he was searching for would be in there. He moved fast, not paying any attention to the contents of the chest, outside of the distant thought that these sorts of belongings would not be left in a random guest's quarters. But he didn't much care who the owner of the room was. It was theirs for the night.

He continued digging until he caught the glint of a blade out of the corner of his eye. He pulled the fancy dagger free with a wolfish grin. Standing, he slowly turned and held his pilfered prize up.

Reyna huffed out a laugh. "Guess I'm not wearing this dress again."

"It served you well while it lasted," he said, stalking back over to her and notching the tip of the knife along the seam at her hip.

He didn't wait for a response before carefully sliding the blade up.

Reyna held perfectly still, the wild flutter of her pulse the only clue that she was not as unaffected as she appeared.

Neither was he.

With each inch he cut away, more of her creamy skin was revealed, and it was the battle of a lifetime to keep his eyes trained on his task instead of allowing them to roam over her exposed flesh the way he wanted to. His breaths were uneven, pulse racing, and it was only a lifetime of focus that kept his hand from shaking with the unfilled need to touch her.

Once the bodice of her gown was cut up one side, he took the halves in each hand and tore the rest of the way down. The move brought him to a crouch at her feet as the now ruined dress fluttered to the ground.

A needy groan escaped him as he gazed up at his wife. "Fuck, kitten. You undo me."

She was a work of art posed against the door, clad only in tiny scraps of transparent black silk and lace that did little to hide her beaded nipples or the dampness between her legs. Her arms were stretched above her head, her back arched, a leather harness slung low on her hips and ringing each of her thighs. He couldn't get over the way those strips of leather framed her pussy.

That is definitely staying on.

His mouth watered as he rose up on his knees and forced her legs wider apart. "Don't forget to purr for me," he breathed, leaning forward and dragging his tongue along the barely-there piece of lace.

He pressed one palm to her quivering stomach, the fingers of his other hand sliding between her legs to pull the damp fabric to the side, baring her slick center to him. He allowed himself a single second to take in her perfection before he dragged his tongue along her seam all the way to that swollen bundle of nerves at the top. He sucked hard, letting his growl of pleasure vibrate through her.

Reyna threaded her fingers through his hair, grasping onto the sides of his skull as she writhed against his face. "Ronan, oh . . . fuck."

He didn't let up but repeated the movement, over and over, adding his fingers and beckoning them inside her until she was a mess of broken moans and desperate cries. When her quaking thighs clamped around his ears, he leaned back.

"No! Don't stop. I'm so close."

He smiled up at her. "I know."

"Then . . . why?"

"Because I'm going to bring you to the edge several more times before I finally push you over it."

She gaped at him, her pale hair wild around her shoulders, her cheeks flushed, and her bottom lip swollen from biting down on it. But it was the haughty cock of her brow that had his stomach clenching with anticipation. "What makes you think I'm going to let you?"

Their battle of wills was his favorite kind, especially when they took place in the bedroom. And the hint of challenge in her voice was all he needed to know the latest round had just begun.

He surged up, grasping her by the hips and lifting her easily.

A surprised screech left her as she grasped his shoulder to maintain her balance. "What are you—Ronan!" His name was an exasperated shout as he tossed her back on the bed, already moving to grab several of those silk scarves he'd spotted in the chest.

She scrambled up, but he was already right there, catching her ankle and pulling her down the bed so he could loop the scarf around her and tie it to one of the pillars.

"Ronan . . ."

He grinned at her, taking a second scarf and setting to work on her other ankle. "What's wrong, kitten?"

"What do you think you're doing?"

"Isn't it obvious? If I tie you up, I don't have to worry about you trying to take matters into your own hands."

"You're always drawing things out. I just want you inside me."

Trailing his fingertips up her side, he took her arm and lifted it up so he could repeat his efforts on her wrist. "And I just want you mindless with pleasure. Is that really so bad?"

She gave a little tug, a pout on her full lips when they didn't give. "If you really think I can't get out of these, you're deluding yourself."

He moved around the bed to the other side, tying off her other wrist before he leaned down by her ear. "You're forgetting that I know your secret."

Her breath caught, and her eyes went wide. "What secret?"

His fingers danced down the center of her body, and she followed the touch by arching up into it. "You don't really want to get free. You want me to have my way with you. You want me to be in charge of your pleasure because you trust me to make it good for you."

"Oh, *that* secret," she breathed when he skimmed the tip of her nipple and then pinched it.

"You have others?"

"No," she answered too quickly.

"Reyna . . ."

"Why would I lie? I'm an open book."

He would have laughed at the absurdity of that statement, but he was far more curious why she felt she had to keep anything from him after what they had already faced together.

"Shall we make a game of it? I don't let you come until you tell me whatever it is you're trying to hide?"

"That's a terrible plan."

He laughed, running his thumb over her bottom lip and pressing it lightly into her mouth to gather some of her wetness before taking it back out to trace circles over her other nipple. The delicate scrape of lace combined with the moisture had her panting.

"You aren't playing fair."

"When it comes to you, I will never play fair. Only to win."

Her exhale was heavy as she tried to turn her face away from him, displacing some of the strands of hair that had fallen across her brow.

"Tell me."

She shook her head. "There's nothing to tell."

"Be very sure you want to play this game with me, kitten."

"You're the one playing games."

Ronan took her face in his hand, bringing her eyes back to his. "Remember that you asked for this."

"I did n—" She broke off on a moan as he joined her on the bed. His mouth found her nipple as he resumed his sweet torture.

He took his time working his way down her body, his fingertips running along her sweat-dampened skin. Sometimes he paused, digging in to rub tense muscles; other times he kept his touch a featherlight tease. And when he found a particularly responsive place, he would lick a trail across her skin just to go back and blow across it and watch her squirm.

There wasn't an inch of her he didn't caress, either with his hands or his mouth. He tormented them both, ramping up his own arousal until there was no ignoring the heavy erection tenting his trousers. It wouldn't take much to send him toppling over the edge; just a squeeze of her hand over him would likely do the trick.

But he was a man on a mission.

"Are you ready to tell me?"

She struggled to open her eyes, a little shake of her head the only answer she could manage.

"You know you can tell me anything, don't you? There's nothing you could say that would make me think less of you or run away from you. You're mine now, wife. Forever. In this life and all others, remember?"

Her throat flexed as she swallowed. Her eyes were bright as they held his.

"All right. I guess it's time to take things up a notch."

She whimpered when he pulled away to remove his clothes, her gaze shooting down to stare as he took himself in his hand and slid his fist along the thick length.

"It would feel better if you let me do it," she rasped.

"That it would, but it's you, not me, keeping us both unsatisfied."

"Please, Ronan. I want my husband inside me."

His hand spasmed as he let out a pained groan. "You know what you have to do first."

"You told me you wanted me to beg."

"That may have been the goal when we started, but then I found out you were trying to hide something from me. Now I simply require the truth, and then I'll give you everything you want."

"All I want is you."

"You have me."

"Not the way I want," she groaned, tugging at her restraints.

Ronan would have laughed, but he was feeling the same restless desperation she was. He moved until he was kneeling on the bed between her spread thighs.

"You really do look beautiful like this."

"At your mercy?"

"Oh, kitten, I'm the one at yours."

"It doesn't look that way from where I'm lying."

"All I want is to take care of you. I'm dying to be inside you. To be one with you. But I don't want there to be any secrets between us. There's no reason for there to be." As he said it, he skimmed the tip of his cock through her glistening folds.

Reyna cried out, her hips bucking beneath him. He repeated the motion, coating himself in her slickness.

"Tell me."

She shook beneath him, After the repeated denial of her climax, every touch from him brought it roaring back to the surface.

"Tell me, or neither of us will find any relief tonight." *And what a fucking tragedy that would be.*

Instead of refusing him, she surprised him by blurting, "Would you really deny the mother of your unborn child?"

"Yes, I would." His head snapped up. "Wait, what did you just say?"

She smiled, her eyes glittering. "We're going to have a baby, Ronan."

His hands trembled as he reached out and rested both palms on her belly, the edge of the harness pressing into the heels of his hands. "We are?"

"We are. Helena told me right before I walked down the aisle. I wasn't intentionally keeping secrets from you. I just wanted to find the right time to tell you."

Ronan reached up and immediately untied her, pulling her into his arms.

Mother's tits, she's pregnant. I'm going to be a father. His head was spinning. Of all the things she could have told him, that wasn't even a possibility. The sheer joy he felt at the news, along with a surge of protectiveness, practically bowled him over.

"Are you all right? I didn't hurt you, did I?"

Her laugh was a gentle tease. "Not in the way you mean."

He pulled back, aghast. "I'm so sorry, I didn't—"

"No, Ronan." She laughed and shook her head. "I knew this would happen. That's why I wanted to wait until after. Now all you're going to do is be gentle with me when I want you to fuck me so hard I see the stars."

His cock gave a happy twitch, eager to do just that. But a new worry had him pulling away instead of sinking inside her to the root.

"Is that . . . safe?"

"Of course, it's safe. The baby is probably only the size of a pin. He's not even going to feel you."

"He?"

"Or she."

"She would be good."

"You want a daughter?"

"I want everything with you."

Reyna melted into him and then laughed. "Can we at least start with orgasms? I feel like you owe me at least a dozen by now."

"You've just given me the world. I could deny you nothing." He pulled her astride him, his arms banded tightly around her waist as she sank down onto his length. "Is this okay?"

She clenched around him, drawing pained groans from them both. "So okay."

"You'll tell me if I'm hurting you?"

"I'll tell you, but I promise you won't." She wove her arms around his neck, kissing him as she started to slowly ride him.

He kept his thrusts slow and easy, one of his hands tangling in her hair when her head fell back. After the way he'd teased them, they were both more than ready, and it wasn't long before her needy cries filled the room. When she began to tighten around him, he urged her on.

"That's it, love. Give it to me."

"Ronan!"

He tugged her head up so he could crush his lips to hers and swallow the sounds of their joint climax.

She peppered kisses over his face, her fingers idly playing with his hair when she finally rested her forehead against his. "Are you happy?"

"I'm the happiest fucking man alive. I have everything I could have ever wanted right here in my arms."

"Me too. I love you, Ronan."

"I love you too, kitten."

Her fingers skimmed the lines of his Jaka, her lips curling in a smile he was coming realize spelled trouble for him. "So by my count, that was only—"

The door crashed open, making Reyna freeze as an angry-looking man with a red knit cap and inky curls glared at them. "Just what the hell do you two think you're doing? These are the captain's quarters."

Her shoulders shook with laughter. "Oops?"

"Get out!" the man in the knit cap shouted, pointing an enraged finger out the door.

"And go where, exactly?" Ronan asked, his voice even despite the fact he was still balls deep in his very naked wife. Another time, he might have responded with threats, but Reyna was pregnant and in his arms. The only thing he was interested in was keeping her there.

"I don't fucking care, just so long as it's not here. Stars, I'm going to have to clean everything," the man lamented.

Ronan considered their options, not all that keen on anything that would give the man an eyeful of either of them. "Hold on tight, love."

"Ronan, what—"

He stood slowly, the shift in position far more erotic than it had any right to be with the way that man was shooting daggers at them with his eyes. With Reyna pressed firmly against him, Ronan strode out of the captain's room, her accompanying laughter the sweetest sound he had ever heard.

Make that second sweetest.

"We're going to have a baby, Ronan."

A new wife and a babe on the way. Even a day ago, Ronan wouldn't have believed this fate could be his. For once, it finally seemed the Mother's favor was shining down on him.

As soon as the thought occurred, a shiver rolled down his spine.

But how long would it last?

CHAPTER 24

EREBOS

A wordless bellow of pure, unadulterated rage whipped around the room as Erebos picked up his bed and hurled it straight through one of the stone walls separating his personal suite from his study. That travesty in the temple had been entirely too close for comfort. A handful of Chosen dogs should not have been able to best him and a room full of guards. Yet here they were.

Dovina peered at him through the hole in the wall, the slight reddening of her eyes the only allusion to her grief. "Still sulking, I see."

His lip peeled back in a snarl, shadows exploding out of him and spreading across the wall behind him. He wasn't sure what shape they took, but when she gulped and took a step away, he assumed it was something appropriately terrifying.

She raised both hands in surrender. "I spoke out of turn. Forgive me, my liege. My twin is dead, and I find myself out of sorts."

Out of sorts.

A dark laugh escaped. The bitch was so cold she couldn't even admit to feeling more than 'out of sorts' over her own flesh and blood's passing.

Instead of acknowledging her apology, he snarled a question of his own. "Where are they?"

She cleared her throat and shifted uncomfortably, her usual composure missing in the wake of his temper. For the first time, Dovina seemed to realize that she wasn't dealing with a mortal man but something far worse.

"There's a ship—"

"There's a damn port. Of course there's a ship. Tell me something useful, Dovina, or you'll be reunited with your brother far sooner than you think."

She swallowed and struggled to hold his unwavering stare. "This one is different. Pirate. Its flag is . . . foreign. Southern, most like. And it's anchored several miles offshore."

Erebos raised a brow, barely holding onto the ragged remains of his patience as he waited for her to get to the fucking point.

"A woman was spotted aboard. Based on the description of her hair and her dress, she's presumed to be the Lady Shadow."

Finally, something interesting.

"How long ago was she spotted?"

"Less than an hour."

"And the ship hasn't set sail?"

"No, High Lord."

What are you up to, Luna?

"And her . . . *rescuers*?" he gritted out, his anger spiking dangerously at the mere thought of Ronan and Luna's other meddling children.

The darkness around the room quivered, responding to his displeasure and eager to do his bidding. Even though he'd only initiated the harvest of his celestial essence from Shadow, the overflow of godly power surging through his mortal vessel was unwieldy and barely restrained. He was like a hair-trigger, his magic looking for any excuse to be set free.

Soon.

Dovina glanced around warily, recognizing that the flickering darkness wasn't like the enthusiastic tail wag of a well-trained dog but rather the warning rattle of a snake. Danger lurked in these quarters, and right now, she made for an easy target.

"Best we can tell, they're all with her. And at least another hundred or so besides . . ." Dovina's pause was weighed down with the words she struggled to set free.

"What aren't you telling me?" he growled, more thick shadows rippling off him and reaching for her.

She scuttled backward. Smart girl.

"They got married. Her and your Champ—the prisoner."

Erebos stilled, the audacity of the act making him bark out a laugh of pure disbelief. That lowborn, dirt-eating piece of shit thought he could replace a god? He wasn't fit to lick the sole of his boot, let alone take his place as groom. Not that Erebos gave a single fuck about the sham of a marriage, but it was the principle of the matter.

What little light existed in the room guttered out as he embraced his rage. It was time to rid the world of these entitled, mewling brats once and for all. The sea made for a perfect grave, and he wasn't feeling particularly precious about how or where it happened. So long as the night ended with them dead and him swollen with his reclaimed power, he didn't care about the particulars.

"Well then, I suppose we should stop by and pay our respects."

Dovina's brow furrowed. "You pay your respects at a funeral . . . not a wedding."

"Exactly."

~

KIERAN

CONVERSATION FLOATED to him like sound through water. It was distorted, the volume uneven. Some pieces came in loud and clear; others were garbled. But he heard enough to get the gist of it.

He was running out of time.

Despite what felt like nonstop attempts, he hadn't managed to regain control of his body. There were a couple of moments when it felt like the usurper could hear him. Minor disruptions in speech. A sudden change of plans. An overwhelming surge of anger that didn't belong to him. But those were fleeting and few and far between.

If desire was the only requirement for success, Kieran would have succeeded ages ago. But it would seem what he wanted didn't remotely factor into the equation. Unfortunately, he couldn't figure out what *did*.

Even though he'd been able to break through that first barrier and free his consciousness, he couldn't find the key he needed to take back possession of his physical form.

He'd hoped the woman who'd woken him would return and provide additional guidance, but no matter how many times he called out for her, only silence answered. Maybe silence *was* the answer. Either that, or she'd said all she had to say on the matter.

As it did every time he chased that well-worn thread, her lone piece of advice rippled through him.

Fight.

"I'm fucking *trying*."

Frustration swelled, and he wished he could pick something up and chuck it as his body snatcher had. If for no other reason than the rush of satisfaction that accompanied senseless destruction. It didn't have to be a bed. A table would do. Or a book. Elder's sagging sack, even a matchstick could be broken into several tiny bits.

Without conscious thought, all attention shifted from the conversation taking place to the items sprawled across the desk that would suit his needs. A quill—easily snapped in half. A piece of parchment—made for tearing. A pillar of wax—perfectly smashable. He was so focused on reaching them, touching them, he didn't immediately realize the index finger of his right hand moved in an effort to do just that.

But then came the silence, the surge of fury that wasn't his own, and he knew.

That tiny twitch had been *him*.

His desire. His intention.

Giddy excitement replaced frustration as his mind buzzed with what he'd just discovered.

Fool. You've been thinking too big. Trying to take back the whole when you should have been focused on conquering piece by piece.

Now that he realized his error, Kieran assumed it would be easy to replicate.

He was wrong.

The squatter must have realized he was up to something because it was like a wall had slammed down between them, shoving Kieran back. Or at least that's what he assumed happened until he reached out to test the new barricade and found that it was not so much a cage as a net. Tightly woven, certainly. But far from solid.

Curious, he sent a little nudge to one of the thin strands. Just to see what would happen. Instead of strumming like a lute string and sending waves of vibration outward, as he'd expected, the strand reacted in the most peculiar way. It reached back, attaching itself to him—his awareness. The sensation was disconcerting, like ice down his spine or prickles of numbness in his foot.

Kieran gave a mental shake, an instinctive attempt to fling it off him, only to realize he'd already absorbed it. That thin tendril was *part* of him. He could feel it, separate but very much there. It was a stain in his mind, ice cold and inky black, but oh-so-responsive. He only had to reach out to that darkness, and it all but vibrated with excitement. A lover's shiver in response to a heated caress. A silent demand for more.

It *wanted* to be played with. Used.

He might have been locked away for the better part of a decade, but everything his body experienced was still there. As was all the knowledge his mind absorbed while at the citadel. Which was why, despite having no magical affinity of his own, it took no effort at all to identify that little strand.

It was raw, untamed power.

The hitchhiker's power.

The Lord of Death's power.

And it was attuned to *him*.

Mother's tits.

Having never experienced anything like this, Kieran could only guess *how* it even happened. When the only possible explanation came to him, he wanted to laugh at the sheer absurdity of it. By selecting Kieran as his vessel—a living, breathing extension of his godly self—Erebos made it impossible for his power to distinguish between them. Meaning it was the bastard's own oversight that allowed this unintentional theft to occur in the first place.

Meaning there was nothing stopping Kieran from stealing more.

The temptation to be greedy, to reach out and blindly grasp all he could of these magical strands, was immense. But caution stayed his hand. One strand could be overlooked. A single drop in the ocean. But several would definitely be noticed.

He needed to use this gift before the one wearing him like a damned suit realized what had happened.

But how?

Think, Kieran. Think . . .

What possible way can you make use of Death's power?

It's not like killing yourself is an option. He'll flee the body, leaving you to die in his place. So, what then?

Death isn't his only title.

The reminder floated through his mind, but not in his voice. There wasn't a chance for him to respond before the meaning clicked into place.

Dreams.

His first title is Father of Dreams.

Could it really be that simple? After all, he *was* the Dreamer. So maybe the answer really did lie in dreams. Specifically sending someone a dream. That was how Erebos had taken him; it stood to reason that with the aid of his power, he could do the same. So why not use the god's most basic skill to undermine him? And who better to test the theory on than the current object of his obsession? If anyone was susceptible to his gift, surely it was his other vessel, the Shadow Queen herself.

Reyna.

Well, Kieran, this will either be the key to victory or the final nail in your coffin. Either way . . . at least it's a new way to fight.

And with that, the Dreamer set about weaving a dream.

CHAPTER 25

REYNA

The glade was filled with dappled sunlight and the sound of her daughter's laughter. Ronan's arms tightened around her waist, his lips at her forehead. "She's fearless, just like her mother."

Watching their little girl leap from the branch she'd skillfully walked across, she couldn't help but agree. As soon as her feet hit the forest floor, she ran full speed to jump into the next, pulling her agile body up and into the tree. With the black swirls of her ancestry painting her chubby cheeks and her red curls flying out behind her like a banner, she was the best of both of them. "She's got her father's fierce spirit."

"And her mother's wild heart."

"She's going to be a handful."

"I welcome the challenge."

"What about her future suitors?"

Ronan scowled. "She's five. Let's not worry about that until we must."

"Mmhmm. And this not worrying about it . . . is that the reason you had her up at the crack of dawn working on drills with you?"

"It's never too early to learn the proper way to handle a weapon."

"Uh-huh."

"She's a warrior in the making. If she wants to live up to her mother's legacy, she has to start sometime."

"Five doesn't strike you as a mite young?"

"We were younger than her when we held our first blades."

Reyna couldn't argue with the truth of that. Nor could she deny the wistful longing in her heart at the unclouded joy on her daughter's face. "I want a different life for her. One of peace and prosperity. I don't want her to fight for every scrap of happiness as we did."

"We don't get to make that choice for her."

She squeezed his forearm. "I know. But a mother can hope."

"As can a father."

Feeling their gazes on her, their little miracle came barreling at them. "Catch me, Daddy!"

Without missing a beat, she leapt up and Ronan dropped down, the move seamlessly executed from years of practice. He caught her and lifted her up high, then swung her down low, filling the clearing with her belly laughs as they 'flew' around the trees.

Contentment unlike any she'd ever known settled in Reyna's bones, and with her hand pressed to her heart, she watched the greatest loves of her life play.

The wind kicked up, and she shivered, tightening her cloak around her as the first of the clouds appeared overhead. Shading her eyes, Reyna glanced up, surprised to find the once blue sky shrouded in black.

No. These do not belong here.

As if summoned by her thought, a face appeared in the clouds. Or at least the suggestion of one. She could just make out the hint of two eyes, the edge of a nose, and the flare of a mouth.

The wind whipped through the trees, sending several leaves falling and bringing with it the sound of her name.

"Reyna."

No. Not here. Not in this place.

She looked away from the face, searching for her husband and daughter, but they were nowhere to be found.

No! Give them back. Give them back to me!

"Not safe."

Fear curled down her spine, filling her veins with ice. Hands fisting at her sides, Reyna glanced back up at the man in the clouds. "Why not?"

"He's coming."

"Who?"

Even as the word left her lips, she knew. There was only ever one who stalked her. And Death could only be outrun for so long.

The wind swelled once more, the roll of thunder accompanying the gust. *"Too late."*

Rain pelted her. This was no summer's gentle storm, but an icy tempest.

Shielding her eyes once more, she tried to blink past the beads of water to make out that face. Were those tears? Was he crying?

"He's already here."

REYNA JOLTED AWAKE, her heart frantic beneath her ribs.

"Ronan! Ronan, wake up!"

"Issit morning already?" he asked, his voice thick with sleep, his limbs still heavy on top of her.

She gave him an insistent shove. "Erebos is coming."

His eyes snapped open, suddenly alert. "When?"

"Now!"

"We have to warn the others."

They each dove out of bed, tossing articles of clothing back and forth in search of something that fit along with whatever weapons they could find in their borrowed accommodations. Reyna's trousers and tunic were made for a much larger man, but what was loose on her strained over Ronan's bulkier form. It would have to do. Thankfully, they each had their own boots, so they didn't need to contend with ill-fitting shoes as well.

As one, they raced for the door.

"Do you know where the others are?" Reyna asked as they poured into the hall.

"No clue."

"Banging on random doors it is," she muttered. "I'll go left, you go right."

She didn't like the idea of splitting up, but time was a luxury they didn't have.

Ronan and Reyna each began to pound their fists against the various doors, their shouts ringing out as they did.

"Attack!"

"Sound the alarm!"

More than one groggy, bleary-eyed head peered out at them.

"What are you yammering on about?" a grumpy brunette with pale green eyes asked.

"We're under attack."

Ronan's echo of, "All hands on deck!" seemed to do the trick because the pirates snapped to attention. Thankfully, no one seemed inclined to ask too many questions, that magical phrase all they needed to know as they rushed to obey in various stages of dress.

Finally, at the end of the hallway, Reyna was greeted by a familiar pair of aqua eyes. "He's coming," she panted. "Erebos. He might already be here."

Helena nodded, expression grim, as if she'd been waiting for such an announcement.

"Do you know where Effie and the others are?" Reyna pressed, the urgency she'd felt since waking an anxious buzz beneath her skin.

"Don't worry about them. We need to get you somewhere safe."

"Somewhere safe?" she scoffed. "Helena, I will never be safe so long as he lives. We are connected. I may as well be a damned beacon."

"Regardless, we cannot have you standing out in the open ripe for the plucking. You are the one he wants, which means you are the one he cannot have at all costs."

"I will not hide while people I love stand and fight."

"Sometimes queens are faced with impossible choices—"

"No, you aren't hearing me. I. Will. Not. Hide. Not now, not ever."

The respect was impossible to miss as Helena's eyes rippled from blue to a swirling iridescent. "Very well." Without looking away, she called over her shoulder. "It's time."

Von appeared behind her, his silver eyes simmering with violence. "Excellent."

Reyna tilted her head. "You say that as though you've been waiting for this."

"Preparing for, more like," Von said.

"Does that mean you have a plan?"

Helena grinned, and there was something ancient and not wholly of this world in the expression. "Effie and I have been working on something."

Right then.

"Well, let's go finish this, shall we?" Reyna asked, glancing over her shoulder to check on Ronan's progress.

"Aye," Von said, joining her in the hallway. "And may the Mother have mercy on that poor bastard's soul, for I will not."

Reyna didn't get the impression the Mother was particularly interested in mercy. Especially when Helena's voice, swollen with her power, intoned, "Neither will I."

CHAPTER 26

RONAN

The deck of the *Lorelei* was a far cry different from the last time he'd seen it, and it wasn't just the hint of dawn creeping across the sky casting the ship in a wash of pale light. The mood was tense and somber, the celebratory atmosphere of the night before wiped away in the face of the impending threat. If any wedding decorations remained, it was impossible to see them around the nearly two hundred armed men and women crowded on the galleon's upper level. If not for the fact that most stood beside him, he wouldn't have been able to make out his friends in the fray.

"Any sign of him?" Ronan asked Caly, since Jagger and Buttercup were acting as lookout.

"None," she answered. "The fog rolled in, and now we can barely see further than we can spit."

His lips dipped down as his eyes scanned the horizon. Fog was right, but like none he'd ever seen. The dense gray mist clung low to the water, obscuring the breaking waves gently rocking the boat. The tickle of a memory scratched at the back of his mind, but there wasn't time to follow the thread before something wiggled in his periphery, drawing his attention sharply to the left.

"Is it . . . moving?" Reyna asked, her focus following his.

The fog was *definitely* moving. Shapes writhed just below the surface, not yet fully formed but filling him with sick dread.

More heads snapped in the direction they were looking as a shout rang out. "Incoming! Port side!"

The fog pulled apart, limbs appearing, followed by heads. But not human heads. There was *nothing* human about the army crawling out of the fog. These creatures—these *nightmares,* as Reyna called them— were all monster. Some were little more than mist-coated ooze with bits of human bone floating around in them to indicate it might have once been a living creature. Others were barely more than torsos crawling forward with two stumps that might have been arms, but the bone structure was all wrong and bent at ungodly angles. Others still seemed like they were the spectral reincarnation of sea creatures that had long since died, with fins for arms and huge overextended heads filled with all manner of teeth. Whatever these fiends were, none of it was good or natural.

One particularly gruesome fiend managed to reach the ship and crawl on board. A member of Lawless's crew swung their cutlass, the blade swiping right through. In response, the creature opened its maw wide and let out an unearthly wail. The unhinging of that jaw was so unnatural, less opening of an actual mouth and more a stretching of the fog to make room for the unfurling of a foot-long tongue and dozens of writhing . . . teeth? *Did that thing's tongue have fucking teeth?*

Ronan's brain was trying to apply words to a creature that defied explanation.

"How the hell are we supposed to fight these things when our blades are useless?" Bronn shouted.

"Fire's usually a safe bet," Von called back as multiple flaming orbs flew into the wall of fog-born creatures. Helena, Von, and Joquil had already summoned a second wave, the molten balls hovering above their palms in case the theory proved correct, but other than a symphony of those inhuman shrieks, nothing happened. The night- mares just kept coming. One becoming a dozen that again multiplied into hundreds. They stood on the surface of the water, supported by the fog that birthed them, and all of them were heading straight for the *Lorelei*. More of them were already crawling up the side.

"Any bright ideas, kitten?"

Reyna swallowed, eyes wide as she shook her head. "I've seen Erebos's creatures many times over, but nothing like these."

One of the creatures pulled its entire body up onto the boat. There was a flurry of strikes as Tiny, Bronn, and Caly tried their best to cut it down, but again their blades harmlessly passed through the mist.

"We're thinking of them as flesh and blood creatures. We need to treat them like what they are. *Fog*." It was rare that the Kiri's Advisor made an appearance on the battlefield, preferring his books to weapons, but Timmins's astute assessment proved once again he was every bit as valuable as the rest of them. Especially in a situation as inconceivable as this one.

Before he finished speaking, Ronan had crafted a spear out of Air and sent it hurling toward the lumbering form. Just as the mouth stretched open and took a threatening step toward Tiny, the bolt of magic exploded through it, causing the misty figure to dissipate and flow back off the ship to rejoin its unholy brethren.

The minotaur looked shaken as he stared at the place the creature had been. "Th-thank you," he stuttered, removing his glasses and giving the lenses a wipe before placing them back on his snout.

Ronan could only nod his acknowledgment as Helena's shout rang out.

"Air! We can knock them back with Air!" Her hair danced on the wind as she called up a storm. The ship rocked as she gathered huge gusts, adding them to the magical funnel she was creating.

"And what are the rest of us supposed to do?" Kael shouting to be heard over the squall.

"Keep an eye out for Erebos. He won't be far behind," Reyna answered.

"This is only the first wave, a distraction," Effie added. "More will follow. We need to be ready."

A creature jumped up and out of the mist, arching up and then over the ship, drawing more terrified cries. At first blush, the creature appeared almost like a whale, but the physicality was all wrong. Outside of the wide head and long mouth, the body was female in structure with a series of tentacles as the back end. Everyone was so distracted trying to make heads or tails of this abomination that no one was prepared when its mouth opened and closed around five of Lawless's pirates, swallowing them whole as it dove back into the mist-shrouded water.

"Mother's tits," Ronan whispered, staring hard at the place where the pirates had been not even a second earlier.

"How is that even possible?" Lucian asked. "If the creatures are too insubstantial for a blade to pierce, how can it pick up not one but several grown fucking men?"

"It's the magic of dreams," Reyna stated. "Anything is possible in a dream."

The wind roared so loudly, all that could be heard were the creaks and groans of the ship as Helena unleashed her storm, a raging cyclone that ripped through the fog creatures and sent their screams of fury blasting outward. If not for that small window of visibility before the fog could roll back in, Ronan would have missed the creeping shadow.

He'd seen its like before, on a different ship and in different waters, but once witnessed, it would never be forgotten. It moved like a ghost, rippling along the top of the water before dipping out of view. He didn't know what the shadow preceded, only that it was a portent of something deadly.

"Look out!" he shouted, pointing to the starboard side.

But his warning came too late. The shadow was no longer confined to the water but crept over the side of the ship, just as the other creatures had done. With the more obvious threat of the fog army, no one cared about a seemingly innocent patch of darkness. It had no shape, no discernible form, allowing it to snake through the throng of bodies unseen.

Or mostly unseen.

"Ronan," Reyna called, her hand gripping his the only outward sign of her fear.

"I see it."

"He's here."

The certainty in her voice sent twin spirals of rage and panic through him. It wasn't the battle he was worried about, but what Erebos might do to Reyna. The god's connection to his wife was an unknown quantity. There was no telling how he might be able to manipulate her, especially since he'd recently harvested more of her power. Ronan might hate the whoreson, but he didn't dare underestimate him.

"Helena!" He spun around, seeking the Kiri's chestnut curls, knowing if any of them had a chance against him, it was her. As his gaze skimmed over the deck, he spotted Von and the others with access to the Air branch engaged in keeping the fog at bay, but Helena and Effie were gone. The women had hinted at a secret plot but hadn't gotten the chance to share the details. He could only hope they were in the middle of putting said plan into action. Which meant it was up to the rest of them to keep Erebos busy until the Voice and Vessel made their move.

Ronan turned back toward Reyna. "Are you ready?"

"For what?"

"To fight."

"I'm always ready for a fight." Her accompanying smirk lacked a bit of her usual swagger, but her voice was steel.

Ronan raised their joint hands to his lips and pressed a kiss to the back of hers, his lips brushing over her wedding band. Her eyes held his as a silent 'I love you' passed between them. Filled with resolve, Ronan looked away in time to see the shadow ripple. Adjusting his grip on the blade in his free hand, he took a deep breath and vowed, *One way or another, this ends here.*

There wasn't time for more than that because the shadow was no longer moving across the planks. It was morphing and growing until it was no longer a shadow at all but the Lord of Death himself.

"Attack!" Ronan shouted, pointing at the place where the god now stood.

All around him, people spun, their eyes wide at the sudden appearance of this stranger. Some looked more inclined to risk their luck in the briny deep. Others seemed to welcome the chance for a fair fight, incorrectly assuming that the human-looking man would be easier to deal with than the mist monsters. The poor fools hadn't the first clue about who or what they were dealing with.

Jagger was the closest to Erebos, the boson and his protector standing near the ship's wheel, a level up from the rest of them so as to keep an eye out. The extra bit of distance might as well have been a chasm because there was no time for help to reach him.

Buttercup shrieked in his ear, the finch's tiny body going up in flame and swelling in size until it was no longer a bird but a person fully grown with transparent wings the color of living flame. For the second time that morning, Ronan had no word for the creature before him. It didn't matter anyway; within seconds of their transformation, Erebos shot his hand out, dark tendrils of his magic bursting through the protector until all that was left was shimmering dust.

"No!" Jagger roared, lurching toward the place Buttercup had just occupied. His movements were clumsy, his arms sweeping out blindly as if to catch what he could of the dust.

"Is that the best you can do? Pathetic," Erebos sneered. "Maybe you simply require a bit more motivation."

With a snap of his finger, the misty fiends surrounding the boat converged, becoming one towering, clawed hand. Even as it formed, the hand swept out, the same way a giant might swat at a flea. In one fell swoop, almost the entirety of the *Lorelei's* passengers were flung into the ocean. Tendrils created of shadows shot up from the depths to pull the unfortunate souls under.

Ronan was stunned. He couldn't believe what he was seeing. In less than a minute, Erebos had killed well over a hundred pirates. A swift scan showed most of his friends had managed to remain on board. Though there were a few notable exceptions. Helena and Effie were still nowhere to be found. Calypso and her crew were gone. As were Kael, Kragen, and Timmins.

His stomach sank in the wake of the truth.

The Lord of Death had arrived. And he wasn't taking any prisoners.

With a slow, menacing grin, he crooned, "Who's next?"

CHAPTER 27

HELENA

"Are you sure this is going to work?"

Helena spared a glance over her shoulder to look at Effie a few rungs down. "Sure? No. Confident? Mostly."

"That's not as reassuring as you'd think."

Helena would have laughed, but she fully understood and shared her friend's reluctance. But as with everything she'd done since finding out she was destined to become the leader of the Chosen, she was relying solely on instinct. It's not exactly like there was an instruction manual she could follow, as much as Timmins tried to convince her otherwise.

Looking back up at the ladder she was climbing, she continued, "It's like you said. For the first time in history, the Vessel and the Voice are together. That's not a coincidence. Especially not with the appearance of another god on our realm for the first time in living memory."

She was almost to the top of the crow's nest and the little walled-in perch that would allow the two of them to remain high above and out of sight. Given the unknown nature of what they were about to attempt, it seemed safest for everyone involved if they were as far away as possible, while still being able to keep an eye on what was going on below. She trusted her Mate and the rest of the Circle to handle things in her absence, but she felt better knowing she was nearby. Just in case.

Helena climbed into what Effie referred to as 'the little bucket.' The Keeper had not been overly impressed with Helena's suggestion to hide out here, claiming that the crow's nest, which, to be fair, did appear to be as small as a bucket from the deck, wouldn't hold one of them, let alone both.

"See, it's practically roomy," Helena said when Effie threw her leg up and over the side. She spared her a baleful look but didn't say anything as she unceremoniously climbed inside.

"So, how do we—"

Lucian's cry rang out from below.

The women glanced at each other, speaking as one. "He's here."

More shouts reached them, these terror-filled and abruptly cut off. They looked over the edge just in time to see over half of their numbers knocked into the sea by a misty hand.

"Luna above," Effie gasped.

Helena growled, and an angry roll of thunder echoed across the sky.

"Do something. Save them."

Effie's desperate pleas were mirrors of her own desire. Helena didn't have the heart to tell her it was too late, that those men were lost the second they fell into the mist-shrouded water. Grief would come later. All she could do now was protect those who remained.

Staring hard at the deck below, Helena's mind whirled with possibilities. Alone she was no match for the Lord of Death. He was a one man—one god—army. What she needed to do was even the playing field a little and offer those below a fighting chance until she could rejoin them.

Biting her bottom lip, she looked to the writhing mass of misty bodies reforming around the ship as the god-hand disappeared. With his nightmares, he wasn't just an army; he was legion. If she could force him to fight on his own, without their aid, maybe it would be enough to tip the scale in the Chosen's favor. That required destroying them, or at least getting out of their range, which seemed like the easier of the two options. At least in theory. Since the fiends could crawl across the ocean's surface, it's not like moving the ship would make much of a difference.

Unless . . .

Hands curled around the rail of the crow's nest, inspiration struck. She didn't give herself time to overthink it. They needed to act *now*. Either it worked or it didn't, and if it didn't, they'd just have to try something else.

Taking a deep breath, she dove deep into the endless pool that contained her magic. Picturing what she wanted, Helena summoned Air, weaving it with small threads of Fire and Earth. Then she pushed the elements out of her hands and into the *Lorelei*, pumping the ship full of magic to reinforce its boards, lighten its considerable weight, and help propel it upward.

"Helena? Helena! This isn't exactly what I had in mind!" Effie shrieked when the ship shuddered and started to lift up.

Hair fluttering in the breeze, like the sails billowing as her power continued to pulse from her into the ship, Helena grinned as she infused it with her gifts.

Sailing through the sea wouldn't help them escape the fog creatures, but sailing through the sky might.

At least for a little while.

And a little while was all she needed.

EREBOS

"WHO'S NEXT?"

It was laughable how pathetically weak these mortals Luna so loved were. There was nothing any of them could do to him, no way any of them could hope to overpower him and his monsters, and yet their need to fight back was ingrained. Even when they didn't have a fucking prayer of winning.

His gaze landed on Shadow as she pushed her way to the front of what was left of her would-be rescuers. The fury burning in her gaze was almost enough to have him consider taking a step back.

The temptation to lash out was intense, but she was off limits until he drained her dry, and now that the eclipse was over, he had to bide his time until the next celestial event. Which meant Shadow was safe . . . for now. The same could not be said for the rest of them.

Lifting her chin in defiance, she called out, "Me."

"Reyna, no," Ronan's urgent cry went unheeded as the Forsaken queen tugged on the thread of power connecting her to her maker. It barely scratched the surface of his magical reservoir, but he still felt that thread between them pull taut as she called on his realm and passed through it.

"What do you think you're doing, moonbeam? You cannot use my own power against me."

"Watch me," she snarled, her mouth at his ear and her blade at his throat when she reappeared behind him.

The ship lurched, throwing her off balance and sending her dagger falling harmlessly to the wooden planks at his feet.

Erebos laughed, using the distraction to shove her away. "It's not your time, Shadow mine. Wait your turn like the obedient slave that you are."

"I am no man's slave."

"Ah, poppet, you forget. I am not a man."

The ship moved again, this time less of a rocking and more a steady and continuous glide . . . upward.

Erebos's brows furrowed, his gaze sweeping across the deck as he tried to discern which of the magic users was capable of such a diversion. Given the confusion on their faces, they were as surprised as him, but rallying quickly as they prepared their attacks.

A ripple of color above caught his eye, and he dipped his head back, spotting Luna's Vessel. He should have known.

She was the one he needed to deal with. Once he removed her from the board, the battle would be as good as won. The Chosen were nothing more than sniveling babes without their leader. She was the source of their power as much as their misplaced bravado. The loss would be devastating, a crippling emotional defeat before they faced their own demise.

How poetic.

Men with weapons drawn rushed him, their battle cries nearly lost in the roar of wind as a funnel of Air and Fire took shape. It was nothing like the firestorm that had been unleashed in the temple, but then, these men were a pale imitation of the woman they served. Hardly deserving of his efforts at all. Still, they were an avoidable nuisance. He could just kill them outright, as he did their comrades, but where was the fun in that? Especially that red-haired arsehole. His was a death worthy of drawing out. Celebrating. Something special that made full use of his gift and required his undivided attention.

He'll be last. Forced to watch all the others fall at my hands until he buckles under the weight of their death along with his own failure.

But in the meantime, he could have a little fun.

Erebos's gift crackled around him, shooting out like dozens of black lightning bolts in search of targets. As one, the half dozen or so remaining men fell to the ground. Out cold, trapped in the prison of their own nightmares.

Sweet dreams.

With a low, booming laugh, he called the shadows to him and stepped through his realm up to the little landing at the top of the mast where his quarry hid.

"No!" Reyna screamed. "What have you done to them? Get back here, you coward!"

Her frustration made his grin stretch. It really was almost too easy. Maybe he *would* draw it out a bit, foster a false sense of hope before dashing it all as he killed them off one by one.

He reached the crow's nest, the ball of his foot poised on the small railing, one of his hands grasping onto some rope to keep him balanced.

Erebos expected gasps of shock and awe. Words of protest and denial. Maybe an insult or two. What he did not expect was to find two women in a vortex of their own making. Hands clasped together, eyes filled with lavender light, their hair whipping around them in a breeze that had nothing to do with how high up they were. A breeze created by the raw, undiluted power cocooning them. He recognized the jets of color that poured out from them. The warm red of Fire, and cool blue of Water, and so on. One for each of the elemental branches.

They were feeding it. Allowing the power they'd been gifted to flow out of them in what was essentially a willing version of what he'd been attempting with Reyna.

But why would they . . .

The thought didn't have the opportunity to fully form.

That ball of power exploded outward in a stunning display of light and pulsing energy. Erebos threw his arm up to protect his vessel's fragile mortal eyes.

The achingly familiar and wholly unexpected aroma of wild-flowers and rain reached him, along with the sharp scent of pine and sunshine. He would have sworn he heard bird song, or maybe the buzz of insects. But they were at sea, far away from all of those things. Which could only mean . . .

"Luna?"

"Hello, husband."

CHAPTER 28

KIERAN

*S*ending the dream took more out of him than he expected. With his consciousness focused on linking to Reyna, Kieran had unintentionally allowed his connection to his physical body to fade. Meaning he'd had to claw his way back to the surface once he severed the link.

There was no way to know how much time he'd lost, but considering his body was now precariously poised on a far-too-narrow piece of wood, he was going to guess it was too long.

He also hadn't been prepared to find himself face-to-face with the two women responsible for his being here. One who'd hunted him across a desert, and the other he'd chased through his dreams.

Once upon a time, Effie had been his reason. Full stop. Looking at her now, all he felt was a tidal wave of grief for what she'd suffered because of him. Or because of Erebos. The culpability was muddy at best, but he regretted the part he played in all of it. She hadn't deserved any of it.

His regret was a surprisingly strong motivator, and it helped cement Kieran fully in the moment. Although his eyes were blocked against an explosion of light, he was aware of the breeze against his face. The sudden thundering of his heart. The sweet scent of flowers cut through with the crispness of evergreen.

And then there was a voice. *The* voice. The one that had reached him in the abyss and helped guide him out.

"Luna?"

Luna. The mother goddess. Of course.

"Hello, husband."

If Kieran could have cowered in some way, he would have. The woman floating—for that was the only word for it—in front of him was a literal force of nature. He had the dual urge to weep and beg for forgiveness.

Her hair was woven from strands of starlight, a crown of what had to be actual pieces of stars sitting atop her head. Her eyes were swirling galaxies, her lips the exact shade of pink the sky turned when the sun began to rise. She was nude, her flowing hair all that concealed her lush, feminine curves. But it was the anger pouring out of her that struck him most. Her quiet ferocity was akin to the rumble deep in the earth before it cracked in two.

He wasn't given the chance to do anything.

Instead, Luna reached out, her palm connecting with his chest and sending sparks shooting out from where she touched him.

His—technically, Erebos's—hold on the rope slackened, and he was flung through the air and back down to the deck, his limbs windmilling as he tried to catch himself on nothing. Erebos reached for the shadows, warping through them to slow the fall, but not even his gift was enough to protect him from the force of Luna's touch. The crack that reverberated through his body when it collided with the wooden boards was enough to stun him.

Luna followed, streaking through the sky like a comet as she came to kneel beside him. "What's wrong, lover? You wanted my attention. Now you've got it." Reaching out, she wrapped her hand around his throat, and Kieran's entire body pulsed like a current racing through his veins.

Those swirling eyes pierced straight through him, seeming to bore into his soul. He thought it a trick of his mind, for how could she be looking at *him* while talking to Erebos? But then her voice rang out loud and clear, *"Now, Dreamer."*

Time fractured as he worked independently of the conversation happening around him. Kieran focused on reaching for the dagger lying beside his hand while the god who'd stolen his body chatted up his wife.

"Luna, darling. And here I thought you swore never to touch me again," Erebos croaked as her fingers flexed harder around his throat. The show of power didn't remotely faze him. It may as well have been foreplay.

"Trust me, *darling*. By the time I'm through with you, you're going to wish I kept my promise."

"You can't kill me," he spit out.

"No. Nor you me. But I can make you beg for death."

He laughed. "Death is my domain. There's nothing about it I fear."

"You always have been short-sighted," she said with a sigh that sounded like the breeze rippling through blades of grass.

"Is that so?"

"Even after millennia, you are woefully easy to see through. You know what it is you fear, Erebos? Being alone, with only yourself for company. It's why you cling to me so fiercely. Why you destroy everything that threatens your monopoly on my time."

"Leave it to you to miss the point entirely."

Kieran had to tune out their bickering as his attention zeroed in on the discarded blade. Just like he did with the items on the desk, he willed himself to reach out and *touch* the dagger. Distracted as he was talking to Luna, Erebos put up no resistance to Kieran's order. This time it wasn't just a finger twitch, his whole hand obeyed, and the god didn't even realize he wasn't in control.

Holding Kieran's gaze, Luna dipped her head in the barest hint of a nod. *"Keep going."*

His fingers curled around the hilt, his hand trembling as it grasped the weapon. He felt nothing but relief as he registered the cool and heavy weight of it against his palm.

Now what?

"The choice is yours, Dreamer."

Kieran didn't hesitate, didn't stop to consider the consequences of his actions. Luna said herself there was no way to kill a god. But Erebos couldn't exist on this realm without a body—his body—so he'd just have to take that instead.

Please tell her . . . I'm sorry.

With that endless scream he'd first used to break free blasting through his mind, Kieran lifted the dagger and stabbed himself straight through the heart.

CHAPTER 29

REYNA

*S*he must have hit her head harder than she thought. That was the only explanation for the madness taking place in front of her. Not only was the ship fucking flying, but Erebos was carrying on a damned conversation with the ball of light that chased him as he fell to the ground while an unholy storm raged above them. The predawn sky had been hidden behind angry black clouds. Rain hadn't begun to fall, but with the continuous roll of thunder and flickers of lightning, it was only a matter of time.

She sat up with a low groan, one hand cradling her belly, the other lifting to the back of her head and coming away coated in blood. It was hardly her first concussion. One didn't grow up amongst the trees without falling from them a time or two, but she couldn't recall one ever causing her to hallucinate before.

Pain weighed her head down, but she focused hard on Erebos as he sneered, "Leave it to you to miss the point entirely."

Who is he talking to?

When she heard a woman's voice answering him through the roar of the wind and the growl of thunder, she knew she was losing the plot. Either that or the ball of light beside him was actually Luna, here to make her husband answer for his crimes.

"Do you really expect me to believe that you've done all of this out of some misguided declaration of love? Please. You don't even know what love is."

"And you do? You who turned your back on the one being capable of understanding you? Was it love when you locked me away?"

The fork of lightning was so close the entire ship lit up. "Yes, damn you! You were supposed to learn from your mistake, not break free and go on a murder spree."

"What else was I supposed to do? It's not like I had any other choice. My other half cast me aside. You betrayed me."

"Betrayed you? What else was I supposed to do, Erebos? You were slaughtering my children to make me pay for a crime I didn't commit. You keep saying I turned my back on you, but we were always supposed to rule together. Your jealousy blinded you and built the wall between us, not me. I never wanted to do any of this alone. I locked you away, hoping that with time would come clarity and eventually my mate would return to me."

For the first time, Erebos seemed truly shocked. "You . . . you wanted me back?"

Before Luna could respond, Erebos's arm rose, Reyna's fallen dagger glinting in his hand a second before he drove the blade into his chest.

"No!" The enraged bellow rocked through Reyna, rattling her bones. "You traitorous bitch!"

The hand around the dagger twisted, and a soundless roar was all Erebos could manage as his vessel was destroyed.

Reyna's understanding of vessels was limited, but she knew they were required as a way to bind the immortal spirits to the mortal realm. Without one, Erebos would be forced to return from whence he came.

Black mist poured from Kieran's mouth, the shadows flowing out of his body to crawl along the floor. Erebos's voice raged around the sounds of the gathering storm.

"Lies. All of it. You never wanted me back. You only said that to distract me. To use my love for you against me. All you ever do is betray me!"

"This. *This* is what you never understood. It is not betrayal to stand against injustice, even if that injustice is *you*. I can love you and abhor your actions, but what I cannot do is turn a blind eye to them. You must be stopped, Erebos. I will not allow you to continue your mindless slaughter of innocents."

As if it could sense Reyna watching, the shadow seethed and turned toward her. For a second, she would have sworn she saw a man's face just below the surface. He was beauty in its most terrifying form. Dark hair swept back from a regal brow, eyes crafted from darkness, sensual lips curled back in a sneer. "I will not fall for your lies. This time you are the one who will learn a lesson."

Erebos. This was the Lord of Death's true form. Or as much of it as her mortal mind could comprehend. Just as the ball of light was Luna's.

She'd gotten so caught up in their conversation, Reyna had forgotten about the very real danger she was in. Pushing to her feet, she attempted to stand, but the blow she'd taken to the head made that a harder feat than it should have been. She dropped back to a crouch, her hands pressed flat against the sea-sprayed boards, unable to do more than brace herself as the shadow reached out for her.

"Erebos, what are you doing?"

"You seek to stop me, but Death cannot be stopped."

"There is nowhere for you to go, husband. Your vessel is dead."

"I will make another."

"You know that is not how it works. Already we are being pulled away from this plane. It was not made to contain us. We cannot stay."

"What if I refuse to go?"

"That is not your choice. This is their home. Not ours. We don't belong here."

The wall of shadow moved into her. She could feel the eternal cold trying to attach itself to her bones and seep all the way into her soul. *"Let me in."*

Erebos was trying to claim her body, possess her the way he did

Kieran. Reyna had no idea how one resisted the call of a god, but with every cell in her body, she attempted to cast him out. To deny him what he was trying so hard to steal.

She wasn't sure if she spoke actual words, but she screamed out anyway. *No! You cannot have me. I will never again be your puppet.*

It must have worked because the shadow peeled away from her, writhing like an angry worm.

"I told you it wasn't that easy."

"But she is mine, more so even than the other was. There's no reason she should be able to resist me."

"That might have been true once, but no longer."

"What do you mean?"

"Her soul belongs to another. She's immune and has been ever since completing the soul bond. Any hold you once had over her is long gone. You know as well as I that a pure soul is impervious to compulsion, and a soul who's reunited with its other half is the purest of all."

"No. No!" Erebos shouted, the thunder so loud Reyna feared the very ship would crack in half under its force. "This is your doing!"

"Of course it is."

He seemed taken aback by the admission, almost as if he'd expected her to deny it.

"My children have always been made in our image. Their soul bonds are an echo of what you and I share, my gift to them. A blessing of Spirit for those who have proven themselves worthy. But also, it would seem, the ultimate protection. For not even death, husband, can come between eternal love."

Reyna didn't realize she was crying until the trickle of her tears splashed onto her knees.

For a second it appeared that the light overpowered the shadows, and some of the raging wind died down. Luna's voice was soft as a spring rain as it said, "It's over, Erebos."

"Death cannot be defeated!"

"And yet, today it was. You have lost, husband, because despite whatever you may believe, it is love, not death, that will always prevail."

At some point during the gods' conversation, the ship had slowly drifted back into the water, and Reyna watched in absolute awe as all the bodies of those Erebos had tossed into the sea floated up. Bast. Jagger. Buttercup. Caly. Each and every one of her friends she'd thought lost was rescued from their watery grave. Her breath hitched, and her heart filled with hope as they were all gently lowered onto the deck.

"If that was true," Erebos started bitterly, "you and I would still be happily going about our business. You never would have locked me up, and none of this would have ever happened."

"I'll prove it to you. Come home with me, Erebos. Leave my children in peace. I am the one you are angry with, not them."

"You cannot mean that."

"I do."

"After everything I've done, you'd welcome me back just like that?"

"Just like that? No. I'm furious with you, and likely will be for ages to come. But it is as you said, you are the other half of me. The darkness to my light. I could no more deny my need for you than I could cease to exist. The only way to get past what has been done is to face it. Together."

"How do I know this isn't a trick?"

"I suppose that is the risk you must take, but I promise you, Erebos, this is your only chance to find out. Because the alternative is to never know. I will not make this offer again. So, what will it be? Are you going to give up this madness and return with me? Or is your need for revenge stronger than the love you proclaim to feel?"

Reyna never heard Erebos's answer, but she could guess it, because the balls of light and shadow winked out as if they'd never existed at all.

Luna and Erebos were gone.

As soon as they vanished, all those who Luna brought back gasped and bolted upright, seeming for all the world as if they'd simply been dreaming. No one seemed to realize what had happened. Some jumped up and spun around as if they were still in the midst of battle. Others scanned the ship in search of the enemy. It wasn't until shouts of "He's dead!" rang out that anyone seemed to realize it was over.

"Reyna!" Ronan called, searching for her among the throng of sailors.

"Here!" she called, but her attention was on the too-still figure lying a few feet away from her.

Ronan shoved the others aside as he dropped down, cupping her face in his hands. "Are you all right?"

She nodded. "I hit my head. I'll be fine."

"And the babe?"

Her heart squeezed at the worry in her mate's voice. He'd lost so much, he was afraid to hope, but ever the resilient thing, it was there. Burning as bright as his love for her.

"I hit my head, not my womb."

Ronan laughed and then kissed her. "Never do that again."

"I will always fight to save the ones I love."

"As will I, but now you're carrying one of them. So have a little care, kitten, for what you do while in possession of my heart."

Cupping his face, she pulled him back for another soul-soothing kiss. "I'm sorry. I'll be more careful. I promise." Then she pulled away and pushed to her feet, clumsily making her way over to Kieran's body before collapsing back on her knees at his side. She alone knew what had happened here. What the man had sacrificed so the rest of them could live. More tears trickled down her cheeks as she pressed her hand to Kieran's chest.

"You'd mourn for the madman who sought to kill you?" Von asked, the Kiri's Mate pushing through the crowd to stand beside Ronan.

Reyna shook her head, not quite able to find the words to explain.

Thankfully she didn't have to.

"Her tears are not for him," Effie said, she and Helena appearing as if from nowhere. "She weeps for the Dreamer."

CHAPTER 30

EFFIE

Helena knelt beside Kieran's body, her eyes falling closed as she pressed one hand to his chest wound and the other to his brow.

"Is he dead?" Effie asked, sending the thought directly to Helena's mind.

The Kiri responded in kind, her thoughts flowing back through Effie's Guardian link. *"His spirit lingers, but the body is fading fast."*

"So only mostly dead then."

Helena's lips twitched. *"Not too dead to save, if that's what you're asking."* She opened her eyes, as if seeking permission.

"Do it."

When Helena came to Effie with her idea, she hadn't been convinced it was sane, let alone possible.

"I'm sorry, you want to what?"

"Manifest Luna."

"How would we even begin to do such a thing?"

"I got the idea from Erebos, actually."

"You want to harvest our power? Is that wise? What if it doesn't work, and we're powerless when it comes time to face him?"

But as she'd asked the questions, the warning buzz of premonition ignited beneath her skin. That not-so-gentle nudge from her gift, combined with the vision she'd stolen from Erebos, made it clear that *this* was their path. The reason they'd been put here, in this time and place, gifted with not only Luna's powers but her Guardian gifts to transform reality as well. It was going to take everything they had to pull this off, but it was the only play they had. How else could they hope to defeat a god?

So after the wedding was over, they'd plotted. Coming up with a way they could reverse what Erebos had done to Reyna. In the end, it was less of a power harvest and more of an offering. Helena called forth her magic, drawing it out of her body, while Effie gave it form, weaving the various branches together and envisioning the goddess as she'd been the first time she came to her. In some ways it was a bit like creating a portal, although instead of tethering one place to another, it was a place to a person. And though it was far from a perfect science, it worked.

The moment Luna stepped through and accepted the magical offering, Effie and Helena were no longer in control of their own bodies. With their combined power in use by the goddess, they'd essentially been trapped in place, unable to do anything but wait. If not for their connection to each other and Effie's gift of sight, they would have been as in the dark about what had transpired between Luna and Erebos as those he'd sent to his realm. Or realms, as the case may be.

Instead, they Saw everything, their ties to Luna allowing them to act as her witnesses.

It was for that reason alone they knew of Kieran's actions and deemed him worthy of redemption. Namely, how he'd broken through at the most crucial moment and saved them all. That his remorse was pure, his sacrifice truly selfless, and in that final moment, his thoughts—while of her—had been only on making amends.

A mere heartbeat after Effie gave Helena the go-ahead, Kieran's eyes fluttered open.

"Welcome back," Effie said, happy to find that she meant it. Anger and heartache, even when justified, were a heavy weight to bear. It was nice to finally be rid of them.

"Well done, Dreamer," Helena added.

Kieran blinked and stood with a groan, causing the others to rise with him.

While the face was technically the same, Kieran's expression lacked Erebos's arrogance. It was soft now with confusion, his green eyes uncertain. But even without those distinctions, the voice would have given him away. Erebos's seductive croon had been replaced by Kieran's smoky rasp.

"Why didn't you let me die? I don't deserve to be here."

"Yeah," Ronan said, his eyes filled with suspicion that was mirrored in the others' as well. "Why *did* you save him? Last I checked, whatever name he goes by, he's still a rutting bastard that belongs behind bars."

"Your actions today prove otherwise," Effie answered before proceeding to fill the others in on what he'd done. The explanation mollified most, but Ronan and the Guardians seemed to be struggling with how to come to terms with this change of events. Which wasn't surprising, really, seeing that they were the ones most deeply wounded by his actions—regardless of which entity was responsible for them.

It was Reyna, ultimately, who swayed them. She reached out, taking his hand in hers. "Thank you for sending me the dream. If not for your bravery and keen mind, today's battle could have ended far differently."

"What dream?" Effie asked, just as Ronan muttered, "What battle? He handed us our arses and then put us to sleep. I didn't even get to fight." Sighing, he added, "I was really looking forward to repaying his hospitality and watching the life drain from his eyes." His gaze darted to Kieran. "No offense."

"None taken. If it would make you feel better, I'll give you a free shot. I was there for . . . some of it . . . you've certainly earned the right to seek restitution after the things he did to you."

Ronan's brow furrowed. "Those times he stopped. That was you, wasn't it? I'd wondered why he'd suddenly piss off out of the blue, but it makes sense now if he was trying to grapple with you for control."

Kieran rubbed at his neck and nodded. "Yeah. I think that's about the gist of it."

"In that case, I guess I owe you my thanks as well."

"So, you're not going to punch me?" he asked, looking as though he was braced for it.

"Not today, princeling," Ronan said with a dark chuckle. "But if you want your bell rung that badly, I know a few people who might take you up on the offer." His eyes drifted to Lucian, whose lips curled in amusement.

Reyna glanced over at her husband. "You should be thanking him for a whole lot more than that. Erebos was never a fight we could win. I'd go so far as to argue it was never *our* fight at all. It was his." She jutted her chin in Kieran's direction. "As for the dream," she continued, finally answering Effie's question. "Kieran found a way to forewarn me of Erebos's approach. It's because of him we weren't caught completely unaware."

The looks sent Kieran's way were now tinged with begrudging respect.

"Still, isn't it a risk?" he asked. "Leaving me alive if he can just take over again?"

This time it was Helena who answered. "You've proven your heart isn't weak anymore. Even if he were to return, it was your bitterness and jealousy that gave him his foothold, and now neither exists. You are free, Kieran. Not only of Erebos's influence, but from any charges that once existed against you."

"Free? Just like that?"

"I would argue that you have more than paid the price for your sins. And I know for a fact that you have learned your lesson. As far as I am concerned, your life, once again, is yours. What shall you do with it?"

He was truly stumped by the question. "I . . . uh . . . I don't know. I can hardly go back to the Keepers." He flushed and couldn't quite meet Kael or Lucian's gaze as he said it.

"If you seek a place among us, Kieran, you may have it," Effie promised. "But I will not lie to you. The road will be hard earning back the trust of those who remain."

"Not so hard as you might think once they learn the truth," Kael said.

Kieran was clearly surprised by the show of support. He stared up at the Guardian, but eventually cleared his throat and shook his head. "I thank you for the offer, but I do not believe my place is there. I only joined the Keepers in search of . . ." His flush deepened, and he abandoned the thought.

Lucian's thoughts brushed against her mind. *I'm glad to see he's not fostering any hope of winning you back.*

"There was never any chance of that."

"Perhaps not, but I'd hate to kill him after you and Helena worked so hard to save him."

Effie swallowed a laugh and shook her head. *"You're incorrigible."*

"You love me."

"So much I require infinite lifetimes to express it."

His answering smile made her belly flutter, and Effie had to force herself to look away from him when Helena asked, "Elysia, then? Would you like a place in my court?"

"If I never set foot in a court again, it would be too soon," he answered baldly.

"So where will you go? Will you seek out a new life in Empyria?"

Kieran opened his mouth, but then his face dropped, and he shook his head. "I don't know, Kiri."

"I might have a suggestion, if you'd like to hear it," Lucian offered.

"Lucian . . . be nice."

"Do you have so little faith in me, fledgling? I'm always nice."

"You are rarely nice, and that's with people you actually like."

This time it was Lucian who swallowed a laugh.

Kieran seemed wary but eventually nodded. "Sure."

"What if I could send you home?"

"Home?" There was no missing the longing in the lone word. "You mean to Eatos?"

"The very same."

"But the gateways are closed. There's no way back."

Lucian tipped his head. "Maybe not for you. But for a Guardian, no realm is closed to us, so long as we've been there once before."

Tears misted her eyes as Effie realized what Lucian was really offering. A portal. As the only other person who'd ever set foot on Eatonian soil, he, and he alone, had the ability to send Kieran back to the one place he might actually be able to start over.

"You would do that? For me?"

"After what you did for us, I would be happy to."

Even a month ago, the words would have been filled with double meaning, but today they rang only with sincerity.

"I . . ." Kieran blinked a few times and then rubbed at his eyes as he struggled against a wave of sudden emotion. "That is, I would very much like to go home. Please."

Lucian's eyes flared blinding bronze as he summoned it then and there.

Before anyone had a chance to react, a woman with a mass of silvery hair and tawny catlike eyes shoved her head through the portal.

"Who dares open me gateway without permission?" Her eyes darted to the left, landing on Lucian. "I remember you. You were there the day that princeling—"

"L-lady W-Witney?" Kieran stuttered, shock robbing his face of color.

She stepped fully through the portal, her head snapping his way. "Well, elder's rotting teeth, it's the princeling himself. I'd always wondered what happened to you." Her eyes narrowed. "Centuries later, and you're still causing me bones no end of headaches." She tsked and shook her head. "Wait until Cyril hears about this."

"Cyril? He's still around?"

"Sure as my tits are perky. That one's fit to outlive us all."

Effie snorted, more than a little enchanted with this Lady Witney already.

"Well then, are yous coming or wot? I don't leave my gate open for anyone. Not even the Lost Prince of Eatos."

"Lost Prince? I was denounced."

"Lots has changed since you left, princeling. That pretty sister of yours is on the throne now."

"Liyah?" His voice cracked around the word. "She's alive?"

Witney's eyes met Effie's. "Issn't that wot I just said? Is he a bit damaged"—she wiggled her fingers around her head to indicate he might have suffered some sort of blow—"or is he just hard o'hearing?" Not waiting for an answer, she simply raised her voice. "She's the flouncing queen. Now, for the last time. Yous coming, or wot?"

Kieran cleared his throat again and nodded. "Definitely coming."

"Well then, 'urry up. Haven't got all day. You interrupted me in the middle of polishing me jangles."

Kieran glanced around at everyone, torn between the desire to say goodbye and his need to be reunited with the family he thought was lost.

"It's okay, Kieran. Go. You deserve a chance to find your own happy ending."

His gaze found hers, and he offered her a smile that was as bittersweet as it was hopeful. "I always knew you were my destiny. I just never realized finding you would lead me back to the one place I never thought I belonged. Go figure."

"Fate is exceedingly tricky that way. May the Mother watch over you, Prince Kieran of Eatos."

He dipped his head. "And you as well, Guardian." He gave her a little salute and a saucy wink that was much more in keeping with the boy she first met. "Guess I'll see you in my dreams."

"Not fucking likely," Lucian grunted.

With a laugh, Kieran ducked through the portal, disappearing from view. Effie couldn't help but smile as the portal faded and the Dreamer, once lost, finally found his way back home.

CHAPTER 31

RONAN

"So, where's our portal?" he asked, suddenly eager to get as far away from this fucking place as possible.

"In a hurry, are you?" Reyna asked with a laugh.

He wrapped his arms around his wife, pulling her in close. "I got what I came for. What's left for us here?"

"I take it that means a life of piracy is out of the question," Calypso said, she and a few crew members joining their group.

"Tempting, but I'm going to have to pass."

"Pity, we can always do with a strapping lad like you on board."

"And what are we, Caly?" Bronn asked, jerking a thumb between himself, Tiny, and Jagger. "A couple of squids?"

"An unavoidable nuisance. Not you, Tiny," she was quick to clarify, reaching out and resting her palm on his meaty fist. "You're a joy."

"My thanks, cap'n," he said, bashfully ducking his head.

Ronan would never wrap his head around the sweet-natured minotaur, with his love of manners and fashion, who'd ended up spending his life as a pirate—which is to say, the exact opposite of the things he embodied. But he knew he'd remember him fondly. His time on the *Revenge,* while short, had been one of the highlights of his adventure. Caly and her men were among the few things he'd miss about this place.

"Keep it up, woman, and I'll make good on my threat to take Glinta up on her offer."

Ronan looked to Bronn. "You'd give this up to be a fish merchant?"

The quartermaster's aghast expression said it all. He had no intention of ever giving up his life at sea. "Never. She needs someone she can trust to oversee a new venture in the south."

"And she came to you?" Sebastian asked, shaking his head with a gusty sigh. "That was her first mistake."

"Watch it. Or you'll find yourself kicked off this ship."

"On whose authority?"

"My own."

Sebastian scoffed. "It's not your ship. It's not even *her* ship," he said, jutting his chin toward Caly. "Which means you have no influence, *mon ami*."

"Technically, it *is* my ship," she muttered, but the men were too focused on each other to hear her.

Bronn pushed up his sleeves and took a threatening step forward. "Perhaps not, but I can toss your arse overboard."

Bast grinned. "I think we've all had enough of that for one day."

It was easy to laugh about now, but Ronan knew the memory of the day's battle would stay with them all. They'd won in the end, true, but only just. It had been the Mother's intervention that saved them, not any skill of their own. Though few realized it.

Given the jovial nature of those wandering around and preparing the ship to set sail, he'd hazard that most didn't recall how close they'd come to meeting their maker. Only those who Erebos hadn't swept into the sea knew what really happened, which was a mercy, really. The army of nightmares they'd had to face was more than memorable.

"What will you do, Caly?" Reyna asked. "Now that you don't have to worry about us?"

The captain's eyes drifted toward the dark-haired pirate who'd just walked onto the deck. As if he could feel her gaze on him, Lawless turned fathomless eyes on her. Calypso immediately turned away, but her lips curled in a devilish smile. "Oh, not much, really. Just a bit of mutiny."

"Mutiny?" Effie asked. "Sounds dangerous."

"Aye, it is. But I'm taking my ship back, and there's nothing anyone can do to stop me."

Ronan had little doubt she'd be successful. The woman was as brazen and fearless as they came. And a brilliant captain, to boot. If she'd set her mind on retaking the *Lorelei,* then Lawless was about to find himself with one hell of a fight on his hands.

"Good luck with that," Effie said with a little laugh.

"Oh, luck has nothing to do with it."

"It rarely does," Lucian agreed, his eyes blazing bronze as he opened his second portal.

"I guess that's our cue," Ronan said, releasing Reyna so he could clasp hands with Caly. "Thank you, captain. For everything."

"The pleasure was mine. I'm glad you found your treasure." She winked at Reyna. "And that all those sparks didn't end in bloodshed."

Farewells chorused all around them as the Chosen said goodbye to their new friends. There was a flurry of limbs as young Willie rushed to Reyna, throwing his arms around her waist and hugging her tight.

Reyna shot a surprised glance at Ronan before carefully returning the boy's embrace. "What's all this for?"

Willie stepped back, his cheeks pink. "Just w-want to s-say g'bye."

"Boy's got a bit of a crush," Cookie rumbled, curling an arm around the boy's neck and tugging him back. "Isn't that so, mite?"

Willie's eyes went round, and they darted between Reyna and Ronan. "N-no," he stammered before struggling free of the cook's hold and scampering away.

"I'm surprised you don't have anything to say about that," Reyna said with a lift of her brow.

"Why would I be jealous of the boy? Of course he fancies you. What lad wouldn't? You're pretty as they come and can gut a man in less than a second."

"Ronan, that might be the sweetest thing you've ever said to me," she teased, feigning a swoon.

"I doubt it."

"Still, I thought for sure you'd have felt the need to stake your claim."

"I married you. My claim is staked. Besides, I know I don't need to be worried unless your dagger makes an appearance."

"Wait. Why only then?"

"Because that's when I know you fancy *him*."

"What? Why would I pull a dagger on someone I wanted?"

"Dunno, but you did it with me. And look where we ended up."

Reyna laughed and shook her head. "You're ridiculous."

"And right, don't forget that part," he said, taking her in his arms again so he could press a kiss to her temple.

"You won't let me."

Warmth trickled through him. Ronan couldn't believe he got to spend the rest of his life doing this. Sparring with her. Holding her. Loving her.

He couldn't fucking wait.

Catching his eye, Effie smiled at him before darting through the portal. More of their ranks followed her, and Ronan craned his neck, realizing someone had grown suspiciously silent.

Bast hovered behind him, eyes downcast.

"What's the matter with him?" Ronan asked.

"I think he's waiting for you," Reyna said softly.

"For what?"

"To say goodbye."

"Why? He's coming with us."

Reyna's smile was gentle as she shook her head. "I'm not so sure about that. Have you actually asked him?"

Frowning because he'd just assumed it was a foregone conclusion, he asked, "Where else would he go?" Not waiting for a response, he stalked over to the other man. "You ready?"

Bast looked up. "I can't go with you, Ronan."

"Why the hell not? What's keeping you here?" Ronan spotted Camille hovering just behind Bast and couldn't help but wonder if she was at least part of the reason. "If you're worried about Cami, I promise there's room enough for both of you at the palace."

"I thank you for that, *mon ami*. The offer means more than I can say, but you know I must stay and find him."

Loren. Of course.

Ronan's adventure in Empyria might be over, but Bast's was just beginning. He had his own rescue to embark on.

Well . . . fuck.

He hadn't banked on having to say goodbye to Sebastian. After everything they'd weathered together, it felt wrong to leave him behind. But he couldn't exactly go with him either. His place was with Reyna. Maybe she'd . . .

"No, Ronan. I can tell what you are thinking, but it is past time for you to go home. You fought many years for this moment. For her. Go. Enjoy it. You have earned your happily ever after."

Ronan had to clear his throat, unable to deny the truth of his words, though his heart ached regardless. Bast and Cami were the first friends he'd made in Glimmermere. Both of them were a huge part of the reason he was even standing here now. How was he supposed to just leave them?

"It's okay, Ronan. I'll keep an eye on him for you," Camille said, stepping forward and taking Bast's hand.

"You do make a pretty good guardian angel," Ronan said gruffly.

Camille smiled. "And you as well. I am better for having known you, Ronan."

"And I'm alive because of you."

"Seems like a fair trade."

Ronan shook his head as he stepped in and hugged her. "Hardly fair. You got the short end of the stick."

"That's a matter of perspective."

As he pulled away, he released a gusty sigh. "So, I guess this is goodbye then."

"Never goodbye, only farewell. We will meet again, Ronan. I know it. Besides, for friends such as us, we are never far apart." Bast tapped two fingers over his heart. "I will carry you here. Always."

"Not friends," Ronan said, voice thick. "Brothers." He pulled Bast into him, hugging him tightly. "Thank you, Sebastian. None of this would have been possible without you. You are one of the best and most loyal men I know."

Bast hastily wiped a tear from his cheek as they pulled apart, his eyes shifting to where Lucian and Von waited beside the portal. "Quite a compliment coming from you."

"Just the truth."

They smiled, but it was bittersweet.

"May the Mother watch over you, Bast."

"She is," Camille said.

"Here," Von said, surprising them both when he walked over, holding out a glittering purple stone.

"What's this for?" Sebastian asked, brow furrowed.

"It's a Kaelpas stone. You can use it to travel great distances. That stone has enough charge to bring you to the palace gates."

"Oh, yes, I remember. Effie used one of these to bring us to Smuggler's Rock."

"But Bast has never been to the palace. How will he be able to activate it?" Ronan asked.

"Allow me," Lucian said.

The Guardian must have telepathically sent Bast the palace's image because the blond man's eyes flew wide, and he let out a little squeak.

"*Merde.*"

"Think you can remember that?" Lucian asked.

"Without a doubt."

"Good," Von said. "Then if you ever find yourself in need, use that stone. All you have to do is hold it in your hand while envisioning the palace, and it will bring you straight to us."

Seeming to realize what a rare and precious gift he'd just been given, Bast swallowed, his fist closing tightly around it. "Thank you."

"Yes, well. How else are you going to make good on your promise to Ronan?"

Ronan raised a brow, seeing straight through Von's excuse. Bast had grown on him too. Fungus indeed. Was there anyone the popinjay couldn't win over?

Somehow, knowing Bast had a way to reach them if needed made it a lot easier to go.

"Until we meet again, Bast," Ronan said.

"Bon voyage, mon ami."

As he turned away from Sebastian, Reyna was right there to take his hand. Together, they walked to the portal, all but Lucian having now gone through. "Ready to go home, husband?"

"As long as I'm with you, I'm always home, wife."

REYNA

"**Y**ou're going to have to come out sometime, kitten."

"Don't be so sure about that," she grumbled, glancing in the mirror as she adjusted the veils for the thousandth time. In the month since they'd returned to Elysia, her husband had taken her in every possible way, yet *this* made her nervous.

"You're the one who lost the bet, sweetheart. Now get that sweet arse out here and pay up."

"If you laugh . . ."

"I promise you, laughter's the furthest thing from my mind."

Closing her eyes, she took a deep breath and tried to calm her racing heart.

Come on, Reyna. Woman up. You've done this at least a hundred times. You're a freaking expert, for darkness's sake.

Yes, but I've never done it for him.

Ronan had been begging her to perform the dance of the veils for him practically since the night he found out what Salome was. She couldn't blame him. She'd certainly painted an erotic picture. Why wouldn't he want to experience it for himself?

Shaking out her limbs, Reyna picked up her zills—small finger cymbals that would help her keep the beat—and began. Sweeping her leg out around the screen separating her from the rest of the room, she tapped her fingers together, the resulting trill filling the chamber, signaling the start of the dance.

Without making eye contact, she rocked her hip out, letting her body follow the swaying movement like a wave as she left the safety of the screen behind. She continued to tap her fingers together, setting the beat of the song that her body followed, her hips and shoulders creating a serpentine pattern as she moved about the room.

It was hard to feel nervous after that, her mind falling silent as her body took over. She'd always loved the sensual simplicity of the dance. A roll of the hips. A twist of the leg. A subtle tug as one of the veils fell away.

True to his word, Ronan didn't laugh. He was rapt, his eyes ravenous as they caressed her body. At first, he'd leaned back in his chair, legs spread wide, fingers running through his beard. But once the veils started to come off and more of her skin was exposed, he sat forward, elbows braced on his knees, gaze hot on her.

When only one veil remained, Reyna twirled until she stood just in front of him. Then she lifted her right knee, swiveling her hips as she brought her leg across her body and then swept it back out, the ball of her foot poised on the edge of his chair by his thigh and the transparent length of silk all that separated him from her.

"Would you like to do the honors?" she whispered.

Ronan audibly swallowed, his palm warm as he slid his hand up her thigh to the little belt at her waist holding the fabric in place.

With a tug, it fell free, the barest whisper of friction over her slick center enough to make her tremble. She'd done this countless times, but never had it been such a tease for her. She was so turned on she burned with it. Her thighs were slick with her arousal, her nipples tight aching points, her skin so sensitive that every brush of the silk or her hair over her skin left her panting. She couldn't recall a time she'd ever been so aware of her body.

Ronan's breath left him in a hiss. "Fuck, Reyna. You grow more beautiful every day. You're the most perfect fucking thing I've ever seen in my life. And I'm the luckiest bastard in the world, because you're all mine."

He grabbed her then, his large palms cupping her ass and pulling her to him. She wasn't sure what he was intending, because with Ronan, one could never know. His lovemaking was as varied and adventurous as the man himself. He could as easily stand and enter her in one quick thrust while carrying her across the room as he could go down on her until she saw stars.

This time he pulled her onto his lap until she straddled him, his rigid shaft an absolute tease as he dragged her along its length.

"Kiss me," he ordered, his hands curling around her thighs and sliding down to grip the back of her knees.

She brought her mouth to his but didn't give him what he asked for, delivering a demand of her own instead. "Get naked first."

His deep chuckle washed over her lips. "My hands are busy."

"Unbusy them."

"No, I don't think I will." He dragged them up her legs, twisting his grip so his fingertips were skimming her inner thighs. When his index fingers brushed along either side of the place she wanted him most, she moaned.

"Ronan?"

"Hmm?"

"In case you haven't noticed, I want you to fuck me." She feathered her lips over his. "Now."

"Isn't that what I'm in the middle of?"

"No. You're teasing me."

"What's wrong with that?"

"I already teased both of us."

His laughter rumbled deep in his chest. "Always in a hurry."

"No, I'm making up for lost time. I spent too many years waiting to have you."

Ronan groaned, one of his hands releasing her to fumble with the ties of his pants. As soon as the swollen length of him sprang free, Reyna sank down.

"If it meant knowing what it feels like to have you clenched around me, I'd have waited my whole damned life."

"You almost did." She cupped his face in her hands and sealed her lips over his.

"I'd do it again. There's nothing I wouldn't give to have known this moment. To be here right now, with you."

"Ronan," she whispered, blinking back a wave of emotion. Pregnancy had made her exceptionally sentimental, and these days it hardly took more than a sweet word to send the floodgates wide open.

"I mean it, kitten. I love you with everything that I am."

"I love you too."

Ronan's hand tangled in her hair as he brought her mouth to his, lips urgent as they moved against hers. She would never tire of kissing her husband. Every time felt like the first. From the butterflies taking flight in her belly to the resulting flood of arousal, he consumed each and every one of her senses.

"Sweetheart?"

"Hmm?"

"I'm going to fuck you now."

The 'finally' she'd been about to utter was lost to her passionate cries as Ronan made good on his promise.

And then he did it a second time, just because he could.

Seven Years Later

"Hurry up, sweetheart. Stella is waiting for you."

"Mummy, why can't I go with you and Daddy?" Shay, their precocious five-year-old daughter, asked, blinking her big blue-green eyes up at her.

"Because you're a baby," Jameson, their even more precocious seven-year-old responded.

Ronan hadn't gotten the daughter he was after the first time, which is why he'd immediately set out to try again. Reyna never called him on it, but she knew regardless of what the outcome was, he'd have done the same.

"I am not a baby!" she shouted, stomping her foot. "Daddy said so."

"There now, what's all this?" Ronan asked, sweeping into the room.

"Shay wants to come with us," Reyna murmured, trying to fight a smile. This same song and dance happened every time they had a bounty that took them away from home. Shay didn't look exactly like the red-haired girl from her dream, but she was every bit as spirited. Reyna knew this was her penance for the endless headaches she'd caused her own mother. And she wouldn't have it any other way.

"Is that so?"

"I'm tough. You said so."

"That you are, wildheart. Which is why I need you to stay behind and look after your brother."

"Hey!" Jameson protested, earning him a conspiratorial wink from his father.

Reyna ruffled Jameson's raven-colored hair. "Why don't you grab your packs? They're by the door."

"When will I get to go with you?" he asked, failing to suppress his own sulk.

"When you're older."

He kicked the ground with a little huff.

"I thought you'd be happy to spend time with your godfather and uncle Lucian," Reyna said.

"I am. Von said he'd teach me how to set my sword on fire, and Lucian said I could train with him."

"Oh, did they?" Ronan asked, his voice deceptively calm.

Reyna shook her head, keeping her amusement from her expression as she asked, "So why the long face then? It sounds like you're going to have a wonderful time."

"Because I'm going to miss you," he grumbled, seeming embarrassed by the admission.

"Me too," Shay said, her lower lip trembling.

Reyna's heart cracked in two. As it did every time they had to leave the children behind. "Oh, my little loves. I promise your father and I will miss you more."

"You will?" Shay asked.

"Of course we will. Why do you think we're always in a hurry to get back?"

Jameson looked to his father for confirmation. Ronan gave him a very serious man-to-man nod.

A knock sounded on the door, cutting the time for goodbyes short.

"That'll be auntie Helena. Come, give me a hug." Reyna crouched down and held out her arms for her daughter to fling herself into. She was quick to squirm away, proving that she was more excited to spend time with her cousin than she'd let on.

"Hey, where's mine?" Ronan asked when she tried to rush past him.

"Oops!" Shay said with a giggle, rushing back and jumping up so he could catch her and spin her around.

"That's more like it. I can't go catch the bad guys without a good luck kiss from my best girl."

"I thought Mum was your best girl," Jameson said.

"Best girls are like best friends. You can have more than one."

"You mean like you and Uncle Bast and Von?" Jameson asked, his face scrunching up adorably with his confusion. "But don't they fight all the time?"

"Just a little brotherly bickering. They don't really mean it."

"That's not what it sounded like…"

"He's onto you," Reyna said under her breath as she walked by him to open the door.

"It's the truth," Ronan protested.

"Just wait until your son uses that 'you can have more than one' excuse on someone in a few more years."

Ronan let out a strained laugh, finally realizing his mistake. "I'll make sure to explain it to him before he earns himself a kick in the shin."

"Pretty sure any girl he tries that on won't aim for his shin," Reyna murmured.

Helena stood in the door, her eyes wide and a laugh on her lips. "What did I miss?"

"Ronan is explaining how best girls are like best friends, and you can have more than one."

"Uh-oh."

"Exactly."

"Is this what you mean by them ganging up on you?" Jameson asked, not quite managing to whisper as he looked up at his dad.

"The very same," Ronan agreed as he set Shay down.

"Noted."

"Yes, *noted*," Reyna said, giving her husband a pointed lift of her brow. "All right, time to go. You two behave while we're gone, understand?"

"Will you bring me something back?" Shay asked, her hand already tucked in Helena's.

"Don't I always?"

Shay's grin was as wide as her whole face as she nodded and made to scamper off.

"Love you, wildheart," Ronan called after her.

"You too, Daddy! I hope you catch all the bad guys!"

"Not *all* the bad guys," Jameson corrected. "Save some for me."

"I'll be sure to do that," Ronan promised, face solemn but eyes dancing with mirth.

With a final nod, their son rushed out to join his sister.

"Thanks again for doing this on such short notice," Reyna said.

"Please, it's no hardship. We love having them. Stella especially. So, who are you going after this time?"

Ronan's grin turned wicked as he pulled Effie's missive out of his pocket. "She found Nightshade."

Despite his short stint in Helena's dungeon, the Bargainer had managed to escape. It had been a sore spot for both Ronan and Helena ever since.

Eyes glittering with iridescence, Helena matched Ronan's bloodthirsty smile. "Ooo, the one that got away. You two must be itching to get out there, so I'll leave you to it."

Ronan and Reyna linked hands. As much as they loved being home raising their family, retirement lost its shine after only a few months—just as Reyna predicted. Which was why, as soon as the children were old enough, they began taking bounties.

The hunt was in their blood. They had a true knack for it. So much so that the pair were whispered about in fear. Rumor had it there was even a lullaby going around warning children of what would happen if the Butcher and his Shadow caught them.

With her free hand, Reyna pulled up the hood of her cloak, hiding her pale braid. Beside her, Ronan did the same, his teeth flashing as he grinned. "You up for a bit of an adventure, killer?"

"Every day with you is an adventure, husband."

"True, but this one might get a bit bloody."

"My favorite."

"Here I was, thinking the Butcher was the bloodthirstiest bastard in town. Looks like he's met his match."

"Consider me your faithful Shadow. Where you go, I follow, husband."

He squeezed her hand, then leaned down to steal a quick kiss. "In this life, and every one after."

EPILOGUE

KIERAN

Ten Years Later

"Would you please stop hovering? I'm old, not infirm."

Kieran laughed. Old was an understatement when it came to the elder. Ancient might be more accurate. Decrepit, more so. Not that he was about to correct the man.

"You heard what the healer said, Cyril. Strict bed rest for the next few weeks until your hip has time to fully recover." He paused in the middle of unfolding a blanket to look up at him. "Why did you insist on testing those, what did you call them? Ice skates?"

Even lying down, Cyril somehow managed to peer down his nose at him. "Because unlike you, I still enjoy a bit of fun."

"Yes, because shattering your hip is the epitome of a rousing good time. Anyway, the healer mended the break, but for one such as you—"

"You mean an old man."

"Exactly. For an old man such as yourself, these things take a bit

249

more time. So, consider me your errand boy until you receive a clean bill of health."

Cyril laughed as Kieran tucked the blanket over him. "If anyone knew the future king was waiting on me hand and foot . . ."

"We've been over this, Cy. I don't care what Liyah says. I'm not going to take her place." He had absolutely zero interest in going anywhere near the Eatonian court. He still had nightmares of his time as Erebos. Just being back among his family was enough for him, more than enough. He could spend the rest of his days transcribing Cyril's exploits, as he'd taken to doing upon his return, and consider it a life well spent. He'd had his grand adventure. Now all he sought was peace.

"We'll see about that," the elder said, laying back on his pillow and pulling the blanket up to his chin. Then he scowled, took great pains to smooth out his beard, and then clasped his hands.

"There's nothing to see. I don't want it."

"Want means little in the face of duty, young prince. And technically, the throne is yours."

"*Technically,* I was disowned, so I'm not a prince. Nothing is mine."

"Your father never got around to making the edict official. So, *technically* you weren't, *young prince.*"

"Elder's swinging scrotum," he said with an exasperated shake of his head.

Cyril wheezed out a laugh. "Where in the seven hells do you come up with such odious expressions? And why must you always pick on the elders?"

"What would you rather I say, Cy?"

"A good, fervent fuck never hurt anyone."

Kieran joined in his laughter. "No, it certainly did not." At this point, good, fervent fucks were the thing of legend. He'd been celibate so long he was fairly certain he'd regrown his virginity.

"So, Cyril. How would you like to pass the afternoon? Shall I read you a story?" he offered, idly scanning the shelves for something of interest.

"I left one just there, yes, the blue one—"

A knock at the door of Cyril's little farmhouse interrupted them.

"You didn't tell me you were expecting company."

Cyril shrugged. "I must have forgotten."

"You haven't forgotten a thing a day in your life," Kieran muttered, setting aside the book Cyril had indicated and heading for the door.

He wasn't prepared when the beauty swept into the room, her dark hair pulled back and an elegant set of spectacles resting on the bridge of her pert nose. She was pretty in a quiet, bookish way. Ink staining her fingers, cheeks and eyes bright from the wind, her attire practical instead of fashionable and still dust-stained from her travels.

"Do something with this, would you, farm boy?" she asked, barely looking at him as she shoved her bag into his hands. "Uncle, when I sent you the skates for your name day, I did warn you not to try them without me."

"Farm boy?" Kieran mouthed a second before nearly dropping her bag to the ground. "What in the seven hells do you have in here, woman? Bricks?"

Said woman tossed him an annoyed glare over her shoulder. "My research, if you must know."

"Research?" he said slowly, looking to Cyril as if this was all some sort of joke.

"Yes, and please do be careful. My specimens are also in there, and they're irreplaceable."

"Specimens," he repeated, because apparently he was an idiot incapable of following basic conversation on top of everything else.

The woman seemed to agree because she dropped her voice in what was supposed to be a whisper but didn't do much to disguise what she said, given the small size of the room. "Really, Uncle. Is this the best the palace could find for you? You should summon that girl and request she find someone new. This boy seems rather simple."

Kieran would have been offended if he wasn't so amused. "Uncle, is it?" he asked, tossing the woman's bag on the table and biting back a laugh at her annoyed, "Hey!"

"Ah, yes. Kieran, allow me to introduce you to my niece, Sofia."

"Your niece . . . so you weren't lying about her then?"

Cyril spread his age-spotted hands. "Live as long as me, boyo, you're bound to come across at least one long-lost relative."

Kieran smothered a smile. "So it would seem."

Sofia took one of Cyril's hands as she sat beside him on the bed, already completely dismissing Kieran. "I've made so many new discoveries, Uncle."

"I can't wait to hear them."

She started babbling on, leaving Kieran to either stand there awkwardly or go. Deciding on the latter, he raised a hand to catch their attention. "Well, I guess I'll leave you two to your reunion. I'll be outside if you have need of me," he said, grabbing his coat.

"Oh, farm boy, fetch me some tea before you go, will you?"

Fetch you some tea? He knew he just said he had no intention of taking the throne, but did the woman really not realize to whom she was speaking? If she did, she certainly didn't care.

He paused, staring at her profile, taking in the flush of excitement on her cheeks and the passionate glimmer in her eyes as she resumed prattling away. She really was something. Filled with an inner fire and purpose he recognized but long lacked. His gaze shifted between her and the elder and then back again, noting the true respect and affection between them. This might be the first he'd heard of her, but Sofia was clearly special to the man who'd been more of a father to him than his actual sire.

That alone would have been enough to pique his interest, though he'd be lying if he said her brusque dismissal of him, along with her good looks, hadn't already done the job on their own.

Intrigued despite himself, he ultimately shook his head and murmured, "As you wish."

BONUS EPILOGUE

BAST

The portal faded with a nearly inaudible sizzle as the tether linking the two realms snapped. He knew saying goodbye would be hard, but he hadn't expected this wave of sadness to crash over him. Their time together had been short by most standards, but the bonds they'd forged during their adventures were the kind that spanned entire lifetimes.

"I'm going to miss them," Caly said, frowning at the empty space where the portal had been.

"Me too," Bronn said.

Jagger, of course, said nothing, but Buttercup gave a cheery chirp.

"Well," Camille said, linking their fingers. "What now?"

"That is the question, isn't it, *mon trésor*? I suppose we must head off on an adventure of our own."

"Where will you start?" Caly asked.

Bast shook his head. "Loren could be anywhere by now."

"What about home?" Camille suggested softly.

"Home?" Bast hadn't thought about returning to Colvers in years. The place was filled with ghosts, not happy memories.

"Not yours, his."

Sebastian scratched his head. "Knightsgrave?"

"It's where he was heading when you were fleeing Erebos. Perhaps he escaped and resumed his journey. If not, perhaps someone there has spoken with him and can point us in the right direction."

It was certainly plausible, and it wasn't like he had a better idea. "I guess that's as good a place as any to start."

"There is another place you could go," Calypso offered.

"Where's that?"

"Have you ever heard of Ravenndel?"

It sounded familiar, but he couldn't recall where he'd heard it before. "If I have, it's been a long time."

"It's an island in the southeast. Many a lost boy finds himself there."

"Loren is hardly a boy," Bast said with a laugh. "Though he is lost."

Calypso waved a hand. "Boy, man, it's all the same in the end."

"Trust me, it's not."

Caly winked at him. "Lost men, then."

"What kind of island is this? It sounds like somewhere I should have visited by now."

"Certainly seems like your sort of place," Bronn agreed.

Bast was pretty sure he didn't mean it as a compliment, nor did he care. Ravenndel was the first place anyone had mentioned that sent a surge of anticipation through him. The other destinations left him feeling hollow. He couldn't ignore the little voice in his head telling him *this* was his new path.

"Ravenndel it is," he said, though his thoughts were distracted and the words came out thick with melancholy.

"You don't seem very excited," Camille said, her voice soft and just for him.

Bast frowned. It wasn't that he didn't want to see Loren again; quite the opposite. But what if *he* didn't want to see him? What was it Reyna had said? Sometimes the flames are only good for a single night? What if the fire between them had already guttered out?

A heavy weight settled in his chest, and he sighed. "Absence does not always make the heart grow fonder, *mon ange*. Sometimes it just grows forgetful."

And *this* was the reason he'd avoided romantic entanglements until now. Feelings were messy and inconvenient. Sex was so much simpler when it was just about getting off. But simple didn't come close to what he felt when he was with Loren. What started as a casual fling had turned into something far more. They just never got the chance to see what the *more* might be. If anything.

Cami squeezed his hand, drawing his attention back to her. "There's only one way to find out. That is, if you're brave enough to risk the heartbreak."

Was he? Brave enough?

He'd spent so long focused on obtaining revenge, he hadn't really considered what came after or what the future might hold for him. But perhaps it was time to start. Didn't he owe it to himself to find out if the spark between him and Loren remained?

He couldn't quite contain his smile or the hopeful flutter low in his belly when he eventually replied. "True love does seem like quite the adventure."

"The biggest," Cami said, unable to contain her grin.

"What do you say, captain? Are you up for another adventure?"

"With you? I suppose I could be persuaded." Calypso smiled even as Jagger groaned.

"What about Drake? Don't you think he'll have something to say about you commandeering his ship?" Bronn asked.

"Let him try and stop me," she said with a smug grin.

"Aye, aye, Captain," Bronn said. "I'll ready the crew."

"So how do we get there?" Sebastian asked.

Caly pointed to the sky. "We follow the stars, straight on 'til morning."

"You don't mean . . ."

But she did, for it would seem that while the Kiri and her Circle had left, their magic remained. And when the *Lorelei* set sail, it was not through the sea as he expected, but amongst the stars themselves.

Bast, Loren, and Camille's adventures will continue in Prince of Sea and Stars, a standalone MMF romantasy set in the Forsaken world coming January 2024, and available for pre-order now!

256

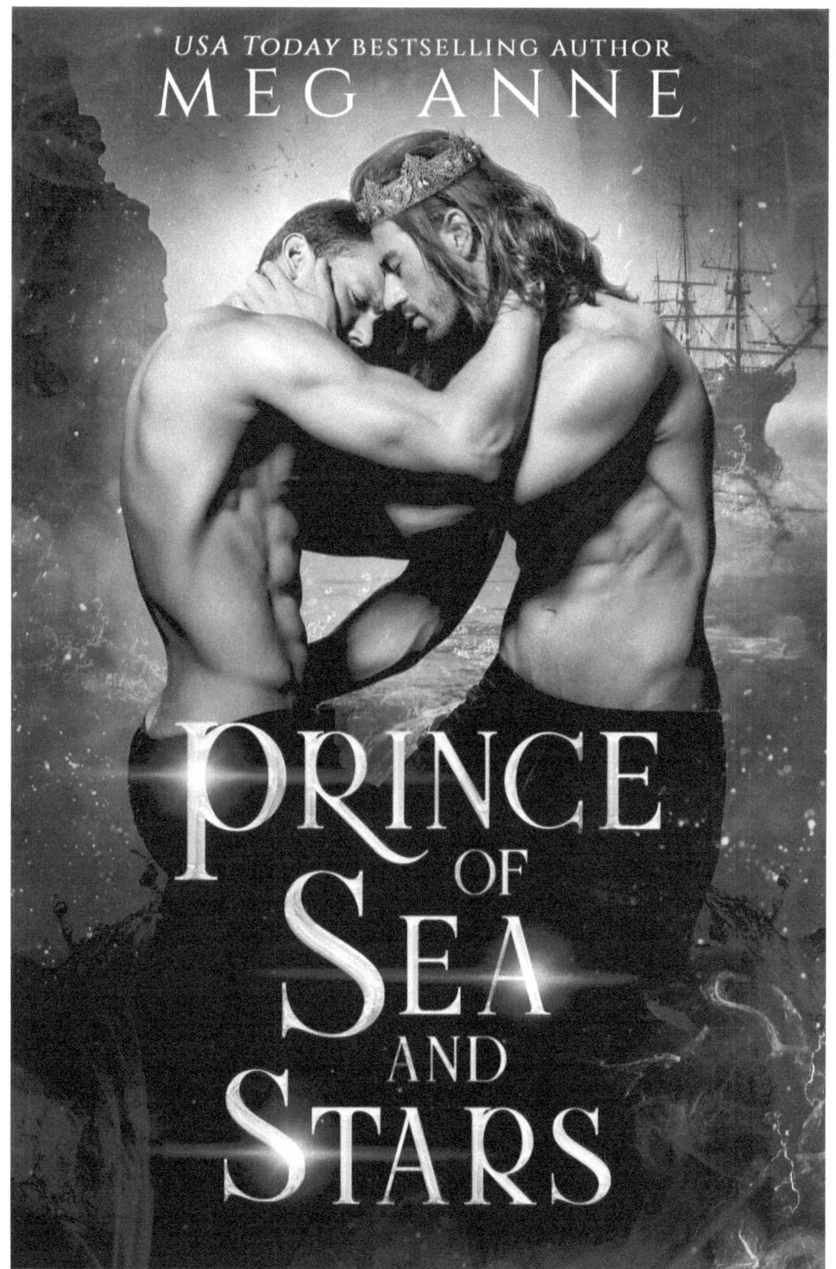
USA Today BESTSELLING AUTHOR
MEG ANNE
PRINCE
OF
SEA
AND
STARS

ACKNOWLEDGMENTS

Oof, this one is hard. Not because I don't know who to thank, but because I don't know if words alone will express the gratitude I have in my heart for them.

As you might have noticed, this book is dedicated to JJ. For the discerning among you, you might have already guessed that is my narrator, James Joseph. This book (honestly this series) would have taken a very different turn if it wasn't for him. I knew from prior projects he was an absolute powerhouse and he was going to bring something really special to the table, but I was not prepared for the absolute magic he created. The second I heard JJ bring Kieran to life, I sat back in my seat and let out a very fervent 'well, fuck' because all of a sudden, I was in love with my villain. And the thought of ending things the way I originally planned didn't sit quite so well any longer. Thus, the mother of all redemption arcs was born. I know now in my bones, JJ was meant to be my Kieran (and my Erebus, and 100% my Bast) because this series ABSOLUTELY ended the way it was supposed to.

JJ you are so much more than my narrator, you were my muse, and along the way you've become a dear friend. Your talent continues to blow me away. I'm pretty sure there isn't anything you can't do and I look forward to many more projects together where we test the theory. I hope you're ready, because I have a list a mile long for you. Thank you, honestly, from the bottom of my heart.

In fact, I have to give a heartfelt shout out to all three of my narrators. Any hope I had for these characters was far exceeded by the absolute master class in performance the three of you delivered.

Stella, Shane, JJ if my words were the rough sketch, yours voices are the color. Together we created something really special. Thank you for the gift of your talent, the world is a better place because of it.

Kimberly Amadeus, you are the Sass to my Sparkle, the Sunday to my Moira, the Quinn to my Lina. Knowing you hasn't just made me a better writer, it's made me a better person. We found each other when I was most in need of a friend, and in the years since you've become so much more. You are my sister, my other (arguable better) half, and I don't ever want to go back to the days before our morning coffee and nonstop messages. I can't wait to be a Golden Girl with you in our haunted mansion. Thank you for loving me. And for spending hours plotting and conspiring with me.

Mom, thank you for proofing the audiobook with me. It was such a joy getting to share the experience with you and get your reaction realtime. It's a rare an author gets to see that with any reader, let alone a daughter who has been supported since day 1 by her mom. I said it before, and I'll say it again, all of this is your fault. I love you forever. I love you for always. As long as I'm living, my mommy you'll be.

Kat, Kenz, Khris, Tara, and Gina. You all bring so much light to the world. You thank us all the time for "letting" you [fill in the blank]. What you don't realize yet, is what a gift *you* are to us. You will never know how much your kind words mean to me, how they always seemed to come when I most needed to hear them. I am so thankful for your friendship and support. #chaosunicorns for life.

Sarah, Suzi, Hannah Banana & Catherine (#teampickle), Vesna, Ruhla, Chris, Jen Favey, Lee Ann, Marla, Stephanie, Michelle, Jodi, Melissa, Niffer, Jackie, Ash & Em, and the rest of the Chosen, Shaneiaks, Hunters, and Hellions thank you. Thank you for loving my characters and books. Thank you for sticking with me and taking a chance on a genre that might not be your favorite cup of tea. I know me and your favorite voices won you over, because I see every post and it fills my heart every time. Oh, and I would be remiss if I didn't send a massive thank you to #poorMike. Seeing the posts about your journey through my series brought me so much joy. I hope all those nights shouting at the speaker are as happy a memory for you as they are for me.

Mo, Dom thank you for polishing my words. No matter how stressed I am, I always take comfort knowing I'm in the best hands.

Tyler @ Plunk Productions, you are an absolute wizard. Thank you for diving in the deep end with me. Creating the power voice with you is one of my favorite things I've done with audio to date. I'm so excited for all our future projects.

Last, but far from least, Gabe. You have been my #1 fan from the very first page. I hit publish because of you. Without your support, without your love, no one would have ever read my words. You do so much for me behind the scenes, you aren't just an unsung hero, you're *my* hero. Thank you feels far too small so instead I leave you with this, 'I will love you. In this life and everyone after.'

And for anyone who's still reading this, thank you for coming on this journey with me. You may not realize it, but you're making some-one's dream come true. It's me, I'm someone.

Until next time, stay safe and happy reading.

THE CHOSEN UNIVERSE

Queen of Whispers & Mist

Court of Death & Dreams

~

(Bast, Loren, & Camille)

Standalone MMF High Fantasy Romance

Prince of Sea & Stars (available for pre-order)

~

ALSO BY MEG ANNE

THE MATE GAMES: WAR

A SPICY PARANORMAL WHY CHOOSE ROMANCE

CO-WRITTEN WITH K. LORAINE

OBSESSION

REJECTION

POSSESSION

TEMPTATION

THE MATE GAMES: PESTILENCE

A SPICY PARANORMAL WHY CHOOSE ROMANCE

CO-WRITTEN WITH K. LORAINE

PROMISED TO THE NIGHT (PREQUEL NOVELLA)

DEAL WITH THE DEMON

CLAIMED BY THE SHIFTERS

CAPTIVE OF THE NIGHT

LOST TO THE MOON

ABOUT MEG ANNE

USA Today and international bestselling paranormal and fantasy romance author Meg Anne has always had stories running on a loop in her head. They started off as daydreams about how the evil queen (aka Mom) had her slaving away doing chores, and more recently shifted into creating backgrounds about the people stuck beside her during rush hour. The stories have always been there; they were just waiting for her to tell them.

Like any true SoCal native, Meg enjoys staying inside curled up with a good book and her cat, Henry . . . or maybe that's just her. You can convince Meg to buy just about anything if it's covered in glitter or rhinestones, or make her laugh by sharing your favorite bad joke. She also accepts bribes in the form of baked goods and Mexican food.

Meg is best known for her leading men #MenbyMeg, her inevitable cliffhangers, and making her readers laugh out loud, all of which started with the bestselling Chosen series.